SWEET VIOLET

The New Covent Garden Tavern in south London was dark and the women were mostly all in leather. They looked a bit scary to Violet – no dancing, no smiling, just lots of standing around looking at each other. After several minutes, a woman came and sat at Violet's table. Violet looked at the newcomer out of the corner of her eye. She was a light-skinned black woman, thin and strong-looking; her hair was cut dangerously short but her face was soft. She had tattoos on her arm.

'So, do you want to have sex or are you one of those feminists?' the woman asked suddenly, breaking the silence between them.

Violet smiled – she liked this place. 'Sure,' she said, her heart pounding. She felt nervous. And very excited.

SWEET VIOLET

RUBY VISE

First published in 1999 by
Sapphire
an imprint of Virgin Publishing Ltd
Thames Wharf Studios,
Rainville Road, London W6 9HT

Copyright © Ruby Vise 1999

The right of Ruby Vise to be identified as the Author of this Work has been asserted by her in accordance with the Copyright, Designs and Patents Act 1988.

ISBN 0 352 33458 4

Cover Photograph by The Attard Photolibrary

Typeset by SetSystems Ltd, Saffron Walden, Essex
Printed and bound in Great Britain by Mackays of Chatham PLC

This book is sold subject to the condition that it shall not, by way of trade or otherwise, be lent, resold, hired out or otherwise circulated without the publisher's prior written consent in any form of binding or cover other than that in which it is published and without a similar condition, including this condition, being imposed on the subsequent purchaser.

ONE

Violet

Sweet Violet, that's what her mother used to call her. She would sing a song, 'Sweet Violet, sweeter than the roses.' Violet looked at her reflection in the tube window and smiled. If only her mother knew. She looked anything but sweet, she thought; if it weren't for her breasts she would look just like her brother. She pulled her jacket closed. She had dressed with great care; she wanted to look cool, calm and collected. She didn't want to look like she had just arrived in London, just turned eighteen, had never been to a lesbian club before and was scared sick.

Violet had never even met a lesbian, apart from Miss Phelps – who had been her PE teacher and therefore didn't count – and Katherine. But now that Katherine was engaged to some boy she had met on the England swim team, she didn't count either.

The tube stopped at Brixton and Violet followed the other people off. *City Limits* said Aphrodite Rising was the place for a lesbian to be on a Wednesday night, so here Violet was. She had looked at the *A to Z* before leaving home and by her reckoning she had to turn left out of the tube station, though her reckoning had been wrong before. This was her first visit to Brixton, but her aunt had told her all about the riots there. She half expected them still to be going on, but there was just a man selling flowers and people hurrying home. Violet also saw some women who might be other lesbians, turning left out of the station, so she followed them.

They stopped outside a building with a large washing machine on the front of it and joined a line of women waiting to go in. Violet joined the queue too and paid her money at the little window, to a pretty blonde woman with spiky hair dressed all in leather. A big woman stood behind her, shaved head and a pierced nose. The women didn't give her a second look, and Violet breathed a sigh of relief. She didn't know what she had been expecting, but it felt like she had passed some kind of initiation test. Inside, the place was a huge barn of a building; it was early so there weren't many women there. Violet couldn't believe there were enough lesbians in the whole of the world, let alone London, to fill the place. As the night went on, she was proved wrong.

She went to the bar and bought herself a beer, trying not to look too shocked at the price. A woman at the bar, waiting to be served, smiled at Violet; she had curly hair and big breasts. Violet took her drink and hurried away, not yet ready to talk to anyone. She found a table in the corner where she could see the women coming in. For nearly an hour she watched them stream in, until it was so crowded she couldn't see any more.

There were all sorts of women there, collecting in groups around the place. Near the stage there were women in tartan kilts and leather trousers, with shaved heads and every visible part of their anatomy pierced. They wore chains and carried whips and some even had dog collars around their necks and were being led around on all fours. Violet tried not to stare too much, because they seemed to be looking around a lot and daring the other women to say anything to them. The other women mostly kept out of their way, and Violet didn't blame them.

By the bar were women in chinos and freshly pressed shirts, with the collars up. Their hair was long enough to touch the top of their up-turned collars and flicked back at the front like Farrah Fawcett-Major's. They stood around with their hands in their pockets, not smiling much. On the far side of the room, as far as they could be from the women by the stage, were groups of women in jeans and checked shirts, or dungarees and sensible shoes. They didn't dance much, but stood with their heads close together, shouting at each other over the music.

There were some women in dresses – short, tight numbers with frills and ruffles, or black lace. They were generally accompanied by women in men's suits and ties, one even wearing a trilby. In the middle of the dance floor, throwing themselves about as if they were the only people there, were some women in long skirts or baggy trousers and bare feet. They were draped in scarves, which they would take off periodically and fling about. One woman was tall and slim and moved through the group like a snake, flicking her tongue in and out. Violet found this last group the most unsettling, although she didn't quite know why.

She went up to the bar and bought herself another beer, and then stood looking down on the dance floor. She noticed a couple of big women tangoing together, cutting a swathe across the floor. Violet smiled – all these women, so many women, all lesbians, all like her. Well, some not the least bit like her, but all lesbians. She grinned from ear to ear.

'Hi.' A woman yelled in her ear over the throbbing music. Violet hadn't heard any music like it before; there were no words, just a beating that seemed to vibrate right through her. She hoped it wasn't special lesbian music, because she didn't think she liked it.

'Hi.' Violet shouted back at the woman. She was one of the Farrah Fawcett hair lot.

'Great, isn't it?' the woman said. Wondering if she could somehow tell it was her first time, Violet shrugged in a non-committal sort of way.

'The name's Hazel.' And Hazel held out her hand, so Violet shook it. 'Never been here before. It's wild.'

Violet smiled and nodded this time.

'This is Val.' She reached behind her and dragged a woman with matching hair and collar around to meet Violet. 'Been together five years now.'

Violet nodded again, but she had suddenly lost interest in Hazel.

If she wasn't chatting her up, then Violet didn't know what she was doing. It was the kind of conversation her mother had when she met friends in Kwiksave, not the sort of thing she expected in a lesbian club.

'Oh, and this is Sue.' Hazel produced another woman from out of the crowd. Hazel winked at Violet. 'Sue has just joined us, and she's single.' Sue pulled away, scowling at Violet. She was obviously annoyed, although Violet imagined that even if she smiled, she would still look unhappy.

'We're from Lambda Ladies, a lesbian social group.' Hazel thrust a leaflet into Violet's hand. 'Come along one night, it's awful fun.'

Awful, Violet thought, that sounded about right. Hazel, Val and Sue disappeared into the crowd handing out more leaflets. Violet turned back to watching the women dancing below her. Tonight, she thought, was the first night of the rest of her life. Tonight, she was going to score.

She searched the floor for any women she might fancy. There was one woman in a flowing skirt with long blonde hair and Violet liked the way she moved, but when she turned around, there was something odd about her eyes, which looked too big in her head. She then picked out another woman, dancing with her arms above her head and laughing. Violet liked her because she looked like she was having a good time. She was plump, with big breasts, wearing a singlet and jeans. Violet watched for a while to see if she was with anyone. There was a redheaded woman with her, but she kept looking around to see if anyone was watching. The rest of the group seemed to be paired off; Violet decided she would risk it.

She moved down on to the dance floor and started dancing close to her, behind her, bumping into her every now and then, and apologising. Soon the woman had turned and was dancing with her. Violet smiled at her and she smiled back. Violet moved in close and shouted 'Hi' in her ear. The woman shouted 'Hi' back. Violet wasn't sure what to do next. It had been so different with Katherine: they'd been behind the pool building having a cigarette, Violet had leaned forward and brushed her lips across Katherine's cheek, like it was an accident, so that if Katherine hadn't liked it she could pull away, but Katherine hadn't pulled away.

Violet stopped dancing. It hurt to think about Katherine; she had come to London so she didn't have to think about Katherine. She had come to Aphrodite Rising to forget Katherine.

'You OK?' The woman leaned towards Violet.

Violet smiled and nodded. She started dancing again, closer to the woman, putting her arm around the woman's waist. The woman put her hands on Violet's shoulders. Violet pulled her in closer and brushed her lips across her cheek. The woman didn't pull away, so Violet kissed her, on the lips – a loose-lipped kiss, which could lead on to other things, if the woman wanted too. Violet felt the woman's breasts against her own, big and soft and very warm.

The woman pulled away a little. 'Let's sit down.'

They found a seat in a dark corner. It was a little quieter, but they still had to shout to be heard.

'I'm Violet,' she said, thinking that if this went any further she should at least know the woman's name.

'Katherine,' the woman said. Violet's heart sank – of all the women in that great, huge club. 'Well, Kathy really; only my mother calls me Katherine.' Violet tried to concentrate; she was nothing like Katherine: her Katherine was tall and slim and had almost no breasts at all; her lips were thin and firm.

Violet kissed her again; Kathy's lips were full and soft. She kissed first Kathy's top lip and then her bottom lip, she slid her tongue along between them. They were nice lips; Violet decided she liked soft lips. Kathy was starting to respond to Violet's kisses, she opened her mouth a little, their tongues touched. Violet moved her arm so that her elbow rested against Kathy's breasts. They were so soft, Violet moved her hand down. She found Kathy's nipple and rubbed it through the singlet. She was wearing a bra. Katherine never had; she hadn't needed to. Violet felt Kathy's nipple harden. It was so big, like a saucer. Violet wanted to see it, to take it in her mouth and suck it.

Kathy moved away slightly, and Violet stopped her massaging. 'God, you're beautiful,' Violet said into Kathy's ear.

Kathy laughed and ducked her head. 'I've got to go to the loo.'

'Me too.' Violet followed her through the mass of women. She watched Kathy's bottom in her jeans wobbling slightly as she walked. She wanted to take one buttock in each hand and squeeze them.

There was a queue for the loo and, in the brighter light, Violet could see Kathy better. She was beautiful. She had a smooth, round face, light brown eyes and shiny brown curls. Violet ran her hand up Kathy's neck and through her hair.

'You are beautiful.' She said it again and kissed her. Standing up, she was taller than Kathy, and it felt odd to have to bend slightly – Katherine had been taller, so Violet was used to having to reach up. Violet pressed her body into Kathy's. She was so soft; Katherine had been thin and bony, all hips and ribs.

Violet pulled away from Kathy. She had to stop it, comparing everything about Kathy to Katherine. Katherine was past, gone – she was engaged, and Violet hoped never to see her again. She had to stop thinking about her, she had to get on with her own life, with other women. She looked at Kathy, who was now looking a bit worried. Violet smiled at her. She would get over Katherine. As many women as it took, Violet decided she would do it.

'You OK?'

Violet kissed her again. 'Perfect.'

Two women came out of one of the cubicles. One was a mixed-race woman with very short hair, who was putting something large and rubbery into her leather-jacket pocket. Kathy looked at Violet and giggled. Violet didn't really understand, but she giggled too. Kathy went in and Violet waited for her – she didn't need the loo, she just didn't want to risk losing Kathy so early in the evening. When Kathy came out and was washing her hands, Violet came up behind her and started kissing the back of her neck. She ran her hands over Kathy's stomach under her singlet.

'Not here,' Kathy said, and they went back out on to the dance floor. Violet rested one hand on Kathy's shoulder and the other on her bottom. They moved slowly together, ignoring the music, surrounded by hundreds of other lesbians.

'This is heaven,' Violet whispered in Kathy's ear. And she meant it: her first night out in London, at a lesbian club, a woman to dance with; it was heaven. If only Katherine could see it, Violet thought – and that ruined it. She pushed Kathy away and turned to leave.

'Fuck,' she swore, as she tried to get through the crowds of women still dancing.

'Violet.' She heard Kathy call her name and stopped. 'Violet, what's wrong?'

Kathy took her hand and they continued towards the door. Outside there were women queuing to come in.

'Come back to my place, it's just up the road.'

The queue of women watched as Kathy and Violet left. One woman, in an old-fashioned black lace dress and matching hat, looked like she was going to Ascot, not into a lesbian club. She caught Violet's eye and smiled at her. For a second, Violet felt a little unsettled, like this woman knew who she was.

'Violet?' Kathy pulled on her hand. 'This way.' Violet turned and followed her up the road. On the way, as they talked, Violet told her a bit about Katherine, and she was very nice about it.

'You'll meet lots of other lesbians,' she said, squeezing Violet's hand. 'That's the best way to get over someone, meeting lots of other women.' She reached up and kissed Violet.

It took them twenty minutes to walk to Kathy's place. 'We're nearly there,' Kathy kept saying.

The house, when they did arrive, was old and run down. 'It's a lesbian co-operative, there are eight of us. It's great.' Kathy started to make a cup of tea. As she filled the kettle from the tap and put it on the hob, Violet watched her.

'You know,' Kathy said, not looking at Violet, 'You're very good looking.' Violet didn't know. She knew that she looked like her oldest brother, and all the girls at her school thought he was dishy. 'And if you want . . . if you still want, you can stay the night.' She looked up at Violet then, shyly, and smiled.

Violet went over and kissed her lightly on the lips, and then on the neck. She pressed her hand into Kathy's breast. She smelt of sweat and soap, not the faint chlorine smell of Katherine. Violet remembered the last time she'd seen Katherine, lying back on the beanbag in the front room, skirt up, knickers off. Her head was thrown back, legs wide apart, fingers gripping the beanbag, waiting for Violet to finish what she had started. Violet closed her eyes tightly. At least she'd left Katherine wanting more.

She pushed Kathy's singlet up and took it off over her head. Kathy's bra was big and grey, fraying in places. Violet reached around and undid it, Kathy's breasts bursting out of it once freed. Violet stared at them; she couldn't hold one in her hands, it was too big, so she put her two hands around a single breast. She bent her head forward and kissed it. The nipple was enormous, and as Violet touched it with the tip of her tongue, it contracted. Violet took the nipple in her mouth and sucked it. Kathy was leaning back against the sink, her breathing faster now. Violet lifted up the other breast and sucked its nipple, then she put one hand under each and rubbed her face between them, her thumbs tracing circles around the nipples.

She straightened up and kissed Kathy – wet, soft kisses, with lots of tongue. She slid her knee up between Kathy's legs and pressed her hips into Kathy's groin. Kathy was rocking slightly against her. Violet let go of her breasts and undid the fly of those jeans. She tried to put her hand down inside, but they were too tight, so she eased them off over Kathy's bottom and down to her ankles. Her knickers were the same grey as her bra and the elastic was coming off in places. Violet tried to ignore that and slid her hand inside. Kathy's pubic hair felt soft and shiny, like the hair on her head. Violet ran her fingers through it until they slipped into the wet, soft flesh in the middle. Kathy breathed in sharply. Violet rubbed her fingers backward and forward through the wetness, resting her cheek against Kathy's stomach. Kathy's breathing was getting faster and faster, and Violet rubbed in time to it.

Kathy's knees were starting to buckle so, without removing her hand, Violet helped her slide down the sink unit until her bottom was on the floor. She kissed her once more and then slid down and put her face in amongst Kathy's pubic hair. Kathy gave a little groan. Violet flicked her tongue into the soft flesh. Kathy groaned again. Violet started licking, and rubbing with her thumb, slipping her fingers deeper and deeper into Kathy, who was leaning against the cabinet door, her head thrown back, her hands clutching at air. She was panting, little high squeaks, and getting higher, higher and faster. Under her tongue, Violet could feel the flesh swelling, getting softer and rounder and wetter. Kathy's right leg started to jerk spasmodically and then suddenly she screamed, a high piercing scream. At the same time her whole body went stiff and started to shake, and Violet felt Kathy tighten around her fingers.

There was a loud bang somewhere behind Violet and the sound of someone shouting, a woman. Violet tried to stand up, but she was halfway under the table and banged her head. She was also having trouble removing her fingers from inside Kathy. Kathy tried to stand up too, but her jeans were still around her ankles and she tripped, ending up on her knees, her chin just missing the edge of the table.

Someone came running into the room, screaming. Kathy tried to stand up again, but now she was laughing too hard to manage it. Violet saw a pair of legs come around the table towards them and stop. She crawled out and stood up with the table between her and the owner of the legs. It was a redhaired woman she had seen Kathy dancing with at the club.

'Katherine.' The woman exclaimed as she knelt down beside her friend.

Violet felt a moment of panic, hearing the name of the woman she was trying to forget and thinking that the redhead was calling her, before she came back to her senses and remembered it was Kathy's full name.

'I'm OK.' Kathy had dragged herself to her feet and was trying to pull up her jeans and put on her singlet at the same time. Then she sat down at the table. 'Oh God, how embarrassing.' She was still laughing, but Violet thought it could turn to tears at any moment. She didn't know what to do, and was starting to feel bad about the whole situation.

'Katherine,' the woman said again, and Violet decided it was time to leave.

'I've got to go.' She headed for the door.

'No, Violet,' Kathy called after her, but she was out the front door and running, all the way back to Brixton.

TWO
Katherine

Katherine chewed the end of her pen. She pushed away the pile of invitations she had finished addressing, one hundred and forty-nine of them, one to go. It was the hardest one of all, Violet's. Katherine chewed the pen some more. Until this moment Katherine had been quite confident that the wedding was a good idea. No, more than a good idea: the best thing that had happened to her. Now – well now she was chewing the end of her pen.

Her mother didn't even want her to invite Violet, but then her mother had never liked her.

'It's not that I don't like her,' Katherine's mother said, when she realised they weren't doing maths homework all those hours in the bedroom. 'It's just that if you go down that path, you'll have a difficult life.' 'That path' meant being a lesbian. 'I just want you to be happy.'

When Katherine met Sean and fell in love with him, her mother had been so relieved. Katherine had been too, and even though they had only known each other three months, she felt so right about the wedding. Until she had written 'Violet' on the one hundred and fiftieth wedding invitation.

'It was just a phase,' Katherine remembered telling Violet. 'There was nothing wrong with it, but I've grown out of it now.' They had sex after that, on the beanbag in the front room, but

Violet left before it was finished and she hadn't seen or heard from her since. She wanted Violet there at her wedding, to show her that she was definitely over it.

'Please do come,' she wrote on the invitation quickly, signing it Sean's name as well as her own. She sealed it, addressed it to Violet's aunt in London and put it in the middle of the pile of other invitations. Then she went to the phone and dialled Sean's number, hoping he was there. He answered.

'Hello?'

'Sean, do you want to come round. Mum's gone out and I thought . . .' Katherine wasn't sure what she thought, she wanted to prove to herself that she was doing the right thing. She wanted to have sex with him. They hadn't up till now, but suddenly Katherine wanted to very much. 'You know what we talked about,' Katherine could feel herself start to blush. 'I thought maybe tonight.'

'Katherine?'

She stopped blushing; who the hell did he think it was? 'No, it's Mother Teresa. Do you want to come round?'

'Are you sure?'

'Yes.'

'You said . . .'

Katherine had said she wanted to wait, and if Sean carried on questioning her then she might change her mind. 'Do you want to or not?'

'If you're sure.'

'Yes,' she said again. Sometimes she wanted to scream at him, he was so considerate.

'All right, I'm on my way.'

Katherine put the phone down. It would take him twenty minutes to drive over, but what was she going to wear? She ran up to her room and opened her wardrobe. All her clothes were so ordinary, there wasn't a sexy item among them. What would Sean think if he undressed her and she had on her old cotton knickers? The only other person she'd had sex with was Violet, and she hadn't been the least bit interested in what Katherine was wearing, but men were different. Her mother certainly dressed up for her boyfriends, lacy underwear, soft slinky dresses. Wouldn't Sean expect that?

And food – the first time with Violet, Katherine had cooked a huge meal, far too much for the two of them. She had burnt the pizzas, forgetting about them as they had sex on a rug in the back garden. Burnt to a crisp they were. Katherine smiled, if Sean was half that good . . . She stopped herself. It would be better with Sean, it would be beautiful and natural and, well . . . normal.

Katherine looked at her little single bed. She and Violet had made love there, and on the beanbag in the front room, and on the sofa, even on a kitchen chair. Katherine didn't want to do it in any of those places with Sean. It didn't leave many places, except perhaps . . . She went through to her mother's bedroom. She was out with Brian, her latest boyfriend, and would probably stay out tonight. Unless, of course, anything went wrong, which it seemed to do quite often.

Katherine looked at her mother's double bed. It was so big, a queen size, covered in a white throw. Like Alaska, Katherine thought. She would take Sean in there.

She caught a glimpse of herself in her mother's mirror. Her hair was a mass of wild curls, and smelled of chlorine where she hadn't washed it properly after training. She ran her fingers through it, but there wasn't time to wash it now. She looked herself over. She was in a T-shirt and jeans, as always. She pulled her T-shirt tight over her breasts and looked at her nipple through the stretched material. She hooked her thumbs into the waistband of the jeans and tried out a provocative pose, pouting a little. She just looked silly.

She opened the top drawer of her mother's dresser, her knickers drawer. She spotted a black lacy pair at the back and pulled them out. They looked like they had never been worn. There was something very odd about them, too many holes. Katherine realised they were crotchless, shoved them back in and shut the drawer. Sean would have to accept her as she was, like it or lump it.

She went downstairs to the kitchen and poured herself a vodka and orange. She didn't usually drink, as her coach forbade it. The vodka was her mother's, the orange juice hers. She thought Sean would probably want a beer, but there wasn't any, so she poured him a vodka and orange too, then drank hers standing in the kitchen. It was fifteen minutes since she had rung Sean, so he would be here in five. She drank his vodka and orange, poured another two and went and sat in the front room, but all she could see was the beanbag where she and Violet had had sex, and the sofa, and the rug.

She went back into the kitchen. The dishes needed doing, but she didn't think that was appropriate somehow, not just before she was about to lose her virginity. She finished the third vodka and orange and stood staring at the fourth. 'Her virginity'. Before Violet, she hadn't had sex with anyone, so strictly speaking she was still a virgin. She looked at her watch again, twenty minutes, where was he? She picked up the fourth drink and started on that. Her legs felt funny, as though her feet belonged to someone else and were far too big, forcing her to walk sideways, like a crab. She hoped Sean would arrive soon, before she fell over, threw up or passed out. That's what had happened the only other time she had got drunk.

She was halfway through the drink when the doorbell rang. She took a deep breath and went to answer it, her feet slapping against the floor tiles. Sean stood there looking red and puffy, sweating slightly as if he had run all the way over. Katherine looked over his shoulder; the car was there.

'Sorry,' he said. 'It wouldn't start.'

Katherine knew he was lying, as he drove a brand new Porsche of which he was inordinately proud, always showing off in it, saying how it would never break down. He stepped inside and gave her a kiss. He smelt funny. He kissed her on the lips and then down the side of her neck, his hands running all over her body. He moved them so quickly that it made her feel dizzy and she pushed him away.

'I thought you wanted . . .' Sean frowned.

'I do. I just need to breathe, that's all.'

'You've been drinking.'

'So?'

'Are you sure about this, I mean I don't mind . . .'

'Come.' Katherine took his hand and led him upstairs to her mother's bedroom.

'Is this OK?' Sean looked around the room doubtfully.

Katherine took off her T-shirt and threw herself backwards on to the bed. Sean stood and stared at her, at her breasts. He stared at them for so long that Katherine wondered if he was disappointed – they were pretty small. She put her hands up to cover them.

'No, don't.' Sean knelt on the bed and moved her hands away. 'They're gorgeous.' He touched them gently with his fingertips, and then leant forward and kissed them. A warmth spread from Katherine's nipples out through her body.

'Do you like that?' Sean looked up at her. Katherine smiled and nodded.

Sean didn't continue to kiss them as she hoped he would. Instead he turned his back on her and started to take off his clothes. Violet never took her clothes off, not even her shoes. Sean moved on to his T-shirt and then his trousers. He folded them on the floor and then stood in front of her in just his socks and underpants. Katherine wanted to laugh: she had seen him in his swimsuit often enough, but in his underpants he looked different, comical somehow. The pants seemed to bulge and Katherine put her hand out to touch him. She had done that a couple of times before when they were kissing and Sean had pushed her hand deeper into his lap. She knew what was there, she had seen pictures, but she had never seen one in real life.

Sean stepped closer, so her hand pushed into the bulge, and moved her fingers, trying to make out which bit was which. Sean closed his eyes and sighed. He leaned over her, so her hand could still fondle him, and started kissing her again. His hands ran over her body, down to the top of her jeans, and he undid her fly. He was breathing heavily now and the bulge had definitely grown. Katherine could feel something sticking out of the top of his pants. She rubbed her thumb over it.

'No.' Sean moved out of her reach.

Katherine didn't understand, she thought men were supposed to like that. Sean was still kissing her, and tugging at her jeans. She helped him take them off her, then Sean lay on top of her, kissing her more urgently now, and rubbing his bulge up and down her stomach. Katherine reached down to touch his bottom, but Sean said 'No' again. So she just lay there, her hands by her side, while Sean rubbed and kissed. He was making funny little grunting noises and Katherine wanted to laugh, but knew she mustn't.

Suddenly Sean got off and sat on the edge of the bed, his back to her, and grabbed his trousers. Katherine wondered what he was doing, he couldn't have finished surely? Then she realised he was putting on a condom. She leaned over to watch him. He had his penis in one hand and was rolling the condom down it. Or trying to, as he seemed to have trouble keeping it still. The idea of touching it made Katherine nervous, she reached out her hand, but Sean pushed it away.

He rolled her on to her back again and spread her legs with his. He slid his fingers inside her, she wasn't very wet so they felt hard and cold. He rubbed them around a bit, but before Katherine could relax and enjoy it, he took them out and pushed his condom-covered penis in. It was bigger than his fingers and at the wrong angle, so it didn't go in easily. Katherine tried to move to make it easier, but Sean was lying on her too heavily. He didn't seem to notice that she wasn't comfortable, he was concentrating too hard on pushing, in and out, faster and faster. In fact he seemed totally unware of Katherine, his face swollen and pink as he grunted with each push. She wanted to tell him to stop, because it was starting to really hurt, but she could see he was nearly there, and she didn't want to spoil their first time together. So she bit her lip and tried not to cry.

All of a sudden, his body went stiff and he jerked a few times and then rolled off. Katherine sighed with relief, as Sean smiled at her and kissed her on the cheek.

'I love you, baby,' he said, then he left the room.

Katherine curled up as small as she could and cried.

Before Sean was back, she heard the sound of a key in the front door. She jumped off the bed and hurriedly pulled on her jeans, tucking her knickers into her pocket. She straightened up the bed, found her T-shirt and put that on. She then ran down the stairs and met her mother going into the lounge.

'Hi,' she said as brightly as she could. 'Sean's here, we were just going over the wedding invitations.' She said it loudly, hoping Sean would hear. Her mother didn't say anything, just sat down on the sofa and stared at the floor.

'You OK, Mum?' It wasn't a good sign, her being home so early.

She still didn't say anything. Sean came downstairs, dressed and looking very pleased with himself.

'You'd better go now.' Katherine pushed him towards the front door.

'But . . .'

'I'll see you tomorrow.'

He tried to kiss her on the mouth, but Katherine turned her head so the kiss landed by her ear. She opened the front door and gently pushed him out, then closed the door quickly. She went back into the front room.

'Cup of tea?'

'Oh, yes, love.' Her mother looked up at her and smiled. Katherine breathed a sigh of relief. If it was something bad, her mother would have burst into tears at the suggestion of tea. She went into the kitchen and put the kettle on. When she went back to the lounge with the tea, her mother had put on some Simon and Garfunkel and was dancing to it. Very odd behaviour.

'Oh, Katherine.' She danced over to her. 'Oh, oh, Katherine, my little angel.' She kissed Katherine right on the lips. 'You'll never guess what.' She did a twirl. 'You'll never, ever guess.' She stopped and looked at Katherine.

'What?' Katherine asked. She had no idea what it could be that made her mother act so strangely.

'He's just gone and asked me to marry him, is what.' She hugged Katherine tightly, making her spill the tea. 'He only wants to marry me, Katherine.' She clung to her daughter and started to cry. Katherine started to cry too. She tried to tell herself that it was happiness for her mother, but she knew it wasn't.

'Two married ladies, we'll be, Katherine.' Her mother wiped

her tears away. 'Two old married ladies.' She laughed and twirled around the room.

Katherine watched her, knowing it was the thing her mother wanted most in her life, always had. She wondered if it was what she wanted, though. She thought about Sean, and the sex they had just had, and she remembered Violet. She left her mother to her dancing and went to bed. She pressed her hand against her still sore fanny and cried herself to sleep.

THREE
Violet

Saturday morning and Violet was feeling very pleased with herself. She had been in London less than a week, already had a job, and was on her way to look at a house. She had been staying at her aunt's in Walthamstow but they weren't wild about having her there, especially after she'd got in at 3 a.m. from Aphrodite Rising. Violet wasn't too keen on cousin Freddy, who was noisier than her twin brothers Jason and James put together. So, she went through *City Limits* and made an appointment to see a flat.

'Fourth woman wanted for women's house N8, NS, veggie, GCH,' the ad said, harmless enough. Violet had her *A to Z*. It was in Wood Green, further out than she had hoped for, but the price was right and they hadn't hung up when she said she was eighteen.

She arrived late, as the tube had stopped for no apparent reason between Seven Sisters and Finsbury Park, and then she had gone the wrong way out of the station. Still, it was only ten minutes. The house was a nice old Victorian terrace with an overgrown garden. A woman in a caftan sort of dress answered the door and looked at her hard and long.

'Sorry I'm late,' Violet said, wondering if the woman was annoyed – the staring was making her feel uncomfortable. 'I'm Violet.'

'More a pinky-orange,' the woman said. 'Anger and hurt. Violet is love.' Violet had no idea what she was talking about. 'We're having our lunch, you can wait in the front room.' She showed Violet into a room painted bright green and purple, with an ugly brown carpet. 'You're the sixth person we've seen today. It is very tiring, having to interact with so many different women, and you build up a big appetite. We won't be long.' She smiled at Violet and left the room, closing the door behind her.

Violet sat down on the sofa, which was cane and very uncomfortable. There were some cushions on the floor and she tried one of those, but it felt rude, like she was making herself too much at home. So she stood instead, by the fireplace, and looked at the pictures on the wall. There was a calendar with lots of stars and moons on it, a horoscope sort of thing, she imagined. And there was a picture of a statue which looked like a woman holding open her bits. On the wall opposite there were some paintings, like children's paintings. Under one was the word 'rainbow', though it looked to Violet more like a flower. On another was the word 'tree', but the picture was of a man stabbing a woman with a big belly like the earth. The third one had 'Julie' on it and was just a mess of colours in lines, circles and swirls.

The house smelt of roast dinners, though Violet was sure the ad had said vegetarian. Every now and then she could hear voices from down the hall. She looked at her watch: 2.35, and they were supposed to see her at two. She looked back at the horoscope calender. She was a Gemini, two-faced and fun-loving, but that was all she knew about horoscopes.

Then she remembered what the woman had said to her at the door: 'pinky-orange' and 'hurt and anger'. Maybe that was something to do with the horoscope – they had asked what sign she was on the phone. The woman had very dark eyes and Violet thought they could see right into your soul, if that was what it was inside you that wasn't flesh and blood. She imagined those eyes looking at her again, right at her. The nose under the eyes was a nice little turned-up one and the lips were red and full. She wondered what it would be like to kiss those lips; she closed her eyes and tried to taste them. It was hard to tell what kind of body she had under that caftan, but Violet imagined big breasts without

19

a bra, soft pink nipples that contracted up into deep red points. She moved down the body: the belly would be round, like in the picture of the woman being stabbed, and under it would be red pubic hair, a soft, full, clay-coloured mound.

She slid her hand down that body, feeling its softness and warmth under her hand, slipped her tongue between those soft lips and cupped the breasts, one in each hand. Pushing her knee between the soft thighs, she felt moisture seep from that mound. She felt the body pushing against her, rocking against her, opening up to her like a sponge when wet. Violet rocked with the body, feeling herself start to open and moisten. Her breathing was starting to shorten, and although she knew it was ridiculous – fantasising about a woman she had only said two words to – she couldn't stop now, so close to something real happening, happening to her.

The door opened behind her. Violet turned round quickly, hot and flushed. Three women came in, the one in the caftan dress, another in tie-dyed overalls and the third in jeans and a T-shirt.

'I was just looking at the pictures.' She clasped her hands behind her back. 'They're great, especially this one.' She pointed without looking, then saw her hand was nearest to the stabbing picture.

'Thank you.' It was the woman in the caftan. Violet felt herself blush.

'I'm Rainbow,' the caftan woman said. 'This is Tree' – she pointed to the one in the dungarees, a big woman with a square face and very short hair – 'and Julie' – who was black with short hair and a bored look about her.

Violet thought Rainbow was joking about their names, and almost laughed, but they all sat down on the sofa and looked at her very seriously. She soon realised they didn't joke about anything.

'Sit.' Tree pointed to a chair opposite the sofa. 'Obviously we have to ask women questions about themselves before we can decide if they are suitable to live with us.'

'We live completely communally, and it's important that we get on,' Rainbow added.

'Physically, emotionally, spiritually,' Tree cut back in.

SWEET VIOLET

'So here we go,' Julie said, smiling almost apologetically at Violet, before they started firing questions at her.

'What is your view on non-monogamy?'

'Who, do you think, is the most infuential writer of the twentieth century?'

'Why do you want to live in a women-only environment?'

'What have you done to address the inherent internalised sexism within you?'

'Do you believe in the mother goddess, despoiled guardian of this planet?'

And 'Do you like cats?'

Violet felt she only got the last one right. Isaac Asimov didn't seem to go down too well as 'most influential writer' nor did 'because men never clean the toilet' in regards to women-only environments. They also seemed to hold it against her that she didn't have a girlfriend, didn't know who Audre Lorde was and wanted to be a fitness trainer. They said something about playing into the patriarchal plot, whatever that was.

It took about half an hour, then Violet was shown over the house. The free room was a large one at the back of the house, overlooking the garden. It was painted pink and orange, with no furniture except for a chest of drawers.

'Helga slept on the floor,' Rainbow explained. 'It's very good for your back.' Violet tried not to look at Rainbow's breasts, although when she leaned to show her something in the bathroom, Violet got a look right down the caftan, and she wasn't wearing a bra or knickers.

Violet left, exhausted, passing another woman who was waiting to be seen. She was in denim dungarees with purple Doc Martens. Violet walked all the way back to Seven Sisters and got the tube from there. At least she had a job.

The job also came from *City Limits*, but that experience was so different from this one. It was with a lesbian removal company, run by two women, Fiona and Judy. Judy was a large woman with severely short hair, Fiona was small and wiry and had long hair in a plait down her back. Judy never smiled and Fiona never seemed to stop smiling.

21

Violet had met them at their flat in Dalston, an upstairs maisonette full of boxes and crates.

'Violet.' Fiona had answered the door. 'Pleased to meet you. Come up, mind the dog.' At that moment a black Labrador came charging at Violet, nearly knocking her over. It chased them up the stairs and stood panting at the top. Fiona pushed past it, but Violet stopped and rubbed it behind the ears, and it wagged its tail wildly.

'That's Well.' Judy stood in the kitchen washing the dishes.

'As in "Well of Loneliness".' Fiona looked at Violet as if she should understand something. Violet had no idea what she was talking about. 'Oh well.' Fiona smiled and the dog turned to look at her, making them laugh. 'Judy, this is Violet. About the job.'

Judy looked her up and down. 'She'll do.'

Fiona offered her coffee and when Violet declined, that was it.

She wished everything was that easy. On the way home from seeing the flat, the tube was crowded with people going to the Walthamstow market. The woman opposite dropped her umbrella as she sat down, and smiled when Violet bent to pick it up. With her pale blonde hair and light blue eyes, she looked a little familiar.

'I don't think you'll need it,' Violet said as she handed back the umbrella. There wasn't a cloud in the sky when she got on the tube.

'Oh I think I might.' The woman smiled again, but then the tube stopped and Violet lost her in the press of people getting off.

She walked along the High Street looking at the stalls. She didn't want to buy anything, even if she had the money to, but she didn't want to go back to her aunt's either. It started to rain out of an almost perfectly blue sky and, as she didn't have her jacket with her, she reluctantly headed back to the house. Freddie was watching TV and her aunt was doing the ironing.

'Oh, Violet.' She stopped on her way up to her room, wondering what she had done now. 'This came for you.' Her aunt pointed to an envelope on the table. 'And someone called Tee, or something like that, rang and said you had the room and could move in tomorrow if you wanted. They left a number.' Violet thought her aunt sounded a bit put out, but she was too shocked to try and figure out why. She didn't believe she'd got the room, and felt sure as she dialled the number that her aunt had got it wrong.

'Hello, Rainbow speaking.'

Violet started to blush again. 'Oh hi, it's Violet.'

'Violet, it's going to be great living with you.' Her voice sounded like honey. Violet tried to pull herself together. By the way Tree put her arm around Rainbow as they said goodbye, it was obvious they were a couple. 'Is tomorrow OK?'

'Yeah, great.' Violet wondered just what she was getting herself into and if it was really such a good idea, but at that moment Freddy came through the hall re-enacting *Nightmare on Elm Street*. She figured it couldn't be worse than that.

Her aunt was almost indignant when Violet told her.

'You can't just move in with complete strangers. What would your mother say?'

'But I can't stay here.'

'Why not?'

'It was only ever till I found somewhere.'

'What will I tell your father?'

'That I'm a grown-up, and quite capable of looking after myself.'

Violet turned and went upstairs to her room. She could hear her aunt dialling her parents' number. Violet didn't care – there wasn't anything they could do. Then she remembered the letter for her on the table. She didn't want to face her aunt again, but the letter looked interesting, clearly not from her mother. She stuck her head out of the door. Freddy was standing at the top of the stairs spitting bits of tissue papaer at his mother on the phone.

'Freddy,' Violet called him over. 'I'll give you fifty pence to go and get that letter for me.'

'Five pounds.'

'Sod off.'

'Mum, Violet swore at me.'

'All right, a pound.'

'Two, and I won't tell Mum you swore.'

'You already did, one pound.'

'OK.' He ran off down the stairs. Violet could hear her aunt being indignant on the phone. Freddy came running back with the letter. He held out his hand for the money, but Violet grabbed it and twisted it up behind his back, taking the letter out of his other hand.

'Mum!' Freddy screamed. She gave him a gentle push, then shut her door and put a chair against it. The envelope was made of fancy paper, thick and embossed with crowns. The writing on it looked familiar. Violet felt her heart race; it was Katherine's writing. She quickly opened it. Inside was a piece of printed paper:

'Mrs Wilson and Mr and Mrs Burton have the great pleasure of inviting you to the wedding of Katherine and Sean.'

There was a handwritten note with it: 'Violet, please do come, Katherine & Sean.'

As Violet stared at the invitation, the word 'wedding' kept coming off the page at her. She knew Katherine was engaged, but to be getting married! She couldn't believe it.

Her aunt was banging on the door. 'Your mother wants to speak to you.'

Violet screwed up the invitation and threw it on the bed. Then she picked it up again and tried to flatten it out.

'So what' she said aloud. 'So fucking what?'

'What did you say?' Her aunt banged on the door again. 'I can hear you, Violet Preston, and I'm going to tell your mother.' Violet heard her footsteps recede down the hall.

'So fucking what?' Violet said again. She picked up a pen from beside the bed. There was gap after her name, where a partner's name was obviously meant to go. Violet took a deep breath, then wrote 'Felicity' in the gap. She wasn't sure why she chose that name, it was just the first one that came to her. Then she needed a surname, and wrote in 'Hope'. 'Felicity Hope' – that's who she was taking to the wedding. She put the invitation under the bible that her aunt had thoughtfully placed beside her bed, then undressed and climbed into bed. Somewhere in London there was a Felicity Hope just waiting to be asked to a wedding and Violet was going to find her.

FOUR
Katherine

Katherine hated Sunday training at the best of times. Today was even worse; she hadn't spoken to Sean since they'd had sex and was dreading seeing him. She was angry with him, in an unfocused sort of way, for lots of different things. For being late, and lying about the reason; for not noticing that she hadn't enjoyed the sex; for not being as good as she thought he would be; and, although Katherine was having a hard time admitting it, she was angry with him for not being as good as Violet.

She changed quickly and got straight in the pool. She swam twenty lengths as a warm-up. The coach, Mr Williams, wasn't very pleased with her at the moment, because she wasn't doing as well as he thought she should be. While the other newcomers to the England squad were shaving tenths and fifths off their times, she was coasting along at exactly the same speed. If she didn't improve, she would lose her place in the squad, but she didn't know how to improve. They had looked at her technique: her start, her turns, everything was fine. Last week, in exasperation, Mr Williams had tapped her none too gently on the forehead with his large hairy finger and said, 'The problem's in here – you don't want it enough.'

Katherine did want it, she wanted it very much. She remembered training with Miss Phelps, in the lane next to Violet. Feeling

Violet there, wanting to beat her, needing to beat her, almost. And as Violet's times improved, so did Katherine's, always half a second ahead, a whole second. Except in backstroke, which was always where Violet beat her. Katherine had given up on backstroke, to concentrate on freestyle and leave Violet something she could win – and she did win. She was also good enough to make the England squad; she had been asked to try out and, unbelievably, said no. Violet claimed she didn't want to be the third best at something, but Miss Phelps said she was scared of failure, of trying for something and not making it.

Katherine stopped at the end of her twentieth length to catch her breath.

'Katherine!' Mr Williams called her over. She pulled herself out of the pool, seeing that he didn't look happy, which meant she was in for a rollicking.

'Katherine.' He didn't look her in the eye, staring instead at her chest. Katherine was aware of her nipples standing up through the Lycra of her swimsuit. She put her hands up to cover them, and then lowered them again.

'Haven't I been like a father to you.' It was a statement, not a question. Katherine nodded, even though she had never had a father and was sure fathers weren't supposed to stare at their daughters' breasts.

'I don't know what else I can do.' He shrugged and was silent for a moment. Katherine didn't know what to say. Mr Williams' gaze ran down her body, down her legs and back up to settle on her crotch. Katherine shifted uneasily, starting to feel hot, despite the cold night.

Mr Williams sighed. 'If you don't take a quarter off your time tonight, you're not going to Paris.' He walked away.

'But . . .' Katherine couldn't believe it, a quarter! Even without a quarter off, she was still quicker than two or three of the girls in the squad going to Paris for the international meet. Mr Williams was gone, off down the pool to shout at someone else. Katherine was furious and humiliated: to stop her going to Paris was outrageous, he couldn't do that; but she knew that he could, and would.

She felt someone behind her, it was Sean. 'Hi, gorgeous.' He tried to kiss her on the cheek.

'Go away.' She dived back into the pool. She wanted to shout, to scream, but it wouldn't be fair to take this out on Sean, even if she was angry with him. She swam under water for as long as she could. She would go to Paris, she'd show them. She reached the other end of the pool and surfaced.

'Out of there!' Mr Williams had his stopwatch ready and there were people lined up for the time trials. Katherine got out and joined the next group. She looked along the line: two of them she could beat with one hand tied behind her back, one was new and thought she was hot stuff, but Katherine could beat her too. The last was a girl called Phillipa, who was a bit older and had a bronze from the Commonwealth Games. She saw Katherine looking and smiled at her, a challenging sort of smile. She was tall and strong, better built than Katherine, and raised one eyebrow at her, nodding her head towards the pool like a dare. Katherine smiled back at her. Phillipa's time was better than Katherine's, but only by a fifth; if she could beat her . . .

Mr Williams blew his whistle for them to get on their blocks. Katherine took one last look along the line at Phillipa, who smiled at her. Mr Williams fired the starting pistol and Katherine dived from the blocks, hit the water, felt it flow over her body. She kicked hard with her feet and drew her arms strongly through the water. She sensed Phillipa, slightly behind her, swimming hard. Katherine increased her kick rate and breathed on every fifth stroke, and at the turn she was centimetres ahead. The last fifty metres, Katherine pushed herself harder than she thought was possible. It felt like she was going to explode with the pressure of it, like there was nothing else in the world but her, the water, and Phillipa, centimetres behind her and gaining ground. Katherine hit the wall hard with her hand and looked over to Phillipa's lane, to see her just arriving. As Phillipa turned to see where she was, Katherine smiled and waved, receiving a smile and a shrug of the shoulders from the woman she had beaten. For a second, in her cap and goggles, it could have been Violet. Katherine ducked under the water, her heart racing from more than just the exertion of the race.

A hand reached into the water and dragged her out – Mr Williams. He was looking at his stopwatch, and only then did Katherine remember her time.

'Well done,' he said, showing her the watch. 'A quarter. I see I just have to be firmer with you.' He put his hand on her bottom and pushed her in the direction of the changing rooms. 'I'll see you tomorrow.'

Katherine showered and changed. Phillipa came in while she was getting into her underwear, stopped and watched her.

'Well done.'

'Thanks.' Katherine tried to cover herself without making it too obvious.

'Where's that little friend of yours?'

Katherine knew she meant Violet, but didn't want Phillipa to know that. 'Which one?'

'The little butch backstroker.'

Katherine had to smile when she heard Violet described like that. 'She's gone to London.'

'Pity.' Phillipa started to strip off her swimsuit, not bothering to cover herself with her towel. 'She was cute.' She disappeared into the shower.

Katherine felt herself blush, but wasn't quite sure why. She was worried that Phillipa might think she was a lesbian, but she also felt a twinge of jealousy – Violet was hers and she couldn't imagine her going off with anyone else. She dressed quickly so she didn't have to face Phillipa again.

Sean was waiting for her in his swimsuit; she could see his penis outlined through the skimpy material and tried not to stare.

'Fancy a drink after?' He was standing too close to her.

'No, I need to go home.' She was going to say that she had a headache, but that was too clichéd.

'Oh.' Sean looked upset.

'It's Mum, she's getting married.' She hadn't meant to tell him and regretted it as soon as she had.

'Your Mum?' He sounded shocked. 'To Brian?' He obviously thought it was funny.

'Yes, Brian,' Katherine said angrily. 'They happen to love each other.'

'Sorry,' Sean said. 'Touchy subject, huh?'

Katherine couldn't stand it any more and walked away.

'Tomorrow? Can I see you tomorrow after training?' Sean trailed after her. He sounded so pathetic that Katherine felt sorry for him.

'All right, tomorrow.'

He rushed over and gave her a kiss. 'I do love you, you know.'

Katherine sighed, 'I know.' And she did know, she just wondered if that was enough.

The next night after training, and after Katherine had taken another fifth off her freestyle time, a group of them went to the nearest pub, a dive called the King's Head. They were all on orange juice, as Mr Williams had banned alcohol till after Paris. Phillipa came too and seemed to catch Katherine's eye every time she looked in her direction, and there was Matt, Sean's best friend. Matt was nearly the opposite of Sean – tall and dark with broad shoulders, loud and funny – and he looked at Katherine in a way that made her feel very uncomfortable.

Katherine sat next to Sean and he put his hand on her thigh under the table. She snuggled up close to him to try and avoid both Phillipa and Matt. Sean kissed her a lot, on the cheek and neck, and ran his hand in circles over her thigh, gradually working his way up to her crotch. Katherine tried to relax under his attention, but it felt wrong in such a public place.

Sean seemed to be reading her mind. 'Come on, I'll take you home.' He pulled her to her feet and winked at her. She got the impression the wink was more for Matt's benefit than for hers, but she didn't resist.

'I've really missed you,' Sean said as they got into his car. He leaned over and squeezed her breast. 'I loved it the other night, being inside you was just amazing.' He kissed her ear. 'I know you didn't . . . you know . . . but I'll make it up to you. I would have done, only your mother came home.' His hands were all over her now, pulling at her T-shirt, kneading her breast. He was breathing faster. 'You have to tell me what you like.'

Katherine couldn't think of anything worse. She couldn't say 'please do this' or 'please do that'. Violet had never asked what she liked, she had just gone ahead and done it. Katherine realised that Sean was at a bit of a disadvantage, being a man, but he couldn't expect her to tell him what to do.

Sean sensed her tension. 'What's wrong?'

'Nothing.' Katherine shook her head. Damn Violet, she had ruined everything; well, Katherine wasn't going to let her. She leaned over and kissed Sean on the lips.

'What I'd like is to go somewhere more private.' She put her hand on Sean's bulging lap.

'Really.'

Katherine squeezed the bulge.

'I mean . . . only if you're sure.'

She started to unzip his fly.

'OK.' Sean started the car and drove too fast to a lay-by in the woods, close to his house. Katherine wondered if he'd been here before and with whom. The idea rather excited her.

Sean got out and came around to open Katherine's door. He pulled her out and leant her against the car, which was cold on her back. He kissed her roughly on the mouth, pushed up her T-shirt and ran his hand heavily over her breasts. Katherine slid her knee up between his legs and rubbed it against his crotch.

'Oh God.' Sean started fumbling with her fly.

'No.' Katherine stopped him and turned him around so he was against the car. She knelt in front of him and started to undo his belt. He looked around.

'Are you sure you want to do this?'

Katherine ignored him and undid his zip, then pulled down his jeans. She didn't know exactly what she was doing – she had read about blow jobs and thought they sounded disgusting, but anything was better than having him inside her again. She pulled down the soft cotton Y-fronts and his penis flopped out. It was quite hard already. She licked the tip of it; it tasted and smelled a bit acidic.

SWEET VIOLET

Sean groaned and she licked it again. It wobbled around under her tongue, so she held the base of it and started licking it like it was an ice cream.

Sean put one of his hands over hers on the base of his penis, the other hand on the back of her head. He was moving his hips, back and forwards, trying to get his penis further into her mouth. Katherine opened her mouth a little, and tried to keep licking in time with his rocking. An image of Violet came to her, on the rug in the back garden, her dark head between Katherine's legs licking her clitoris. She tried to chase the image away, but it wouldn't go. Sean was moving her hand on his penis, up and down, faster and faster. Sean's head was thrown back and his breathing was getting quicker and quicker. Katherine wondered if it felt as wonderful to Sean as Violet's licking had to her.

Giving a blow job wasn't as unpleasant as she had thought, once you got over the smell and the taste, but her neck was getting a bit stiff. Suddenly Sean pushed her out of the way on to the gravel. He was leaning back on the car, his penis straight in front of him, pumping semen into the air, his face red and sweaty.

Katherine recognised the look, the same as when he was late the other night for their first time. So he had stopped for a wank. Sitting on the damp gravel, she started to laugh.

His penis shrivelled. 'What's so funny?' He carefully wiped it with a tissue and tucked it away in his Y-fronts before pulling up his jeans.

Katherine wasn't sure it was funny any more. 'I know why you were late the other night.'

'When?'

Katherine could tell he knew exactly what she was talking about. 'And you pushed me.' Katherine showed him her grazed palms.

'Sorry, I just didn't want to . . . you know . . . all over you.'

Katherine was laughing again. ' "Come". The word is "come". You should know that, that's why you were late! You stopped for a wank.' Katherine was angry now.

'Only so I wouldn't be too fast with you.' Katherine didn't understand. 'It happens so fast sometimes, it was our first time, I wanted to make sure it was . . . well, great. And I know it wasn't, but I will make it up to you, if you'll let me, please.' He looked like a little boy who'd just been told off. Katherine felt so sorry for him, she leant forward and kissed him on the cheek.

'After the Paris meet, OK.'

Sean grinned from ear to ear. 'It'll be the best, you'll see, just the best.'

Somehow Katherine doubted it. 'You'd better take me home.' She felt suddenly very tired.

They drove home in silence and had a long, soft kiss before Katherine went inside.

As Katherine lay in bed that night, she realised she didn't really understand Sean at all, or any men for that matter. They seemed as confused about sex as women were, and maybe it was just a case of telling him what she liked, because how was he to know otherwise? She reckoned men only knew what they liked because they masturbated so often, and she wondered if she should try it more often. She only did it occasionally if she couldn't get to sleep.

She ran her hand down her body and slipped her cool fingers in between her legs. She tried to imagine Sean doing it to her, that her fingers were his. She slid two fingers up inside her and rubbed her thumb over the top of her clitoris. She smelt the faint chlorine smell coming off her skin and before she could stop herself, it was Violet there with her, not Sean.

It was Violet's fingers exploring her, like they used to, then her tongue lapping at her, teasing her. She rubbed her fingers harder, and faster, up and down inside her, just like Violet used to do. She was wet now; her back was arching so her fingers could go deeper. She could feel the pressure building inside her, like it used to with Violet, building as she flicked her thumb across her clitoris and imagined it was Violet's tongue. Then she came, a moment of pure physical relief. It was over in a moment, such a small thing, Katherine thought, but so beautiful. Now that is what I like, she thought, and she fell asleep.

FIVE
Violet

Violet woke on Monday morning and wondered where the hell she was. The ceiling was blue and the walls were orange and pink. Then she remembered it was her new home; not that it felt anything like a home. Rainbow and Julie had greeted her warmly enough, but Tree had laid down a whole lot of rules that seemed rather extreme and unnecessary.

No men; no guns (it seemed that the previous inhabitant of her room had owned a gun and wasn't averse to waving it around when she was angry, which sounded like pretty much all the time); no meat, or products thereof; no honey or dairy products; house meetings to be held weekly and no excuses would be taken for missing them; there was to be a compulsory house outing to a poetry reading the following Friday; no tabloid newspapers; no pornography; no bleach products and, finally, no noise when Tree was meditating, which could be at any time day or night from what Violet understood.

They had all drunk a celebratory glass of organic apple cider and then left Violet to unpack. It didn't take long – she only had her backpack, and there was nowhere to put anything. Julie leant her some sheets and pillowcases and Violet set up a bed as best she could on the floor. Rainbow said she could get some foam from work, and Tree asked them to please be quiet.

Rainbow brought her up a hot-water bottle, and sat cross-legged on the floor to watch Violet set up her bed. She smiled all the time, which made her seem a bit simple. Violet felt nervous in case Rainbow could tell she was having fantasies about her.

'Do you want to know why we chose you?' she asked.

Violet hadn't really thought about it, except to think it was strange.

'I liked you immediately, especially because you are a Gemini, but also you looked very sweet when I opened the door to you, such a clean aura. Tree wasn't so sure, but then she didn't like any of the women we interviewed. Now don't be put off by her stern front, she's really a softy underneath it once you get to know her. Julie of course is so easy going – it's because she's a Libran and they're like that. Tree's Scorpio, of course.' Rainbow giggled. 'It is going to be so nice having you here.' She leaned forward to touch Violet's arm; Violet could see right down her dress to her pubic hair but Rainbow didn't notice.

'It was your aura that did it, it matches this room perfectly.' She hugged Violet, rubbing their breasts together. 'Sleep tight.' She kissed Violet's forehead and left.

Violet got out of her improvised bed and crept into the bathroom. It was cold and smelt of damp; she hadn't noticed it before because of the candles burning in there which had also hidden the fact that the light didn't work. There wasn't a shower, so Violet had an inch deep, lukewarm bath. She crept back to her room and put on her best jeans and T-shirt, because today was the first day of her summer course, a certification in Health and Fitness. Her mother thought she should have gone to Teacher training college and become a PE teacher. But Violet thought about Miss Phelps and couldn't think of anything that she would less like to be.

She set off to the tube and took the Piccadilly Line to King's Cross and changed to the Northern Line for Elephant and Castle. Travelling across town was exciting. She had only been to London once as a child, and they had stayed in Walthamstow and only ventured as far as Oxford Circus. She had to pinch herself now and then to prove she was really living in the capital.

SWEET VIOLET

The tube exits at the Elephant and Castle were very confusing and she managed to be twenty minutes late. She hadn't missed anything: the students were all just sitting around waiting for the course coordinator, who was also new and had also got lost.

The whole of the morning was taken up with introductions; they met the tutors and were shown around the campus. It wasn't what Violet had expected, it was just like school, only there were boys in her classes. They were mostly all muscle types who only seemed interested in girls in the class, and the girls only seemed interested in doing their hair.

They had lectures most days and were expected to get jobs in gyms as practical work experience. They were given sheets and sheets of paper, reading lists; diet and exercise sheets; gym addresses; more reading lists and rules and regulations.

In the afternoon they had some free time and permission to use the gym. The boys played basketball at one end and some of the girls used the gymnastic equipment. One of them was very good.

'She would have been picked for the Olympic team but she was too tall,' a short muscular woman informed Violet.

'Yeah?' The gymnast had a fabulous body, and knew how to use it, not just on the beam either. She was attracting a lot of attention from the men, and clearly enjoying it.

'Ow, I bet that hurt.' A short, slim man was standing beside Violet watching the display. 'I'm Garth, and you're the only interesting-looking person in the whole room – pleased to meet you.'

Violet was flattered. 'Violet.' They shook hands.

'A very firm grip, I like that.'

There was something about Garth that made Violet a bit uneasy, but she couldn't quite put her finger on it.

'So, what's your story?'

'Story?'

'Oh you know, everyone has a story. I was dumped by my boyfriend, hopped on the first bus to London – well, it was a train actually, but bus sounds more romantic, don't you think? And signed up for the first course that would have me. I hate sports, but I figure it's a good way to meet good-looking men and touch them, legally.'

Violet had worked out what made her uneasy about Garth. 'Boyfriend?'

'Yes, a boy who is a friend, I guess you've never had one of those.' Garth smiled, but he looked a little wary too, like he thought Violet might punch him.

'I've got four brothers. Enough to put me off men for life.'

Garth laughed, probably from relief as much as anything.

'Actually I lied, I do like sport. I rowed under-sixteen for England, then I stopped growing.' He shrugged.

Violet wondered how many others in the class had almost represented their country at something.

'I'm out of here, all this testosterone is getting too much for me. Ciao, bella.' He flapped his hand at her and left. Violet stayed and watch the gymnast some more – she didn't know bodies could be so bendy.

After that she went home, stopping at the corner store to buy some milk and corn flakes. She was halfway through the door, when she remembered that dairy products were banned. She sneaked the offending item up to her room, then rang Judy and Fiona to give them her new phone number.

As a celebration for being clever enough to find a flat, get a job and start a new course, and as a way of beginning her search for Felicity, Violet decided to go out for the night. She had read about a pub in North London that had a women-only bar and it didn't sound too far away.

As it turned out, she couldn't have been more wrong: the journey involved two buses and a long walk at the end. When she got there, The King's Knees was dim and quiet. The women's bar was out the back and nearly empty. The woman behind the bar looked her up and down disapprovingly when she bought her beer. She was a pretty woman with short dark hair and lovely skin, but her eyes were cold.

'You know this is an anti-racist pub,' the woman said as she handed Violet her beer.

'Yeah?' Violet looked around the room; she couldn't see any black women in the bar.

'Yeah,' The woman leaned across the bar towards her, 'And anti-SM and all, so you just watch it.'

Violet didn't say anything; she took and paid for her drink and found a seat in the corner.

'Welcome to London,' she thought to herself as she settled down to watch the few other women who were there. The pub filled up gradually and another woman came to work behind the bar. Violet noticed the first woman talking to most of the women she served, in that threatening, lean-across-the-bar sort of way, so it was nothing personal.

The women in the pub were a more homogeneous group than at Aphrodite Rising: jeans and checked shirts, with the odd pair of tie-dyed trousers and a few pressed chinos thrown in. There was one woman Violet thought she recognised, sitting with a group, wearing jeans and a white shirt with a wing collar that made her look like a choirboy. She was deep in conversation with another woman, but when Violet caught her eye, she smiled back like she knew her.

The women all sat round in groups talking to each other, occasionally moving off into other groups. Violet got lots of looks, but no one made a move to come and talk to her. Violet didn't mind, she wasn't much good at talking. She spotted a woman in the group closest to her who appeared to be single. She was a bit older, maybe mid-twenties. She smiled a lot and had curly hair like Katherine's.

Could she be her Felicity? What would Katherine think of her? She was pretty; she looked like good fun. Her breasts were bigger than Katherine's and her hair was nicer – she had nice eyes too, but so did Katherine so that didn't count. Yes, Violet decided, she would do as Felicity.

She tried to make eye contact with the woman; managed it briefly a couple of times and even got a smile out of her. Violet got up to buy herself another beer and brushed past the woman.

'Sorry,' she said. The woman smiled at her again. Violet walked behind her again on the way back to her seat and brushed the woman's hair with the back of her hand; it was smoother than Katherine's.

She sat down. 'Stop it,' she told herself. When was she going to stop thinking of Katherine? For God's sake, it was three weeks since it had all ended. Four weeks since Katherine had come back from her training camp, glowing with good health and happiness, talking of nothing but the camp and the others on it, especially Sean. 'Sean did this and Sean did that and he's so funny.' How he won a medal at the World Championships, how he thought Katherine was so good, and how the coach thought she'd be ready for the next Olympics in Seoul in 1988. It was only two years away.

Violet tried to be pleased for her. Violet could have gone for the team try-out, she might even have got a place as the third-string backstroker. But Violet couldn't see the point in being the third best at anything.

'Excuse me,' the woman Violet had been watching was sitting beside her. 'Is this seat taken?'

Violet had forgotten all about her. 'Yes,' she said, meaning it was free.

'Oh.' The woman looked disappointed. 'Are you waiting for someone?'

'No,' Violet said, realising her mistake, 'and no, the seat's not taken — I meant yes it was free. Sorry.'

The woman laughed. 'I'd offer to get you a drink only I see you've already got one.'

'Yes,' Violet said and the woman laughed again at the monosyllable.

'I'm Angela. You're not really with it.'

'No, I was thinking.'

'Your ex, I bet.'

Violet looked at her. 'No . . . How . . .?' She wanted to get a grip on this conversation.

'I recognised the look . . . on your face. There's a lot of it about. Look.' Angela pointed to a woman sitting by herself across the room, looking into her glass with a bittersweet expression. 'She's thinking of her ex too.'

Violet smiled, seeing another woman alone by the bar. 'And her?'

'Yep.'

'And her?' Violet pointed to another woman by the door.

'Oh no,' Angela said. 'She's thinking about sex.'

'Sex?'

'Yep.' Angela laughed.

'How can you tell?'

'I can always tell when a woman is thinking about sex.'

Violet looked at her, realising she was flirting with her. 'Really?' She asked provocatively, imagining kissing Angela, running her fingers through those curls.

'Yes.' Angela said. She had soft brown eyes and a little nose. Violet leaned forward and kissed her cheek, just a glancing kiss. It was how she kissed Katherine the first time, like it was an accident. But Katherine hadn't moved away and Angela didn't either. Instead, she turned her cheek so that their lips met. It was a gentle kiss, almost chaste. Violet sat back in her seat and Angela smiled at her.

'So, what's your name?'

They went outside, Angela claiming it was too hot. She leant up against the wall and Violet stood in front of her. Angela was about the same height but broader than Violet. She was a teacher at a sixth-form college in Kent, teaching psychology. As Violet listened, she watched Angela's mouth. It was a tidy sort of mouth, not big and soft like Kathy from Aphrodite Rising, but softer than Katherine's. Her breasts under her T-shirt looked bigger than Katherine's too. Violet wanted to touch them, feel them with the very tips of her fingers, and watch their nipples contracting. She wanted to kiss Angela again, a less chaste kiss, with tongues and teeth as well as lips. She wanted to slide her fingers inside Angela and watch her face as she came. But she knew that, first, she had to listen to her talk about herself and even tell her a bit about her own life. She wasn't good at that part of it, but she knew it had to be done before they got to the bit she was good at.

Violet realised she had lost the thread. Angela was looking at her as if she was expecting an answer.

'Sorry,' Violet said. 'I was thinking about sex.'

Angela laughed; she had a nice soft laugh. 'I can see that.'

Violet kissed her then, harder than before, one hand leaning against the wall, the other on Angela's waist. Angela put her hands on Violet's shoulders, which was oddly distracting. Katherine had never touched her when they kissed. Violet wondered now what Katherine had done with her hands. She remembered seeing them clutching the beanbag while Violet knelt between her legs exploring that soft, wet flesh with her tongue.

Now Violet had lost the thread of the kiss. Angela leant back against the wall.

'Sex or ex?' she asked.

Violet didn't understand.

'You were thinking again.'

'Sorry.'

'Only be sorry if it was the ex.' Angela smiled.

Violet smiled back. 'I'm not sorry then,' she lied.

'You want to come back to mine?' Angela held Violet's hand and looked coy.

'Yes,' Violet said, maybe a little too quickly.

'It's not too far.'

Clearly all lesbians lied about how far they lived from the pub or club. It took ages to walk to Angela's, through the back streets of Dalston. Violet was about to give up on her when she announced that they were there. It was an upstairs flat with its own front door.

'I share, but Alan's out tonight. He's gay.' It seemed like a defensive afterthought.

Angela unlocked the front door and then locked it again before she started up the stairs. Violet stopped her halfway up the stairs and kissed her. She pressed both her hands against Angela's breasts and could feel that she wasn't wearing a bra – Katherine didn't either and Violet liked that. She pulled Angela down so that they were sitting on the stairs; then pulled up the T-shirt so her hands were against Angela's skin. She felt the nipples harden.

Violet nuzzled Angela's neck and ran her tongue round Angela's ear.

SWEET VIOLET

'Let's go to the bedroom.' Angela tried to stand up. Violet pushed her back down.

'Haven't you ever done it on the stairs?' Violet lifted Angela's T-shirt again and bent down to lick her breasts.

'I'm worried about slipping,' was the breathless reply.

Violet put her arm between Angela's legs. 'Better?'

Angela didn't answer, but Violet took her silence as a yes. She unbuttoned Angela's white jeans while sucking her right nipple and then her left. She worked her way back up to Angela's face, kissing and licking. Angela put her arms around Violet's neck and they kissed deeply, their tongues chasing each other around, in and out of their mouths. Violet rocked her arm gently against Angela's groin and with her free hand pinched on a nipple.

Angela started moving her hips, lifting and dropping them against Violet's arm. Violet slid her free hand down into Angela's knickers. There wasn't much room in there and her hand was at an awkward angle but she managed to get her thumb into the wet bit and, almost as soon as she touched it, Angela arched her back and let out a low grunt, her body twitched slightly and then relaxed. Violet waited a moment to see if that was it. It was. Angela sat up grinning.

'Mmm,' she said as she took Violet's head in both hands and kissed her on the mouth. 'That was great.' She took Violet by the hand and led her the rest of the way up the stairs to the kitchen.

'I need to pee now. Put the kettle on.' She waved vaguely in the direction of the cooker and disappeared into the bathroom. Violet looked round the small kitchen. It was painted dark green and red, which made it feel very small, and crammed with papers, letters, bills and newspapers. Violet filled the kettle from the tap and put it on the cooker. She looked round for some matches, couldn't see any, walked up the few steps to the lounge and didn't see any in there. She looked in the bedroom. There was a double bed and clothes everywhere, but no matches, so she went back into the kitchen. She was about to call out, when she heard Angela talking very quietly. Then she saw the cord of the phone leading from the table and disappearing under the bathroom door. She crept over to the door and lent her ear against it.

'Give me ten minutes,' Violet heard her say, 'and then come in quietly.'

Violet straightened up and hurriedly sat back down at the table, pretending to read a week-old *Guardian*. There was a flush of the toilet and Angela came out.

'I couldn't find matches,' Violet said.

'It's self-lighting.' Angela pushed a button and the flame came on under the kettle.

'Oh.' The cooker at her parents' needed matches.

Angela came over to Violet and kissed her. 'It's your turn now,' she whispered in her ear as she ran her hand over Violet's breasts. If Angela meant she was going to do it to her now, then Violet couldn't think of anything she would like less. She moved Angela's hand off her breasts.

'Actually, I think I'll go now.' She stood to leave.

'No.' Angela sounded angry. 'No,' she said again, adjusting her tone. 'Please stay.'

'I don't want to miss the last bus.'

'I'll give you a lift home – I've got a motorbike. Really, I want you to stay.' She had hold of Violet's hand and was pulling quite painfully on Violet's thumb. 'If it's because you don't want me to do it to you –' Angela was trying to be coy again and Violet decided it didn't suit her '– that's fine, you can do it to me. I really –' she looked up at Violet through her lashes in a bad Princess Di impersonation '– really liked it.'

'Who's coming in ten minutes?'

'What?' Angela let go of Violet's hand.

'Give me the keys.' Violet held out her hand.

'I don't know what you're talking about.'

'Just give me the keys.'

Angela went into the bathroom and came back with the keys. 'You lesbians are so narrow-minded.' She held out the keys for Violet to take. 'No fun at all.'

If Angela wasn't a lesbian, then what was she? Violet started down the stairs, aiming to be well gone before Alan came back.

Angela followed her down. 'You're missing out on half the fun. No one is all one way or the other, we're all a bit bisexual.'

Violet had the key in the door; she unlocked it and stepped out. She didn't look back.

'There's nothing wrong with being a bisexual!' Angela shouted down the street after her.

Violet laughed. God, she loved London, it was full of crazy people.

SIX
Katherine

On Friday, Katherine climbed on to the coach outside the pool for the journey to Paris, and her first international meet. There had been swimmers from other countries at some of the meets she had been to in Britain but this was her first fully fledged international – important enough to be televised – and she was nervous. It was a long trip and boring; made even more uncomfortable by the fact that Mr Williams had ordered boys and girls to sit apart. The girls had the front of the coach, and the boys had the back, with Mr Williams, Steve the physio and the very unattractive Mrs Jenkins sitting between them.

Mr Williams lectured them for the first hour of the trip on the twin evils of sex and alcohol before a big meet. He left out the lesser evils of cigarettes and too much fatty food, because he was partial to both of those. Katherine tried to catch Sean's eye over Mrs Jenkins' head, but caught Matt's instead and blushed when he smiled and winked at her.

On the ferry they ate under strict supervision. Sean tried to persuade Katherine to join him in a cabin, but she declined. She didn't really believe what Mr Williams said about sex before swimming, but she felt she was lucky to be on this trip and didn't want to blow it.

They were staying in a hotel on the outskirts of Paris and were

SWEET VIOLET

sent straight to bed on arrival. Katherine was down to share with Phillipa. Mr Williams promised them that he and Mrs Jenkins would be up all night prowling the corridors. 'So no one, not even engaged couples –' he looked over at Katherine '– are to be about.'

Phillipa had been to a few international meets before: 'It doesn't matter what city you're in, it's all faceless hotels and swimming pools. The only difference is the language of the signs above the changing rooms.'

Katherine went into the bathroom, cleaned her teeth and changed for bed. She was excited and nervous. She kept telling herself it wouldn't be any different to the meets in England, but it didn't help. Partly she was nervous because she had a good chance at a medal – several if she was lucky, Mr Williams expected big things of her. She snuggled into her cold, single bed. Phillipa was in the bathroom; Katherine could hear her moving about, the toilet flushing, water running.

When the door opened, she pretended to be asleep, though she could see Phillipa walking around the room naked. Then Phillipa sat on her bed cross-legged and started humming tunelessly. After about ten minutes, she got under the covers and seemed to fall asleep.

Katherine was a million miles from sleep; it was ten o'clock and they had to be up for breakfast at six-thirty. There was one way that she knew would send her off, but she wasn't sure about doing it in a room with someone else, even if they did appear to be asleep. If she didn't sleep, though, she wouldn't swim well, and if she didn't swim well, she would be letting the team down. She slid her hand down under the covers and inside her pyjama bottoms. OK then, she thought, I'm doing this for the team. She rubbed her hand over her mound and slipped her fingers inside. At first, nothing much happened. She ran her thumb backwards and forwards over her clitoris, just getting the feel of it. She tried to imagine it was Sean touching her – she knew it wouldn't work, but she felt duty-bound to try. Then she pictured Sean and her in the showers soaping each other down, but Matt appeared from nowhere and joined in. Katherine found this strangely exciting, so she threw in Phillpa for good measure, and without her thinking about it, Mr Williams, Steve and Mrs Jenkins appeared. They were all naked, all touching each other, then she stepped in and they all started touching her: Sean kissing her, Matt rubbing soap over her breasts, Mr Williams rubbing it over her back and Phillipa ... Katherine found Phillipa on her knees in front of her gently running her fingers up the inside of her thighs.

Katherine opened her eyes; the sensation was so intense that she wouldn't have been surprised to find Phillipa there beside her. She wasn't of course; she was in her own bed breathing gently in and out. Katherine closed her eyes again. Now Sean and Matt were kissing, their hands holding each others' faces, their legs intertwined, Mr Williams off to one side watching them, his penis in his hand. Phillipa's tongue was lapping at Katherine's clitioris.

Katherine was getting very wet; she tried to keep her breathing quiet so as not to wake Phillipa, but the more she tried, the harder it was. Katherine found it terribly exciting to be fantasising about someone who was in bed next to her. She had lost Sean and Matt, Mr Williams too, and now there was just her and Phillipa, but soon Phillipa was gone too and there was just her own thumb rubbing, faster and faster. The effort to keep quiet was making her feel dizzy. The tension was building inside her, she rubbed faster and harder, the tension built until it reached a pinpoint, and then it burst like a tiny firework. She let out a long sigh, and waited while the minute contraction in her vagina stopped. She listened to see if Phillipa's breathing had changed, but it sounded the same. Katherine curled up on her side and went to sleep.

She woke in the morning to Mr Williams banging on their door. 'Rise and shine girlies, it's show time.'

Phillipa was still asleep, one arm over her eyes and a half-smile on her face. Katherine slipped into the bathroom and had a quick shower.

Phillipa was sitting on the edge of her bed with her head in her hand when Katherine came out. 'God, I hate this.' She rushed into the bathroom and slammed the door; Katherine could hear her throwing up. Wondering if she should try and help her, she knocked tentatively on the door. 'Phillipa?'

'Fuck off,' was the reply.

'OK.' She went downstairs but there wasn't anybody else about and it felt very early. Breakfast of toast and orange juice was laid out. Katherine helped herself and went and sat by the window. It was grey outside: grey sky, grey building, grey cars going past. Claire, another new girl, came in, picked up some food and then came and sat next to Katherine.

'Nervous?'

'Not really,' Katherine lied.

Claire looked at her dubiously. 'I think I'm going to be sick,' she said. Katherine looked back out of the window. Others started arriving – Sean and Matt came in, laughing and joking. They grabbed some food and came and sat next to Katherine, moving Claire out of the way.

Sean snuggled up to Katherine. 'Sleep well?'

She nodded, guiltily remembering her fantasy.

'On our honeymoon, we'll be in a hotel like this.' He squeezed her thigh. Katherine felt even guiltier, and as if on cue, Phillipa walked in.

'I've got to go.' Katherine stood up. 'To get my things.'

She met Mr Williams by the lifts. 'Where are you off to?' he asked.

'To get my stuff.'

He was staring at her breasts. 'The bus leaves in ten minutes.'

'I'll be there.' In her room, Katherine sat on the edge of the bed. She felt so flustered; she had to calm down. She remembered some breathing technique her mother had tried to teach her: in and out in a figure of eight, very, very slowly. Her mother listened to Japanese music while she did it, all plinky and plonky, every morning. It drove Katherine nuts. She settled herself comfortably and tried it, but it just made her feel giddy and no calmer. It felt like she had done it for ages, but when she looked at her watch it was only five minutes. She cleaned her teeth, packed her bag and went downstairs again. She just had to hope there would be someone in each of her heats with whom she could make it a personal contest, someone enough like Violet.

★

Phillipa was right about the pool: the main difference between it and any other was that the signs were in French. They warmed up for half an hour, then Mr Williams handed them their race schedules: Katherine had two in the morning and then a big gap before the other two in the afternoon. The relay and finals, if she made them, were on Sunday.

Butterfly was her first race; she was in the second heat. Phillipa was in the first and won it. Then it was Katherine's turn; she stood on the blocks and looked along the line at her opponents. She was in lane three, in four was a German girl, built like a tank, the favourite to win. The girl looked Katherine over and then looked away as if dismissing her as competition. OK, thought Katherine, if that's the way you want it. The starter put them on their marks, the gun went off and Katherine threw herself into the water. She swam the first fifty metres hard; at the turn she was just behind the German. In the last fifty she could feel the German pulling away from her, she remembered the look the girl had given her and found the strength from somwhere to catch her up, touching the wall just one-fifth behind her. She was second, and it was a personal best, taking nearly two-fifths off her previous. Mr Williams actually smiled at her.

Sean came over and gave her a hug, Matt slapped her on the bottom. Katherine went to the changing room to put on a dry swimsuit and to get some peace and quiet. Phillipa was sitting huddled in the corner, shivering.

'You OK?'

She nodded. 'Just cold.'

Katherine took a dry towel out of her bag and handed it to her. 'Thanks,' said Phillipa.

Breaststroke was next; it was Katherine's weakest race and she didn't expect to do well, although she had the second fastest time of the England squad. She had a fast heat: a German, two French, two Russians and an Irish girl. She came in third, but with another personal best – or PB as they called it. If she were lucky she would qualify for the final as the fastest third place.

She had an early lunch and watched the other races. Matt won his breaststroke heat and Sean came second in his butterfly. Phillipa bombed out of her breaststroke; Claire came third in the backstroke and cried. There was a team meeting at one o'clock and Mr Williams shouted a bit, then soft-soaped them. Katherine supposed it was good for morale.

She had an easy freestyle race; she was in lane four, the favourite lane and coasted in well under her PB. If Mr Williams shouted, she was going to say that she was conserving energy for tomorrow, but he had moved on to shout at someone else. Phillipa was in the second heat, and came second, to the German tank. Both Matt and Sean qualified for their freestyle finals.

The bus took them back to the hotel, where they had dinner and then an hour of free time before bed. They couldn't leave the hotel and the physio called them in one by one to check them over. Katherine was tired and, after the physio had poked his fingers into her shoulders and declared her fit, she went up to her room. Phillipa was curled up on her bed and Mr Williams was shouting at her; she had bombed out of her two-hundred-metre freestyle race as well as the breaststroke. Katherine waited in the hall until Mr Williams passed her, silently patting her head. Phillipa had locked herself in the bathroom and Katherine could hear her crying.

Katherine went back downstairs. Matt was there, looking very pleased with himself; Sean was off with the physio.

'So?' Matt sat down, uncomfortably close to Katherine. 'You want to play?' He left her wondering what exactly he was suggesting for a moment and then produced some cards.

'OK.'

'Strip poker.'

'How about snap?'

Matt shrugged and they started. Katherine won almost every time – Matt's hand would be a second too late and land on top of hers, staying there just a bit longer than was necessary. When Sean arrived, Katherine was actually pleased to see him. The three of them played until Mrs Jenkins come through and hurried them off to their beds at nine o'clock.

'I wish neither of us had done so well today,' Sean whispered in

Katherine's ear in the lift. 'Then we could have had the night to ourselves.'

Katherine couldn't agree. With so many finals tomorrow and especially the relay, she was more than happy about having an early night.

Phillipa was curled up on her bed. Katherine cleaned her teeth and changed for bed. In the bottom of the toilet were a clump of white pills; she fished them out and took them through to Phillipa.

'What the hell are these?'

Phillipa looked at them. 'Aspirin?'

'Like hell they are.'

'Oh don't be so sanctimonious, everyone takes them.' She put her hand over Katherine's and crushed them into her palm.

Katherine pulled her hand away. 'That's cheating.'

'Oh yeah? Look how much good they did me.'

Katherine went back into the bathroom and washed her hand.

'I should try your method,' Phillipa called through to her.

'What?' Katherine came back into the bedroom.

'A little wank before sleep.' Katherine felt herself blush. 'You can't have thought I was asleep. What was it, you and little Sean on a beach somewhere, the water gently lapping?' Phillipa got off the bed and came towards her; she took hold of one of Katherine's hands and pushed it between Katherine's legs. 'Little Sean and his wham-bang thank you ma'am. If you want a man, and I'm not sure you do, you'd be better off with Matt. Bigger, brighter and altogether much better.'

Katherine pushed her away and headed for the door.

'If you're going to tell Mr Williams about the pills, I wouldn't bother. He was the one who gave them to me.'

Katherine stopped. She hadn't been going anywhere in particular, and although she was almost certain Phillipa was lying, she was deeply shocked by the possibility that Mr Williams could be giving swimmers drugs.

'I'm sorry.' Phillipa's tone had changed completely. 'I just . . .' She started crying.

Katherine didn't know what to do. She still wanted to leave, but she couldn't help but feel sorry for Phillipa.

She went and sat on the bed next to Phillipa, who snuggled up against her. Katherine put her arm around her and patted her tangled hair.

'So why did Violet go to London?'

'She wants to be a fitness instructor.'

'And she couldn't do that in Coventry?'

'She got on a really good course.'

'Maybe she couldn't bear the thought of you and Sean.'

'I . . . we . . .' She was too tired to lie. 'It was over.'

'I bet she was good.'

Katherine started to blush again. Phillipa looked up and saw.

'That good, huh?' She laughed. 'So it wasn't Sean you were thinking about then, last night. It was Violet.'

Katherine felt herself blush even more and tried to get off the bed, but Phillipa held on to her arms.

'Oh my God.' She sat up so her eyes were level with Katherine's. 'It wasn't Violet either.' She moved her face closer to Katherine's and gently touched her cheek against Katherine's. Katherine could feel Phillipa's breath against her skin, she smelt slightly of chlorine just like Violet had. She noticed her breathing was faster and so was Phillipa's. Their lips seemed to be drawn closer together, they touched, just barely touched. Katherine was feeling hot and dizzy; she turned her head to one side. Phillipa's lips touched her neck; her hand was on her neck and moving down towards her breasts.

'No.' Katherine got off the bed. She stood with her back to Phillipa, trying to catch her breath. 'No,' she said again.

She went into the bathroom and cleaned her teeth again, washed her face and sat down on the toilet. She was engaged to Sean, she had five races tomorrow, what the hell did she think she was doing? She tried some of her mother's breathing, in and out, very slowly. After a while she started to feel calmer.

When she came out of the bathroom, Phillipa wasn't there. She curled up in her bed and did some more breathing, till slowly she fell asleep.

SEVEN
Violet

Violet wasn't looking forward to the house outing. She didn't know the first thing about poetry and she didn't relish the thought of spending the whole night with her housemates. Julie seemed OK, although she had only seen her a few times in the week. She was a psychiatric nurse and worked the oddest shifts. Rainbow wasn't too bad either, although she was a bit wet, always talking about auras and star signs. Tree was a nightmare; Violet couldn't do anything right according to Tree.

Violet had mentioned, only in passing, how messy the house was, and didn't anyone ever do the dishes? Tree stopped in the middle of her breakfast. 'That is your issue Violet. We have moved beyond the middle-class need for tidiness, it is a male preserve. If you find the house too messy, then you deal with it.'

Middle class! Violet had never been called middle class before in her life; her father was an electrician.

Over the same breakfast, Rainbow had teased her because she had never been out of the country. 'It's so mind-expanding to immerse yourself in other cultures. Greece is just heavenly.'

That evening, both Tree and Rainbow were stunned and amazed that she had never had hummus, a foul-smelling, grey gloop that they were trying to force on her.

'Guess us middle-class kids aren't fed this stuff.' She was being ironic, but neither Tree nor Rainbow noticed.

Violet decided that they had chosen her, not because of the colour of her aura, but because Tree thought she could mould her into being a proper lesbian. A 'proper lesbian' being a feminist, separatist, man-hating lesbian, just like they were. All other types of lesbians, in their books, were traitors to the cause and didn't deserve the name lesbian. Tree even went as far as calling all men 'fuckers' and refusing to speak to them. She referred to heterosexual women as breeders and gay men as faggots. Violet had only lived with them for five days, but she knew she definitely didn't want to be a lesbian like that.

Still, it was only one Friday night out of the rest of her life and, for the sake of some sort of peace in the house, she was going to go. Tree and Rainbow were taking a weekend out from Greenham to go to the poetry reading, and they let Violet know that she was privileged to have them make such a sacrifice on her behalf. Before that, though, there was college to attend, and she had her first removal job that afternoon.

So far, college had been fairly easy: anatomy lessons, sport psychology, some silly aerobics classes. Garth was about the only one in the class who talked to her, and he was quite funny, in a weird sort of way. Violet didn't really understand how a man could want to sleep with another man, but she didn't feel she was in any position to pass judgement. Still, he made the otherwise boring classes more bearable.

Friday was a half-day, and in the afternoon she caught the tube to Finsbury Park where she was meeting Fiona and Judy. She was early, so she sat on the wall of the house in the sun waiting for them. She remembered waiting for Katherine like this once in Coventry, to walk with her to swimming training. Violet lived right on the opposite side of town, but it was nice to walk with Katherine. They wouldn't hold hands or anything, but Violet thought that the people they passed could see that they were together and she liked that.

Violet sighed. Was she ever going to get over Katherine? She imagined Katherine in white at the wedding, a big hooped skirt, a veil and white flowers strewn in her curly blonde hair. She could see Katherine's eyes, their deep blue and her lips, smiling, looking up at Sean. She had never met Sean, but Violet imagined him as blonde and built, tanned, like someone off *Neighbours*. She pictured the church, decked out with white flowers, Katherine's mother in a blue dress and matching gloves – and there was Violet in suit with bow tie and cummerbund, ready to give Katherine away.

She would get over Katherine, she had had sex with two women already and she had only been in London two weeks. Sure, both times had been a bit strange, but the first two nights she went out she had scored. As it turned out, neither of them had been her Felicity, but it had been easy enough. She wasn't going to be too fussy; she just wanted someone to take to the wedding who would prove to Katherine that she was over her. Someone beautiful, clever, funny, a good body would be nice, and their own car. And of course they had to be good in bed, or under the kitchen table, or on the stairs. Violet didn't think she was asking too much.

The van arrived and Judy and Fiona jumped out.

'Sorry we're late,' Fiona said. 'The traffic was awful.' Judy just growled.

They spent the afternoon loading boxes into the van and then unloading them again halfway across London, or so it seemed to Violet. The women moving were obviously a couple; they argued all the time about almost everything. Fiona and Judy said nothing to each other or to Violet. The house they were moving to was huge. Each box had a room written on it, but one of the women would direct Violet to another room, then the other one would shout at her to put it back in the room written on the box. They were like some comedy double act. Violet wondered what was in it for them to stay together when they seemed to dislike each other so much. She hoped the sex was good.

When they finished they stopped in a small, grim pub for a drink.

'How long?' Fiona asked Judy.

Judy thought about it for a moment. 'Two months.'

'Maybe three.'

Judy nodded and they laughed.

'How long they'll stay together,' Fiona explained, seeing Violet's confused expression. 'Lesbians always split up after moving.'

'Oh,' Violet said, then, 'Why?'

'Because,' Judy got in before Fiona could answer, 'They're bloody stupid. Something's wrong with their relationship so they buy a house together to fix it, like hets having babies. Never works.'

'Oh.' Violet still wasn't sure she understood.

They dropped her home about six. Violet went to her room and got out her reply to the wedding invitation. She put it in its fancy envelope, licked it and sealed it, went downstairs again and out the front door. Just in front of their house was a postbox. She took a stamp from her pocket and posted the invitation.

'See you there then,' she said aloud, and then she looked around, hoping no one had heard her. She went back inside and up to her room, where she got out an exercise book she had bought for her course and not yet started. In it she wrote:

Finding Felicity
1. 1 Sept Aphrodite Rising. Kathy at her house, kitchen floor. Wrong name.

As an afterthought she wrote: 7/10. Then:

2. 5 Sept The King's Knees. Angela, her place, stairs. Too weird, bisexual. 3/10.

She closed the book and put it under her pillow. She didn't want Tree reading it, as she had a feeling it wasn't very politically correct. She felt much better though.

'Come on, Violet,' Julie called through her door. 'We don't want to be late.'

The reading was in Holborn House, a warren of a place that was tucked out of sight off Southampton Row.

'It's run by women for women,' Rainbow whispered excitedly in Violet's ear.

Julie looked around the room and sighed, she was the only black woman there. 'You would think I would be used to it by now,' she said. 'They even asked me to read. I haven't written a poem since I was six. They are that desperate.' She looked around again. 'Guess I'm going home alone again tonight.'

Violet didn't really understand, although she had overheard Rainbow telling someone that Julie only went out with other black women. Violet had been disappointed to hear that, because she thought Julie was very beautiful. Still, it was better not to sleep with your flatmates.

She wouldn't be making any exceptions for Rainbow, either, and not just because she was lovers with Tree, but because Violet found them both disturbingly unclean.

'The council fund this place, it's just fabulous.' Rainbow was bouncing up and down in her excitement. 'I mean, women have achieved so much.'

The women who had organised this event hadn't managed to achieve getting the seats set up or rigging the microphone. They all had to pitch in and help, with Tree and Rainbow spending some time in the lighting box trying to get the induction loop working. In the end it was announced that deaf women could sit in the front to make lip-reading easier. Fortunately, there were no deaf women there; in fact, there were hardly any women there at all.

Violet looked round to see if there were any likely candidates for Felicity. Most of the women there were wearing a variation on the baggy tie-dyed look, with lots of dangly earrings and bangles. Violet couldn't see a single woman that she fancied. They all had that wet look that Violet associated with Patricia Masters, the girl responsible for Violet being expelled from her first school after they were caught kissing. They had met later at swim meets and Violet had heard Patricia and Miss Phelps having sex in the toilets one night when everyone else had left . . .

Violet had caught them by accident. She and Katherine had been kissing behind the swimming pool building after training.

SWEET VIOLET

Katherine had left and Violet needed a pee. She saw the door into the pool wasn't locked so she went in. It was a bit spooky in there alone, so she moved quietly. She heard voices in the changing room but couldn't see anyone. She went through to the toilets and the voices were louder but she couldn't hear what was being said. She went into the first toilet stall and quietly closed the door. As she was pulling down her jeans, she noticed feet under the dividing wall. White sneakers with a pink trim, facing towards the toilet. The voices were still faint and coming in short, out-of-breath sentences.

'Yes, do it,' she thought she heard. The feet moved and she saw knees in white trousers.

'Oh yes,' she heard. The sneakers, she knew, were Miss Phelps's. The voice she hadn't recognised at first. Violet realised that if she stood there, they might see her feet. She couldn't pee, because they would have heard that, but she couldn't leave either.

'Do you like that?' Miss Phelps's voice was muffled.

'Oh yes.'

'Am I good at this?'

'Yes.'

Violet carefully sat down and tucked her feet up under her. She was torn between embarrassment and being turned on.

'Do you want me to stop?' Miss Phelps again.

'No, no.'

'No what?'

'No, please.'

'Please what?'

'Please, Miss, please, please.' The voice got higher and higher and more out of breath. 'Please, Miss, please, Miss . . .' There was some grunting and gasping. Violet got quite turned on by this.

'Oh, oh, oh,' the voice whimpered.

'Yes?' Miss Phelps sounded out of breath too.

'Oh yes.' The yes had sounded like more of a cry – and of pain than pleasure. There was silence for a moment, then sobbing.

'There, there.' Miss Phelps sounded embarrassed. 'Don't cry now.' They left then and Violet was nearly locked in for the night.

Fortunately, Patricia had forgotten something and Violet was able to sneak out as she came back for it.

Violet smiled to herself. Even though Patricia had been eighteen at the time, Violet knew she could have still got Miss Phelps into so much trouble over that. She never quite knew why she didn't.

Julie was asking her what she wanted to drink. There was no beer, only non-alcoholic drinks and some dodgy-looking food: chickpea salad and home-made bread. The others were having carrot juice, which looked grey and lumpy. Violet decided to leave it.

There was lots of kissing and hugging and squealing as if meeting long-lost friends. Tree and Rainbow introduced Violet and Julie to everyone, other women with names like Celeste and Phoenix. They looked her up and down as if assessing her for something, her political right-on-ness, Violet supposed, knowing she failed on almost all counts, even aside from her leather shoes.

They all tried to hug her as if welcoming her into some secret society, and when Violet resisted they seemed offended. One woman called Carol tutted and wagged her finger at Violet.

'That Violet needs to get in touch with her feminine side or she'll fracture,' Violet heard her say to Rainbow.

'I know,' Rainbow whispered back. 'We're going to work on that with her.'

Violet would have said something but the readings were about to start, only forty-five minutes late.

The first woman up had more bangles than most and huge earrings. She read a long poem about a woman bleeding in the desert and meeting some goddess. It didn't rhyme and, although Violet knew nothing about poetry, she knew that particular piece sucked. The same woman read several more poems, fortunately not as long, but equally tedious. As she started on her fourth poem, Violet decided it was time to go to the loo. She stayed there as long as she could, even wetting and drying her hair with the hand dryer.

On her way back in, she noticed a familiar-looking woman at the back of the room, out of place in a black dress and Ascot hat. Violet sat down beside her.

SWEET VIOLET

'Did I miss anything?'

The woman looked at her and shook her head. A different woman was at the front, reading a poem that sounded remarkably like the first woman's poem. Violet wondered if she should just leave. Fiona said the Honey Pot was the place to go on a Friday night. Violet didn't want to waste a Friday night listening to tedious poems, surrounded by unfanciable women – not if her Felicity was somewhere else waiting for her.

The compère announced another reader, Belinda Kelly. The woman sitting next to Violet stood up and made her way to the front, smiled nervously at the audience and started reading a poem. Violet couldn't hear a word of it.

'Louder!' someone near Violet shouted. Belinda looked up, embarrassed, and cleared her throat. The compère mucked around with the microphone and discovered it was turned off. Belinda stood back and watched, nervously. When it was sorted, she stepped forward, smiled and started again.

The poem was short and funny, about her cats and how they were better than lovers. Violet clapped loudly at the end of it, a few women turned and gave her dirty looks. Belinda's next poem was also funny, about a complicated mathematics equation, and turned into a love poem to a mathematician.

Her last poem was called 'Two Fat Ladies'; there was some tutting when she said the title. The poem was about bingo and a woman waiting for the number 88 to come up for a house. It was touching and funny and so cleverly written that Violet could see the woman sitting there, sweating for that last number. Violet clapped and called for more at the end; most of the other women sat in stony silence. Violet couldn't understand it; they had applauded and whistled after the dreadful readers before Belinda. Violet figured there was something more than poetry going on here.

Belinda left the microphone and hurried through the hall with her head down. She collected her bag from beside Violet and left the room. Violet followed her out and found her standing by the lift, staring at the closed doors. She didn't turn when Violet came and stood beside her.

'I liked your poems,' Violet said, trying not to sound too awkward.

'Thanks.' Belinda still didn't look up.

'I'm Violet.' She realised that Belinda hadn't pressed the call button on the lift, so she pressed it for her. 'Do you want to go for a drink?'

She didn't answer and Violet realised she was crying. The lift arrived as Belinda stepped into it, Violet followed her.

'They're very funny, your poems.' Violet was starting to feel embarrassed now. Belinda took off her hat and wiped her eyes. She looked at Violet and smiled weakly. 'Thanks.'

Violet remembered she had a tissue in her jacket pocket. She took it out and offered it to Belinda, who blew her nose. The lift reached the lower ground floor and they both got out.

'Stupid cows,' Belinda said suddenly. 'I don't know why I come.'

Violet laughed – the outburst seemed so out of character, she looked like butter wouldn't melt in her mouth. The woman sitting at the reception desk looked up at them and frowned.

'Come on. There's a pub round the corner,' Belinda said, sweeping past the reception desk. Violet followed her, smiling sweetly at the woman behind it, whose frown deepened. Violet decided she liked Belinda, as anyone who could invoke such disapproval had to be worth knowing.

The pub was genuinely just around the corner, not a twenty-minute walk. Belinda found a seat in the corner while Violet bought the drinks: a beer for herself and a double gin and tonic for Belinda.

She smiled at Violet as she came back with the drinks, a proper smile this time, one that reached all the way to her light blue eyes. Violet smiled back. Belinda wasn't exactly pretty; she was too pale to be pretty. Her hair was on the pale side of sandy and her skin looked almost transparent, but her eyes were lovely and when she smiled properly her whole face sort of lit up.

'So,' Belinda said after downing half her drink, 'what's a nice girl like you doing in a God-awful place like Holborn House?'

SWEET VIOLET

Violet laughed again. 'Oh, I share house with Rainbow and Tree and Julie.'

Belinda cast her eyes heavenwards. 'Those women,' she sighed. 'Why is it that those who harp on the most about being oppressed are the most oppressive?'

Violet didn't know what to say, but Belinda didn't seem to expect an answer. Neither of them said anything for a moment.

'I really did like your poems,' Violet said when the silence seemed to go on for too long, 'especially the last one.'

Belinda smiled again. '"Two Fat Ladies", too right off for that audience. I think they only invite me because I've had things published, to give them some credibility. I'll say no next time, I swear I will.' She finished the rest of her drink.

Violet went and got her another drink. She wondered if Belinda could be her Felicity, but she couldn't imagine making love to her, or that she would want to make love to Violet. She imagined Belinda was a double-bed sort of person, surrounded by candles and champagne and chocolate and an older, more experienced lover. Violet liked that picture. She imagined Belinda slow-dancing in a pale floating dress, with an older woman wearing a dinner jacket, very formal and upright like a couple from *Come Dancing*, smiling into each other's eyes. She couldn't see Belinda letting her take her under the kitchen table two minutes after they had met. Actually, she couldn't see how anyone would let someone do that, but they did.

Belinda was looking at Violet. 'Where did you just go?'

'To the bar.' Violet didn't understand.

'No, in your head.'

'Oh.' Violet felt herself start to blush. She decided to tell half the truth. 'Just ballroom dancing.'

'Do you?'

'Not really.'

'I do. It's lovely, you should try it.'

'I think I will.' Their eyes met and held for a moment. Violet felt as though something had happened but she wasn't sure what. Suddenly Belinda was reaching for her hat.

'Have to go,' she said, standing up. 'My boys are waiting.'

'Your boys.' Violet felt terribly let down.

'Harold and Vincent, my cats.' Belinda laughed and left the pub.

Violet sat on for a little while, finishing her drink and trying to decide what she thought about Belinda. She hoped to see her again but had no idea where. After she had found her Felicity, maybe she would look for her again.

EIGHT
Katherine

In the morning, Phillipa arrived back just before Mr Williams' wake-up knock. She didn't say anything to Katherine about the dramas of last night, just went straight into the bathroom. Katherine went downstairs for an early breakfast and when she came back to the room to pack, Phillipa had gone. She sat on her bed for some more breathing, which did make her feel better – maybe there was something in it after all.

Back at the pool, her schedule for the finals was similar to the heats: butterfly then breaststroke – she had made the final with the fastest third place – and in the afternoon, freestyle and the relay. This time, though, she would be watched all over Europe – the TV cameras were everywhere.

For the butterfly, she was out in lane six with Phillipa in two and the German in four between them. She gave Katherine another dismissive look. Katherine took a couple of deep breaths before the gun went off. On the turn she was behind the German and another swimmer; she couldn't tell where Phillipa was. In the last fifty metres she gave it everything she had, every ounce of strength, and a few more that she didn't know she had. She came in third, another PB, just in front of Phillipa, and the German girl won. As they were presented with their medals, straight after the race, Mr Williams nodded in approval. Matt won silver in the men's butterfly, but Sean didn't look very happy about his own fourth place.

For the breaststroke final, Katherine was in lane one, the loser's lane. She didn't feel fully recovered from the butterfly, but she was determined not to come last. She made a good start and a great turn to come fourth, with yet another PB.

After that, she changed into a dry swimsuit and had lunch. The freestyle was her big one and the physio gave her a prepartory shoulder massage as Mr Williams watched. She expected a speech but he didn't say a word. Meanwhile, Sean was taking the bronze in the men's backstroke.

Suddenly she was up again, on the blocks waiting for the starter's gun. She was in lane four, next to the German; Phillipa was on the other side of her, staring straight ahead. They had a false start, the German being too keen. Katherine hated those; she liked to dive in dry, feel the shock of the water.

Out of the pool and back on to the blocks and they were off properly, Katherine cutting through the water, clean strokes and a beautiful turn. Gliding like she belonged there, just her and the water, then finally the wall, drenching the timekeeper, touching first, a clear heartbeat ahead of the German, with Phillipa splashing in third.

Katherine was over the moon; she hugged Phillipa, pulling her close over the lane divider. She could see Sean and Matt cheering her and even Mr Williams clapping. She climbed out of the pool and Mr Williams hurried her off towards the changing rooms. Sean still managed to land a kiss on her cheek and Matt patted her bottom. The changing rooms were empty and Katherine sat down to try and catch her breath. Mr Williams had warned her that she still had the vital relay ahead of her. She smiled to herself, a gold medal. She had won other golds, but this was the first time she really felt like she was representing her country, beating the German who was the European Champ and twenty-six years old. Katherine wondered if Miss Phelps had been watching on TV. She knew her mother would be, and Violet? Tears welled up in her eyes, Violet could have been here with her! What would she think when she saw Katherine winning?

Phillipa came in looking tired and a bit sick.

'Well done,' Katherine said, knowing it would sound a bit hollow. Phillipa nodded and headed for the showers, still in her swimsuit.

Claire came rushing in. 'They want you for the medals, they're waiting.'

Katherine went and dragged Phillipa out of the shower. 'Medals.' She hoped Phillipa hadn't taken any more of the pills, not just because it was cheating, but because it could louse up their relay.

Phillipa followed her out and accepted her medal, staring at the floor the whole time, dripping wet. Katherine climbed on to the top stand when her name was called. The whole stadium seemed to explode in sound around her. She smiled and waved and shook the hand of the French official who put the medal around her neck. She smiled and waved some more and then it was over.

She went back to the changing rooms, knowing she was missing Sean's big race, because she needed to rest before the relay. Other girls came in and out, getting changed, packing up their bags. She could hear the sound of races going on, shouting and cheering, and she hoped Sean did OK. It would nice if just once he beat Matt, though that seemed unlikely. She fingered her medal on the seat beside her and smiled.

The relays were last and as the changing room emptied out, Claire came to get Katherine. Phillipa was already there with Mr Williams and Beverly; she threw Katherine a veiled look. Katherine soon found out why: Mr Williams had changed the order; he wanted Katherine to swim anchor, the last and most important in the relay. Katherine had started as third swimmer and then worked her way up to second and then first. She wasn't at all sure about swimming anchor, but Mr Williams wasn't having any arguing.

'Sorry,' she whispered to Phillipa, who just shrugged.

The waiting while the others swam was awful. Phillipa gave them a slim lead, which Claire couldn't quite hold on to and which Beverly lost completely, slipping back to third behind the Germans and the French. Katherine was swimming against the German tank, who dived in first with Katherine a clear second behind her. The first fifty metres were a struggle – nothing about her swimming felt comfortable or natural, every bit of her hurt. Her turn wasn't good either; she could see the German half a length in front of her. She suddenly remembered Violet saying 'I don't want to be the third best at anything.' Katherine gave an extra kick; something in her body changed and she was back in tune with the water instead of fighting against it. She made up a foot and then another until she was level with the German and, just at the wall, a fingernail ahead.

She felt like she was going to burst, her head was so tight. The timekeepers were consulting; she wondered if they were going to disqualify someone and worried that she had left the blocks too quickly. Mr Williams was hovering around the timekeeper, his own stopwatch clamped in his hand, following every move of the head judge.

Katherine was too tired to care now. She just wanted to get out of the pool, curl up somewhere warm and dry and go to sleep. The judge said something and Mr Williams punched the air with his fist, the most animated Katherine had ever seen him. They had won, by one tenth of a second. The tank glared over at Katherine, who smiled at her, saying, 'See you in Munich.' She pulled herself out of the pool. Beverly and Claire came running over, dragging Phillipa, to give her a hug, and Claire was crying again.

They all hung around to watch the men's relay. Matt had won a bronze in the freestyle final and Sean had come fourth. Sean was swimming first in the relay; two brothers, Ian and Patrick, swam second and third, and Matt was the anchor. They were second after Sean's hundred, first after Ian's and back to second after Patrick's. Matt swam the first fifty metres well, turning in second, just behind the Irish swimmer, but in the last fifty, the German coasted past him and so did the Frenchman. Mr Williams looked gutted and Sean threw his goggles on the floor in disgust.

The relay medal presentation was very subdued, as a lot of the teams had already left and the English men's team were in no mood for cheering. Phillipa finally smiled, though, and Beverly and Claire didn't stop smiling.

They got straight on the coach after getting changed. Now the swimming was over they were allowed to sit anywhere they liked.

SWEET VIOLET

Mr Williams even produced a bottle of champagne for them and handed it to Katherine first.

Sean came and sat beside her. 'Well done.'

'Thank you.'

Sean was obviously disappointed and quite angry. 'You know what it was? Why we lost that relay?' He checked to see that Mr Williams wasn't within earshot. 'He spent the night banging Phillipa in our bathroom.'

'Who?' Katherine was shocked; she had wondered where Phillipa had gone.

'Matt! That's why he bombed the relay.'

Katherine felt something more than shock, she was angry as well. 'Phillipa swam really well.'

'What the hell's that supposed to mean?'

'Nothing.' She didn't know why she should be angry. Just because she and Phillipa had nearly kissed and then Phillipa went running off to Matt, why should that make her so angry?

'Come on.' Sean said pulling her to her feet.

'Where to?'

'The back seat.'

'Oh Sean, I'm tired.'

'Matt and Phillipa are back there.'

'Then definitely not.'

Sean leaned closed to her. 'It was amazing last night, listening to them. I could hear everything. They'd left the door open so I could see –'

'Sean, I don't want to know.'

'She was bent over the bath and he was on his knees pumping her doggy-style. Here.' Sean put her hand on his crotch; there was a definite bulge there. 'I'm that hard just thinking about it. Matt said it was a real turn-on knowing I could hear it all.'

Katherine could picture the scene: Phillipa's smooth, tanned body against the white of the bath, Matt's hairy bottom bobbing up and down, and Sean crouched on the floor, his eye to the door and his penis in his hand.

'I'm going down there.' Sean stood up again and started down the aisle.

67

Katherine was horrified – fancy eavesdropping on other people having sex! – but the image of Phillipa's thighs and Matt's bottom stuck in her head. She stood up, knowing she had to make sure Sean didn't do anything stupid. Phillipa and Matt were stretched out along the back seat, Matt on top, his hand disappearing up Phillipa's jumper. Sean grinned from ear to ear when he saw Katherine, and let her slide past him into the corner.

'I want us to try again, Katherine. I can do better.'

'We can't do it now.'

'I've got condoms, genuine french letters!'

Katherine heard Phillipa groan quietly.

'I think he's got his fingers down her pants,' Sean whispered in Katherine's ear. Phillipa groaned again. Sean put his hand up Katherine's T-shirt and fondled her breast. Then he slid it down over her stomach to the top of her jeans. 'Let me.'

Phillipa was groaning softly, close to an orgasm. Katherine leaned back so Sean could undo her jeans; he put his hand down inside her knickers. Phillipa's groans had turned to little gasps. Sean's finger slid deeper, through her pubic hair, and found her clitoris, Katherine drew a sharp breath.

'Sorry,' Sean moved his finger away.

'No.' Katherine couldn't believe it. 'That was good.'

'Oh.' Sean put his finger back on it. Phillipa's gasps were getting higher.

'Now move it,' Katherine instructed Sean, when he seemed at a loss. He did so, but too hard. 'Softer.'

'OK.' He did as he was told, rubbing backwards and forwards. Katherine was getting that light-headed feeling, with Sean breathing heavily in her ear and, further away, the sound of Phillipa so close to coming. Then Katherine heard a high sigh and knew that Phillipa had done it. Sean was still rubbing away, but Katherine was suddenly not in the mood any more. She pushed his hand away.

'Sorry, I'm just too tired.'

He sulked for the rest of the trip, but Katherine was beyond caring and curled up in a seat by herself for sleep.

Her mother collected her from the pool where they were

dropped off at nearly two in the morning. She had videoed all the TV coverage and wanted to show it to Katherine along with cuttings from all the papers with Katherine's name highlighted.

'I'm so proud,' she kept saying. 'My little girl, I always said you were a fish.'

'Mother, please, I need sleep.' It was three before Katherine finally got to bed, and she fell straight to sleep with her medals under the pillow.

NINE
Violet

When Belinda left her in the pub, it was still only 10.30. So Violet had found her way to Oxford Street and then down Regent Street to the Honey Pot, as recommended by Fiona at work. There was a small queue and a male bouncer. Inside, everything was plush, red velvet and black chrome. Everyone stared up at her as she walked down the stairs that led to the bar and a poorly lit dance floor. Violet went straight to the bar and bought herself a beer, then found a table in the corner where she could sit and watch.

It wasn't very crowded but more and more women were coming in, so she felt she had timed her arrival perfectly. The women coming in seemed a slightly different lot to Aphrodite Rising and The King's Knees. The most obvious difference was the hair; there was so much of it. Dresses too, big taffeta ones, like something out of *Saturday Night Fever*, with an underlit dance floor to match and lots of loud disco music. At least the songs had words, unlike the Aphrodite music, and Violet even knew some of them.

There was a lot of looking too, with women walking around the room, checking out other women. Several glided past Violet's table and gave her the once over. Violet felt a little uncomfortable, until she realised there was no harm in it, and that it would make it much easier to see who was single.

She was on the lookout for her Felicity, of course. But tonight, after the tedium of the poetry reading, she was beyond caring what they looked like – as long as they weren't tall, with blonde curly hair, called Katherine, or bisexual. On the dance floor in front of her was an almost infinite array of women to choose from. She had liked Kathy's big breasts a lot, the other night, although she could have wished for nicer underwear. And she remembered being disappointed when she peeled back her own dear Katherine's jeans to find little girlie knickers with embroidered flowers on them, having always fantasised about black lace.

A big group of women came in; a sports team of some sort, maybe. They were drinking pints of beer and leering round at the women on the dance floor. There were two big women in the group, who seemed to be the centre of things, racing down their pints and putting the empty glasses upside down on their heads when they had finished. There was lots of back-slapping and laughing. After several beer races, they moved on to the dance floor, clowning around, taking the piss out of each other's dance styles. Violet forgot about finding Felicity for a moment and just watched them enjoying themselves. So many of the other women there looked like they were at a funeral.

Then one of the women spun past Violet and fell over. Violet leaned forward to help her to her feet and before she could object, the woman was spinning her around the dance floor, clamped against her ample breasts. At first, Violet wasn't at all sure she liked being swept off her feet, but the woman was bigger and stronger than she was, so she just had to go with it. As she relaxed into it, she actually began to enjoy it; the woman was a very good dancer, guiding Violet easily around the other dancers. At the end of the song, she escorted Violet back to her seat and bowed deeply. Violet sat down, laughing and shaking her head.

The woman went back to her group and started dancing with the other big woman, a tango that didn't go with the music. They moved so well together that Violet felt they must be lovers. She was disappointed that neither of them could be Felicity, and consoled herself with another beer. It was getting late, if she didn't find Felicity here soon then it wouldn't happen tonight, and she only had two more months before the wedding.

The music slowed down and everyone on the dance floor seemed to be doing slow dances in pairs. Violet watched the couples move together, it seemed at that moment that every woman in the room was part of a couple except Violet.

Suddenly the two big women tangoed through the crowd, scattering couples before them. They came over to Violet, scooped her up between them, and carried on tangoing. Violet had no idea how to tango, but she didn't need to as, stuck between the two women, her feet hardly touched the floor. Then they dipped unexpectedly and she lost her footing completely and tripped. The woman who had danced with her first caught her just before she hit the ground. Their eyes met and for a second Violet thought they were about to kiss, but the woman pulled away at the last moment, dumping Violet on the floor.

'Oh my God, I'm so sorry.' She picked Violet up and dusted her off. 'Listen,' she said, her mouth almost on Violet's ear. 'We're going back to ours to party, do you want to come?' She was still holding Violet's arm, even though Violet was safely on her feet again.

'OK.' There clearly wasn't a Felicity here in the club, she might as well have some fun for the rest of the evening.

The two women were Grace and Peaches (not her real name but that was what everyone called her, and she did look a bit like a peach). Grace was the one who had danced with her first. The three of them squeezed into the back of their friends Rachael and Kim's Fiat Panda. Violet in the middle. They headed north. Rachael appeared to be furious about something and drove like a lunatic, and Kim sat back in her seat and laughed a lot, nervously.

Grace put her arm around Violet and kept squeezing her shoulder, in a friendly sort of way. She was quite drunk; Peaches, even drunker, had her hand on Violet's knee. Occasionally, Grace and Peaches would lean across Violet and kiss each other, pressing themselves against her so she could enjoy being squashed between them.

They were part of a lacrosse team. Violet had no idea what

SWEET VIOLET

lacrosse was and was not much wiser after their explanation which made it sound like a particularly dangerous form of hockey. They also told her that it was Peaches' twentieth birthday. Grace was twenty-five and they had been together nearly a year.

'That's seven in lesbian years,' Grace said, laughing. 'They're like dog years.' She leaned over Violet to kiss Peaches, whose hand moved up Violet's leg to her crotch. Halfway through the kiss, Peaches turned her head towards Violet and started kissing her instead. Violet was a bit surprised, but it was a very nice kiss so she didn't resist. Peaches tasted of beer and cigarettes. Grace was now kissing the side of Violet's neck and licking around her ear, both women pressing their breasts in against Violet's, as Peaches' hand massaged Violet's crotch. Violet was having trouble breathing, for several reasons; she was getting light-headed.

The car stopped suddenly, and they were all thrown forward.

'What the . . .?' Grace pulled herself up off the floor.

'Stop it!' Rachael shouted. Violet thought she must be talking to them, but she was looking at Kim.

'You stop it,' Kim said quietly, but more dangerously.

'Are we there?' Peaches asked. 'I want to get out.' She pushed against Kim's seat. Kim got out of the car and pulled the seat forward, then Grace and Violet got out and helped her out.

'Are we there?' Peaches asked again.

'No honey.' Grace put her arm around Peaches. 'Kim and Rachael are arguing again. We're going to get a cab home.' She was already hailing one.

'Hackney, my good man, and don't spare the horses,' she said as they climbed in. The cabby looked at them and shook his head, then drove very sedately to Hackney.

Grace sat on the long seat and Peaches curled up on her lap. Violet sat opposite them on the fold-down seat.

'What about Kim and Rachael?' Violet asked.

Grace shrugged. 'Who needs them?'

'Yeah, who needs them?' Peaches sat up for a moment and they lay down again. Grace winked at Violet.

Their place was a flat in a mansion block, painted green and orange, with sanded floors and big windows. Grace tossed Violet a beer from the kitchen, which she nearly dropped.

'Not a ball player,' surmised her host.

'No.' Violet opened it. 'More a breaststroker.' It wasn't exactly the truth, as backstroke had been her strongest stroke, but Grace laughed.

Peaches came out of the loo looking more alert than when she went in. 'Party time,' she said before shimmying across the room to the stereo in the corner. She put on a tape of Sade and started dancing. She moved very well.

'Come on.' Peaches pulled Violet to her feet. Violet looked over to Grace and got the nod.

'She's a smooth operator,' Peaches sang in Violet's ear, rubbing her breasts against Violet's. 'A smooth operator.'

Violet felt Grace come up behind and press against her back. 'A Violet sandwich,' she whispered in her ear. Peaches started kissing Violet wetly on the lips; Grace nibbled Violet's ear. She felt a moment's unease at not being in control, even though she was enjoying it. She let the beer and Peaches' kisses wash the unease away. Peaches' lips were soft and Violet opened her mouth to let that tongue reach hers. Grace slid her hands from Violet's waist up to her breasts. Violet put one hand on Peaches' breast, massaging the nipple with her thumb, and slid the other hand back between Grace's legs.

'Coast to coast, LA to Chicago,' Sade sang in the background.

Grace was kissing Peaches over Violet's shoulder now. Violet kissed Peaches' throat, retrieved her hand from between Grace's legs and undid the buttons on Peaches' shirt, pushing it back off her shoulders, before undoing her bra. Peaches' breasts swung free and both Violet and Grace stopped what they were doing to look at them.

'Aren't they gorgeous?' Grace reached over Violet's shoulder and touched them.

Peaches broke from them and threw her shirt and bra on the floor, then danced around the room topless. Her breasts danced a dance all of their own. Violet and Grace stood watching her.

SWEET VIOLET

Peaches danced back towards them, seductively unbuttoning her fly.

'Cool operator,' she sang, although Sade had moved on to another song.

She pulled down her jeans and tried to kick them off, but they wouldn't go over her shoes. She sat down on the floor and took off her shoes and then her jeans. She danced around the room in just her knickers; they were large and pink.

'My knickers,' Grace said, laughing. She was still holding Violet's breasts, one in each hand, which Violet found strangely comforting.

Peaches was slowly lowering her knickers, like a bad strip artist. When they were down to her knees, she started gyrating her hips, like she was playing with a hula hoop, and her knickers dropped to the floor.

Violet had seen girls naked before – the first time she had seen Katherine, she was naked in the changing room. But Peaches was something else. Katherine was tall and straight, barely any breasts or hips. Peaches was all breasts and hip and belly.

'Gorgeous,' Grace whispered again in Violet's ear.

Peaches came shimmying back to them, every part of her moving, to stand in front of Violet, who reached out her hands and gently squeezed Peaches' breast, then bent her head and lifted the breast into her mouth.

'Oh, yes,' Peaches sighed.

Violet took the whole nipple in her mouth and followed the circle of it with her tongue, running her other hand down Peaches' side and around to her bottom. Grace moved away and sat on the couch. Violet looked over to her.

'Carry on.' Grace waved a hand. 'I want to watch.'

Violet looked up to Peaches' face, but she didn't seem worried, so Violet carried on. She moved to the other nipple and sucked it until it was hard under her tongue, then she lowered Peaches to the floor and laid her down. Kneeling beside her, Violet kissed her again, and ran her hand down Peaches' body from her face, over her breasts and stomach to her pubic hair. She felt Peaches' breath quicken. She then followed the same path with her tongue, lingering on each breast and running the back of her hands up the inside of each thigh.

She circled her index finger through Peaches' pubic hair, in smaller and smaller circles until the finger slid wetly inside and Peaches gave a little gasp. Again, Violet's tongue followed where her finger had gone, and Peaches started moving her hips. Violet's thumb and tongue found the soft round bud of flesh. Peaches' hips were thrusting off the floor faster and faster, her breathing short and ragged. She gripped the side of Violet's head, as if she wanted her deeper. Violet could feel throbbing under her thumb.

Peaches was making little gasping noises, higher and higher, and she stopped everything – moving, breathing, everything. Violet stopped moving too, but left her hand and tongue where they were. Suddenly Peaches bucked, like a horse trying to throw a rider. Her whole body convulsed, throwing Violet off her; she let out a loud grunt with it, and then she started crying.

Grace came off the couch and took Peaches in her arms. She held her hand out to Violet and drew her into the hug too.

'There, there.' She rocked Peaches like a baby. 'There, there.'

The music had stopped and the flat seemed suddenly very quiet. Peaches' sobbing died down and she fell asleep. Violet helped Grace carry her through to the bedroom and watched as the sleeping girl was tucked into bed.

'You're good,' Grace said to Violet. 'Takes me hours to get her there.'

Violet didn't know what to say, so she didn't say anything.

Grace sat on the bed, one hand on Peaches' head. 'I asked her what she wanted for her birthday, tonight in the club.' She smiled down at Peaches, and kissed her on the cheek. 'She said you.' Grace looked up at Violet. 'You don't mind, do you?'

Violet shook her head.

'You *are* good,' Grace said again.

Peaches stirred in her sleep and Grace kissed her again. She held her hand out to Violet.

'Want to snuggle up between two fat dykes?'

Violet had never heard a lesbian call herself a dyke before. It was one of the names that children had shouted at her as they followed her round the playground.

'Come on.' Grace pulled Violet on to the bed. 'She won't mind sharing her birthday present.'

Grace's body was softer than Peaches', her breasts even bigger. Violet pushed Grace's T-shirt up and found her bra already undone. She squeezed Grace's nipples between her fingers with one hand and slid her other hand down to the top of Grace's jeans, finding them undone too. Grace was already wet; Violet slid her fingers in and out slowly, enjoying the feeling of Grace's soft, wet flesh. Grace put her hand on top of Violet's and started moving it faster and faster until it was just a quiver. Grace then clamped her legs around Violet's hand and, with nothing more than a big sigh, came. Violet felt Grace's muscles contract around her fingers, then relax again. Grace patted Violet on the head, rolled over and went to sleep.

Violet lay between them, Peaches sighing in her sleep and Grace now snoring gently. She suddenly felt very lonely but didn't understand why. Here she was, in London just two weeks and she'd had sex with four women and met loads more. She had a flat and a job and her course; everything was going swimmingly, except that Violet felt miserable. She wanted Katherine, she wanted to be curled up in Katherine's single bed, watching her sleep, not with two women she hardly knew.

Violet got off the bed carefully, so as not to wake them. She let herself out of the flat and then the building with no idea where she was, she instinctively turned left out of the house, left again, and walked. She didn't have a watch on but figured it was around 4 a.m. After about forty-five minutes of walking, she saw a sign for Wood Green saying three miles.

She got home by six to find an angry note on the table from the housemates she had last seen at the poetry reading.

'We are deeply hurt by your unsisterly actions of tonight. The evening was to be a house-bonding session and you showed a total lack of respect and understanding by disappearing halfway through it. We feel it was a passive-aggressive act, aimed at undermining, consciously or not, the entire structure and premise on which living in this house entails. We therefore insist that you attend a house meeting on Sunday evening at 6.30 to explain your actions.'

Violet screwed up the note, left it on the table and went to bed.

TEN
Katherine

Mr Williams had given them three days off from training, which was just as well – Katherine had never felt so tired in all her life. She was using the time to catch up on her neglected college work, although that was proving a bit difficult because whenever she sat down in the library, someone would come up and congratulate her on her medals. She had to keep her studies up to pace during the summer months too; but if she tried to work at home, her mother was in and out, pestering her.

Her mother could talk about nothing but their weddings with her and Brian's coming up in two weeks. It seemed unduly rushed, but her mother said she didn't want to upstage Katherine's, which was in two months. Katherine figured it gave Brian less time to change his mind. They had booked the registry office; she had chosen her dress, shoes and hat, but wasn't sure about the flowers. They were having the reception in a local pub and had invited about thirty people, mostly her mother's friends, as Brian didn't seem to have any of his own.

She wanted to take Katherine shopping to get a dress. 'You having nothing to wear to my wedding and you haven't even thought about a dress for yours have you?' Katherine hadn't. 'We can choose them both at the same time,' said her mother.

Katherine hated shopping almost as much as she hated dresses.

She couldn't imagine there was a wedding dress anywhere in which she would look good, and certainly not in Coventry.

'I suppose you want to get married in those jeans?' asked her mother.

If she thought she could get away with it then she would, but Katherine knew it wasn't possible. So on Wednesday afternoon she went with her mother to try on wedding dresses. Coventry had three bridal shops, all with the same dresses, at the same prices – ridiculously expensive. They all hung on her like tents and made her skin itch.

'Oh, that's lovely,' her mother said of all of them, except the one that Katherine disliked least: 'I don't know, it's a little plain.'

Her mother found a skirt in Chelsea Girl that Katherine grudgingly agreed to wear to the first wedding. It was pink taffeta, gathered at the waist. Her mother found a peasant blouse to go with it and Katherine was too tired to argue. They had coffee in a cafe opposite the sports shop where Matt worked, before trying out the last bridal shop.

'Isn't that where Sean's friend works?' her mother asked. Katherine nodded. 'Let's pop in and see whether he knows of anywhere else that sells wedding dresses.'

'No, Mother.' After Phillipa, Matt was the last person Katherine wanted to see, and she definitely didn't want to talk to him about wedding dresses.

'Come on.' Katherine's mother marched in and found Matt behind the counter. Katherine stayed outside and watched through the window but Matt saw her and waved her in.

'Actually, Mrs Wilson, you might not be able to tell by looking at me, but I'm a bit of a wiz at choosing wedding dresses.' He winked at Katherine in a friendly sort of way. 'What about your daughter then, two golds and a bronze?' He put his arm around Katherine, brushing her bottom on the way up. Katherine was sure he had done it on purpose.

'I don't know where she gets it from.' Her mother laughed. Matt laughed too, leaning forward so his hand brushed against her breast. She felt a buzz of excitement; an image came to her of him taking her from behind over the edge of the bath. She moved away from him.

'Come on Mum, there's one more shop to see.'

'Oh, he's lovely,' her mother said as they left the shop. 'So tall and well built.'

'Mother!'

She shot one last look over her shoulder. 'I bet he's a goer.'

'Mum!' Katherine couldn't believe it.

'Brian's built too, if you know what I mean.'

'I don't want to know.'

'But ever so gentle.'

'Stop it.'

'I hope Sean is too.'

Katherine shot her mother an angry look which silenced her for a moment.

'I just want to know . . .'

Katherine hated these conversations. She wished her mother could be like everyone else's, with a husband and a cat, and no interest in sex.

'I don't know what you and Violet got up to, but I don't want it to have spoiled things for you.'

'No, Mother.' Katherine wanted to hurry her up and get the conversation over with.

'Sex is meant to be a beautiful thing and it's meant to be between men and women. When you're young it's all right to . . .' She searched for the right word. Katherine looked at her feet and wondered what shoes she could wear with her new skirt.

'. . . experiment.' Her mother found the word.

'Finished?' Katherine looked at her mother.

'OK.' Her mother smiled. 'I just worry about you. I just want you to be happy.'

'Yeah, yeah.' Katherine had heard that all her life.

In the last shop at the end of the last rail, Katherine found her dress. It was a white silk tunic, split up the sides with matching drawstring trousers.

'I don't know,' her mother said.

'I do, I'm taking it.'

They measured her for the alterations and arranged a date to pick it up.

On the way back to the car, they passed Matt's shop again.

'Let's just tell him we found one.'

'No, Mum.' But it was too late; she was already in there. Katherine trailed in behind her. Matt was at the counter talking to Phillipa of all people; Katherine hid behind a football display stand.

'Hi, Katherine,' Phillipa called out to her. Katherine pretended she was looking at the balls, while her mother described the dress to him.

'Lucky Sean,' Phillipa said. Katherine couldn't quite read her tone. 'We're going for a drink, do you want to come?'

'No thanks.' Katherine said it too quickly. 'I've got so much work on.'

'Oh, one drink with them would be nice.' Her mother couldn't stop interfering.

'Come on, Katherine, even your mother says it's OK,' Phillipa teased her.

'I'll drop her home,' Matt added.

Katherine watched her Mother's face fall as she realised the invitation didn't include her. 'Fine, I'll see you later then.' And she marched from the shop. Katherine wanted to run after her and beg her to take her home, but that would have been desperate and she didn't want Matt and Phillipa to think she was desperate.

'OK then.' Phillipa slipped her arm through Katherine's. 'We'll see you over there.' She blew Matt a kiss and they left the shop.

The pub was around the corner. 'So, how's the golden girl then?' Phillipa asked as they waited to get served. Katherine still wasn't sure if she was taking the piss or not.

'Fine.'

'Wedding dress shopping? Exciting stuff.'

'Not really.'

'Can I be your bridesmaid?'

Now Katherine knew she was teasing. 'I'm not having any.'

'Maid of honour then?'

'None of those either.'

'Just as well, I'm not very honourable.'

SWEET VIOLET

They got their drinks and sat down, Katherine with an orange juice and Phillipa with vodka and tonic – 'While I still can,' she said, grinning at the fact that the swimmer's alcohol ban was temporarily lifted.

They sat in silence for a while, then Phillipa said, 'I'm sorry about the other night.'

'It's OK.' Katherine didn't want to talk about it.

'I was just mad at myself for bombing out of the race.'

'It's not a problem.'

'And I'm sorry you wouldn't let me kiss you.'

Katherine felt herself start to blush; she didn't want to be having this conversation. She pushed her chair back to leave but Matt was behind her and put both hands on her shoulders.

'Where are you going? I haven't bought you a drink yet.' He went off to the bar.

Phillipa was looking at Katherine, too intensely for Katherine's liking. She played with her glass.

'Sorry,' Phillipa said again. 'It's no big deal.'

Matt came back with the drinks. 'Here's to you, kid,' he said as he raised his glass to her. Katherine took a mouthful of hers. It wasn't just orange juice, there was vodka in it – a lot, by the taste of it.

'Sean said you liked vodka.' Matt winked at her again, but it didn't feel so friendly this time, and Phillipa giggled. 'Mind you, what does Sean know? Doesn't know a good thing when he's got it.' He was sitting very close beside Katherine on the bench seat, his arm along the back, just touching her hair.

Katherine leaned forward.

'Don't tease her,' Phillipa said quite sternly.

Matt shrugged; he leaned over the table and took Phillipa's hand. 'Sean reckons you're the reason I bombed the relay.'

Phillipa laughed. 'I probably was. What did the trainer in *Rocky* say? "Women weaken legs".'

'So, you're giving him the cold shoulder this week?' Matt turned back to Katherine.

'No, I just have so much work on for college.'

83

'But you've got time for a drink with us.' His hand was playing with her hair.

'I was rather forced into this.'

'No!' Matt and Phillipa said it at the same time, and then laughed.

'Another?' Phillipa headed for the bar.

'I have to go.' Katherine tried to stand up too, but Matt put his hand on her arm. She felt another buzz of excitement run through her.

'You're wasted on Sean.' Matt ran his hand up her arm and put it under her chin. He tilted her face up and kissed her very lightly on the lips, but Katherine pulled away.

'What about you and Phillipa?'

'Oh that.' Matt waved his hand dismissively. 'Just two lonely people.' He leaned forward to kiss her again, but this time Katherine turned her head.

'I hear you give good head,' he whispered.

'What?' Katherine was pretty sure she knew what he meant, but she couldn't believe he was saying it.

'Blow jobs,' Matt said. 'He tells me everything.'

Katherine was furious; how could Sean do that to her?

'That's why I let him watch.'

Katherine downed her drink; she wanted to punch someone.

Matt continued: 'Not that he seems to learn anything, from what he said about your first time.'

Katherine banged the glass down on the table, sending Matt's drink flying.

Phillipa arrived back. 'What's going on?'

'Katherine's upset. I think it's because I told her Sean tells me everything.'

'About him watching us?' Phillipa obviously knew too.

'Now *that* seemed to interest her.'

Katherine couldn't believe it. She stood up. 'Get out of my way.' She tried to push past Matt.

'Oh, sit down.' Phillipa pushed a drink across the table to her. Katherine sat and started to cry, feeling humiliated. Matt put his arm around her and wiped her tears with his sleeve; Katherine let

SWEET VIOLET

him do it. He kissed her softly on the neck, then along her chin till he reached her mouth. Katherine opened her lips to his tongue and let him slide it deep into her mouth. She could feel the kiss right through her body, from her head down to her toes, through her nipples but mostly right between her legs.

It was Matt who broke off the kiss, and Katherine leant back in her chair feeling a bit dizzy. Matt smiled and pushed her drink towards her. Katherine drank it.

'Let's go.' Phillipa leaned over the table and took Matt's hand.

Katherine felt all the warm feelings she had been enjoying suddenly desert her. Matt finished his drink and stood up, then turned back to Katherine and held out his hand. 'Coming?'

Katherine was so confused. She was engaged to Sean and Matt was his best friend, his best man even, the person to whom he told everything. She finished her drink and stood up. 'OK.'

Matt drove them in his old BMW, in silence, to Phillipa's flat, near the hospital where Phillipa was doing her physio training. Inside the flat was bare and clinically decorated, apart from the bedroom, which had a huge double bed. Phillipa kicked off her shoes and flopped down on it on her back. Matt pulled Katherine to him and started kissing her again, his hands on her bottom. Katherine could feel the bulge of his penis against her stomach; his tongue and lips were soft and wet. He moved his hands up her back and pulled her T-shirt off over her head, stepping back to admire her.

'Oh boy.' He touched her nipples with his fingertips. Katherine was aware of Phillipa watching from the bed. Matt started kissing her again, flicking his tongue in and out of her mouth and rolling her nipples between his fingers. Katherine could feel her clitoris throbbing.

Matt pulled her towards the bed, still kissing her; he sat down on the edge of the bed and pulled her to kneel in front of him. He let go of her with one hand and reached out for Phillipa, who snuggled in beside him and started kissing his neck. Katherine could feel her cheek touch Phillipa's every now and then, and these touches made her feel even more excited.

Matt stopped kissing her and pulled her even closer, leaning forward to take her nipple into his mouth. She closed her eyes and tipped her head back. It felt like her whole body was on fire; she was short of breath and starting to feel dizzy. She was aware of another hand touching her, a softer hand. She opened her eyes and Phillipa was reaching over Matt, running the back of her hand over Katherine's stomach.

Matt pulled his head away, sucking out the nipple until it stung. He took off his T-shirt and Phillipa took off her own. Matt pushed her bra up over her breasts and Phillipa pulled it the rest of the way over her head. Katherine didn't do anything except stare. She had seen Phillipa naked before, but had been too embarrassed to look; now she couldn't stop looking. Phillipa had the most perfect breasts, round mounds with small dark nipples so tight that they looked like they must be hurting.

Matt held one of them and licked it and Katherine reached out her own hand – she wanted to touch them too. Phillipa closed her eyes and leant towards Katherine who rubbed her cheek over those breasts and breathed in Phillipa's musky smell. Phillipa groaned quietly.

Matt stopped stroking Phillipa and moved to undo Katherine's jeans. She stood up to let him pull them down and her knickers went with them. Matt leaned forward and put his nose to her stomach and breathed in.

'Oh boy,' he said again.

Katherine slipped off her shoes and stepped out of her jeans. Matt pulled off his boots; Phillipa helped him unzip his trousers and pulled them down. He was wearing boxer shorts which were sticking out at the front.

'Naughty boy,' Phillipa said as she squeezed the bulge.

Matt slapped her hand away playfully and peeled her jeans off her but Phillipa pushed him out of the way and finished the job herself. Katherine and Matt watched her do it. She was wearing red knickers and she peeled those off too, slowly swivelling her hip, obviously enjoying the attention.

Matt put his arm around Katherine and pulled her on to the bed facing him, then Phillipa lay down behind her.

'A Katherine sandwich,' Phillipa whispered in her ear.

'Yummy,' Matt said, kissing her throat and collarbone. Phillipa put her arms round Katherine and started softly kneading her breasts; she pushed her pelvis into Katherine's bottom and kissed her behind the ear. Matt continued kissing her, working his way down her front, stopping for a moment to suck Phillipa's thumbs, then kissed down Katherine's stomach to her pubic hair.

Katherine could hardly breathe, her whole body was tingling, it was if she could feel every nerve ending in her skin. Matt ran his hand up the inside of her thigh and nestled his nose in her pubic hair; she wanted his fingers inside her. He was running them in circles along her thigh, and then suddenly he pushed the heel of his hand into her mound. Katherine groaned at how good it felt and pushed her hips even harder into his hand.

'She wants it,' Philipa said in her ear. 'Oh God, she wants it.'

Matt rubbed the heel of his hand around and around; Katherine moved her hips in time with him to maintain maximum contact. Then he moved his hand down and slipped a finger inside her. Katherine groaned again.

'Is she wet?' Phillipa asked.

'Drenched,' Matt said, and he ran his tongue up Katherine's stomach.

Katherine tightened herself around Matt's fingers, trying to draw them deeper into her. Matt moved his thumb and flicked it over her clitoris. Katherine gasped; the sensation was so sharp it almost hurt. Her breathing was out of control, ragged and too shallow, but she couldn't do anything about it.

Phillipa was pinching her nipples and biting her neck, grinding her pelvis against Katherine's bottom. Her breathing was hard and fast too. 'Here,' she said, and she took Katherine's hand and guided it back so Katherine's fingers were against her pelvis. Katherine felt her pubic hair and then let her fingers slide inside Phillipa; she was very wet too. Katherine pushed her fingers in deeper.

'Oh yes,' Phillipa panted in her ear.

Katherine searched round with her thumb until she found Phillipa's clitoris and then massaged it gently. Phillipa groaned, just like Katherine had heard her do on the bus the other night.

Katherine groaned too. Matt was rubbing harder and faster,

licking the very top of her thighs, moving closer to her centre. Then suddenly his tongue was in her, licking her, his thumb still on her clitoris. It was almost more than Katherine could bear and she thought she was going to explode, as her whole body seemed to be shaking. From being able to feel every nerve she could now feel only one, the one Matt had his thumb on. She thought she was going to die, and just then, something let go inside her and her whole body went into spasms, jerking uncontrollably.

It took a moment for her body to stop its tremors.

'Oh boy,' Matt said, removing his fingers slowly. They seemed to leave a huge void behind them. Phillipa was still holding her from behind; her body was trembling slightly too. She had come at the same moment as Katherine.

'Oh boy,' Phillipa echoed Matt.

'That was something else.' Matt pulled himself up so he was lying beside Katherine and kissed her softly. Katherine was completely limp; she didn't think she would ever move again; she wasn't sure she would ever even think again. She had never come like that before, not even with Violet. She smiled. Maybe there was hope for her yet, maybe it was just something about Sean that was the problem, not her. Because here she was with Matt, and she'd just had the most amazing orgasm.

Phillipa rolled over and stretched. 'You want a go now?' She was asking Matt.

Matt nodded, leant over Katherine and kissed Phillipa. Katherine could see his penis straining against his boxer shorts. Phillipa reached to her bedside table.

'Look what I've got.' She held up a condom.

'Yummy, yummy.' Matt rolled on to his back and put his hands behind his head. Phillipa came around Katherine, straddled him, and pulled off his boxers. His pubic hair was darker than Sean's and his penis was huge. Phillipa tore the condom packet open with her teeth and started to roll it down his penis in teasing little strokes. Matt held on to the base of it to keep it still, with his head back and his eyes closed.

Katherine rolled on to her side to get a better look. She knew she shouldn't be watching, but it was such a compelling scene that she didn't think she could look away, even if her life depended on it, and she sensed that Matt and Phillipa were enjoying her being there as an audience.

'You like that?' Phillipa teased Matt, running her hand down the condom, smoothing it out.

Matt didn't answer. His face was starting to go red and he looked like he was concentrating hard on something. Phillipa crawled forward over Matt until her bottom was level with his penis, took it in one hand and lowered her sex on to it. Matt grunted, Phillipa moved around a little to get it more comfortable and then slid lower. Matt let out a long breath.

'Hold on, Matt.' Phillipa lifted herself up a little and then slid down again. Katherine watched as Phillipa's thighs contracted and relaxed, thinking how beautiful they looked. Matt brought his hands forward and grabbed hold of Phillipa's waist, helping her, moving her faster. He had opened his eyes and was looking up into her face, but her eyes were closed now, her head thrown back.

Katherine watched as Phillipa's breasts bounced up and down, and sweat ran down between them. She wanted to reach out and touch them, but they were concentrating so hard, she didn't want to distract them.

'Oh yes.' Matt's hips were pumping off the bed now, and Phillipa was having trouble staying on. She leant forward and grabbed the bedhead.

Matt was grunting, and then with a final thrust went stiff. Phillipa seemed to squeeze her whole body together and then she rolled off him. His penis fell out of her and flopped on to the bed between them.

'Oh boy,' Matt said again.

'Oh girl,' Phillipa said, ruffling his hair. 'Men say the oddest things during sex. But at least he doesn't call me Momma.' She laughed and playfully stroked his limp penis. 'I need to pee.' She peeled the condom off Matt and left the room.

Matt half sat up and winked at Katherine. Now that there were just the two of them in the room, she felt suddenly nervous.

'You won't tell Sean?' she asked.

Matt laughed. 'He may tell me everything, but he doesn't know half of what I get up to.'

'So you won't?'

'Not if you don't.' He moved closer to her and kissed her on the shoulder.

Phillipa came bouncing back into the room. 'I'm starving, anyone want to eat?'

'I've got to go.' Katherine got up and started looking for her clothes. She was aware that both Matt and Phillipa were watching her and she felt very uncomfortable. She found her T-shirt and jeans but not her knickers, so she put her jeans on without them, eager to cover herself up.

'I'll give you a lift.' Matt dressed unhurriedly and Katherine went to wait by the front door, starting to feel a bit sick.

'You want to come back later?' She heard Phillipa ask this but didn't hear Matt's reply. Then: 'Thank you for this, I owe you.' It was Phillipa again. Matt emerged into the hallway, smiling.

'Come on.'

They drove to Katherine's in silence. She was embarrassed and worried now about what had just happened.

'You won't tell?' she asked again. 'Not anyone?'

'Don't worry.' Matt put his hand on her shoulder.

But she *was* worried, worried what they would say about her to each other, what other people would say if they found out. She was so worried, she thought she was going to be sick. And as if to confirm her fears, Sean's car was outside her place.

'Drop me here,' she told Matt, before they reached it. 'I don't want him to see us together!'

'Your mother will already have told him you're with me.'

'I don't care, stop the car.' Katherine got out and slammed the door. She had been so stupid, so bloody stupid, and now she was going to pay for it.

ELEVEN

Violet

Violet was woken at 8 a.m. on Sunday by a phone call from Judy, saying they needed someone to help them with an emergency move. She had a shower before Judy came by in the van to take her to Stoke Newington.

'We're slipping you know,' Fiona said to Judy when they got there.

Judy nodded.

'Why?' Violet asked in the ensuing silence, unsure if she was supposed to understand their shorthand conversations.

'We gave them six months,' Fiona said, and Judy nodded. 'It's only been four.'

Judy shook her head. 'Slipping,' Fiona said.

There wasn't a lot to move: boxes of books, a small table, and a new double bed.

'Ah,' Fiona said when she saw it, 'We didn't know about that.'

'No,' Judy said as they lifted it into the van.

'So that's OK then,' Fiona said, and Judy nodded.

Violet liked working with them, she wasn't required to say anything, there was no small talk. Fiona did any talk there was; Judy just pointed at what was to be moved next and Violet moved it.

They drove from Stoke Newington to Tottenham and had to

carry the boxes up six flights of stairs. Violet was ready to fall over by the time she had lugged up the last box. The woman, whose name was Alice and who looked a bit like Alice in Wonderland, offered them tea, and they all accepted. Alice had big, frightened eyes and her hair was held back by a flowery scarf. She looked sad – not like someone who had just that second broken up with her lover, but like someone who had seen something terrible as a child and never got over it.

'You could be in there if you wanted,' Fiona said, nudging Violet in the ribs while Alice was off making the tea. 'She's a doctor.' Violet wondered, a doctor? It would certainly impress her parents, but would it impress Katherine? She wasn't much to look at, not nearly as pretty as Katherine, but now that Violet knew she was a doctor, she could seriously consider her as a potential Felicity. She shook her head; if only she wasn't so tired.

Alice was in the kitchen for ages, and in the end, Violet went in to see if she was all right. She was curled up in a corner crying, shaking with sobs; the kettle was boiling its head off on the gas. Violet didn't know what to do; she went over and crouched down beside her.

'Shall I get the tea?' She stood Alice up, led her out to the lounge and sat her down on the one chair, then went back to the kitchen and made the tea. By the time it was ready, Alice had calmed down a bit. Judy was looking very uncomfortable and Fiona was nodding absent-mindedly as Alice explained the exact ins and outs of the break-up.

'I'm twenty-six,' Alice was saying, close to tears again. 'I'll never find another girlfriend.'

'Of course you will,' Fiona said, not very convincingly. 'Judy was nearly that when we met.'

'Oh.' But Alice wasn't listening. She was watching Violet pouring tea from the pot into four mismatched cups.

'I couldn't find any milk,' Violet said.

'There's some in the van,' Fiona said, but almost before she had finished, Judy said, 'I'll go,' and was out the door.

Fiona laughed. 'We always carry it.'

SWEET VIOLET

'So,' Alice was looking at Violet with her big, startled eyes, 'How old are you Violet?'

There was something about the way she said her name that set Violet's teeth on edge.

'Oh, Violet's just a baby, barely legal.' Fiona said, winking at Violet.

'Come on Violet, tell us.' Alice smiled, it didn't suit her.

'Eighteen,' Violet said.

Alice sighed. 'Oh to be eighteen again.'

'And know what you know now,' Fiona joked.

'No.' Alice looked like she was going to cry. 'If I knew then what I know now, I would never have become a lesbian.' And she fled into the bedroom.

'Now look what you've done,' Fiona said to Violet.

'Me?' Violet asked.

Fiona started to giggle. 'I think we'd better go.' And they tiptoed to the door.

'Alice,' Fiona called into the bedroom, 'Violet will come by tomorrow to pick up the money.' Then she ran down the six flights of stairs, Violet chasing after her.

It was 3.30. Violet didn't want to go home for this evening's house meeting and imagined Rainbow, Tree and Julie sitting around the table, convicting her in her absence. Near King's Cross, Fiona pointed out a pub with a Sunday afternoon tea dance, and Violet saw her chance and asked them to drop her off there. She was a bit early so she sat upstairs and nursed a pint.

People started arriving at four o'clock. Some of the men had frocks on, so did some of the women. There were dance lessons first, but as most of the people had arrived in couples, Violet just sat and watched without a partner. It looked like fun and some of the couples were very good, especially the men.

A man came over to her. 'You want to try this?'

Violet wasn't sure. She had never danced with a man before, but he looked harmless enough, not much taller than Violet, with greying hair and nice eyes.

'You can lead,' he said.

'OK.'

It was harder than it looked and Violet discovered the meaning of 'two left feet'. Eric, her partner, was very patient, and by the end of the lesson, Violet had more or less got the hang of the waltz.

'Don't look at your feet!' Eric told her. 'Relax,' he said repeatedly, and 'Look like you're enjoying it.'

After the lesson, the couples waltzed around the floor to music.

A woman came over to Violet. 'Would you care for this dance, madam?' she asked.

It was Belinda, in a dinner jacket and top hat. Violet didn't recognise her out of her dress. 'I'm not very good.'

'I know, I saw. Still, Eric will have straightened you out, so to speak.' And she laughed.

They went once around the room. Violet was meant to be leading but Belinda kept taking over and, because she was much better at it, Violet let her. She tried not to look at her feet, but if she looked into Belinda's eyes, she would lose track of the rhythm or take too big a step and end up treading on Belinda's toes.

'Sorry,' Violet said for the third or fourth time.

Belinda smiled. 'I've got to go now anyway, before they start the 60s music. I hate it.'

Violet watched her leave, waving to people as she went and giving one woman a hug. She didn't look back.

Violet sat through the 60s music; she quite liked it, but was too tired to dance. She left before the 70s music started. Even if Tree and Rainbow were angry with her, she had to go home and sleep.

They were out and there was another note for Violet but she couldn't be bothered even reading it. She made some toast and took it up to her room. There was the letter from her mother that she hadn't read either. But before she read it, she took out her *Finding Felicity* book and wrote.

3. 8 Sept. The Honey Pot. Peaches, lounge floor.
4. 8 Sept. The Honey Pot. Grace, bed beside Peaches.
8/10 each. Couple and therefore unsuitable.

She ate her toast and thought about Alice. It was just because she was upset that she looked so odd. Once she had got over her break-up and brushed her hair, she would probably look halfway decent. Violet tried to imagine Katherine coming down the aisle and seeing her there and then seeing Alice at her side, a little sad. She imagined giving her a little wave and kissing Alice very lightly on the cheek . . . She couldn't quite make it work, as those eyes of Alice's kept staring at her. But she only had three weeks, and Alice did seem pretty desperate, perhaps desperate enough to agree to be Felicity for the day.

After her classes on Wednesday, Violet climbed the six flights of stairs to Alice's flat. She found that she wasn't really looking forward to seeing her again, despite the possibility that this was her Felicity.

Fiona reported her conversation with Alice: 'She said four is fine, and wanted to know what wine you liked.'

'I hate wine.'

'I thought you might.'

'I'm just collecting the money.'

'Yeah, right.'

'Is she really a doctor?'

'Want her to give you a physical?'

'No, I just wondered.'

'Remember she's just finished a relationship, she needs some TLC, that's all. It wouldn't do you any harm.'

Violet supposed it wouldn't, especially if, in return, she agreed to come to the wedding.

'Nothing much will happen,' claimed Fiona. 'Most lesbians are all mouth and no trousers when it comes to that sort of thing.'

Violet had to disagree. She seemed to have met a lot of fully trousered lesbians in her short time in London – maybe she was just lucky. She knew something was going to happen, because she had seen the desperation in Alice's eyes.

The door opened almost before she had finished knocking. Alice was standing there, the light behind her, her hair down and straggling round her shoulders. Her Indian dress was almost completely see-through, with no underwear beneath it. All that was a little unsettling, but it was her eyes that Violet found most disturbing, those rabbit-caught-in-the-headlights eyes.

'Come in.' Alice didn't move out of the way, so Violet had to brush past her. She smelled spicy, like the Deep Heat ointment Violet would use on aching muscles – back when she still swam.

The flat was still full of unpacked boxes; but Violet caught a glimpse of the bedroom, the bed was made and surrounded by lit candles. It looked like a fire hazard.

'Coffee?' Alice was speaking oddly, her voice sort of husky, like she needed to clear her throat. Violet wondered if she had a cold.

'Ah, no thanks.' Violet said. 'I'll just take the money and be off.' Alice smiled at her, and although she might have meant it to be coy or knowing, it came across as plain mad.

Violet remembered what Fiona had said about it not doing her any harm, but she wasn't sure about that now. Alice was doing something to her dress. Violet looked away, out of the window, wondering if she would survive a six-storey drop. When she looked back, Alice was naked, her dress around her feet.

'I know you want me,' Alice said as she stepped out of the dress towards Violet. 'I can see it in your eyes.'

Violet backed away until she hit a wall, but Alice kept coming at her. Her body was pale and floppy, not fat but with no muscle tone. She put her hand on Violet's shoulder and pressed her body against Violet's. Not knowing what to do, Violet held her hands out in front of her. She couldn't quite bring herself to touch Alice's skin.

The woman had her face on Violet's neck now and was licking her. Violet put her hands on Alice's arms and pushed her away gently; her skin felt cold and clammy. Violet turned them both around so Alice was against the wall, kept hold of her arms and looked at her. Alice was breathing hard, her eyes staring out at Violet.

'I know you want me,' she said again. Violet felt a sudden surge of emotion, anger mainly, but embarrassment and frustration too. She wanted very much to slap Alice, swing the palm of her hand across Alice's face and feel the sting of it. She lifted up her hand and saw Alice flinch, and then she felt bad, knowing someone in her past had slapped her. Violet touched Alice's cheek with the back of her hand. Alice closed her eyes and leant her head into Violet's hand. She ran her hand down Alice's neck to her breast, feeling the skin turn to goosebumps under her touch.

'I know . . .' Alice started again. Violet put her finger to Alice's lips.

'Sh,' she said, suppressing the urge to shove her fist into Alice's mouth. Instead, she pressed her hand hard into Alice's breast.

'Do you like that?' she asked, pinching Alice's nipple.

'Yes,' Alice whimpered.

With her other hand she cupped Alice's pubic bone. 'Do you like that?'

Alice didn't answer. Violet slid two fingers up inside Alice. Alice's eyes flew open.

'Do you like that?'

Alice whimpered again. Violet pushed her fingers further in.

'Do you like that?' Violet repeated.

'Yes.'

Violet added a third finger. Alice was surprisingly wet. 'Yes what?'

'Yes please.'

'You want more?'

'Oh yes.' Alice was panting now.

Violet pushed her fingers as far as she could up into Alice. She rubbed her thumb along the length of Alice's slit until she could feel the fleshy bud. She pushed her thumb into it. Alice's head was rolling from side to side. Her hands were spread out wide; she was clutching at the wall with her fingers, whimpering and panting. Violet moved her fingers in and out, pushing them further in each time. Her other hand was still against Alice's breast, nipple pinched between her fingers. It was the only thing holding Alice up.

Violet pushed harder and faster and Alice's breathing got harder and faster with it. It seemed she was saying something with each out breath, but Violet couldn't quite hear it. She didn't really want to know what it was. She thought that Alice might be saying no.

'Do you like this?' Violet asked again, pushing even harder than before.

Alice let out a high-pitched breath, which sounded like a yes.

'Do you want more?' Violet stopped moving her fingers.

'Oh yes.' Alice looked like she was about to cry, her face red and blotchy, her lips dry and slightly cracked, her eyelids swollen. Violet started moving her fingers again, faster and faster, as well as her thumb. Alice seemed to expand under Violet's fingers, letting them slide deeper into her. The flesh under Violet's thumb was swelling up and then suddenly it seemed to explode, shooting water all over Violet's hand.

She stepped away and Alice crumpled to the floor, whimpering.

Violet left her there and went to the toilet to wash her hand. On the way back past the bedroom, she noticed an envelope on the bedside table with 'Sappho Removals' written on the front, picked it up and left. At the bottom of the six flights of stairs, she stopped and wondered if she should go back and check on Alice. She started up the stairs again and then decided she couldn't face it.

Back home, she did feel a bit bad as she wrote in her book:

5. 12 Sept. Alice, lounge wall. 6/10.
Not suitable because . . .

She couldn't find the right word to explain why she wasn't suitable.

. . . Too desperate.

She wrote this after some thought. It was a pity, because a doctor would have been good.

The scores seemed a bit arbitrary. She didn't know whether she was rating how much she enjoyed it or how much they seemed to. She had left Alice in a pile on the floor and given her a six, but Angela had been much more eager to keep going, and she only got a three. Violet wondered if she could work out a more objective scoring system, something that took account of both her own and her partner's enjoyment levels. That led to the problem of how to judge whether the other woman enjoyed it or not. Violet hadn't really been brave enough to really enquire afterwards. But they certainly seemed as if they had enjoyed it. Though even with Katherine, it had been difficult to tell – the first time they had sex, Violet thought she'd done Katherine some serious damage . . .

They had been in the garden lying on the rug; they had kissed often enough before, behind the swimming pool after training, even in the school loos once. But both of them knew that they were going to go further this time. Katherine's mother was out with her boyfriend and Katherine had cooked up a frightening amount of food, most of which Violet had never heard of. But she wasn't there for the food, she was there for that moment, the one when her hand would reach lower than the top of Katherine's jeans and there would be nothing to stop it going further.

That first time, when Violet had her fingers inside Katherine, it was so amazing. It was like diving into a pool when you are very hot, or having a drink when you're thirsty, it was like Violet had lived all her life up to that point for that precise moment.

Katherine had sighed, which put Violet off a bit, but she soon found the soft bit of flesh that felt like velvet and made Katherine sigh some more. It was when her friend went completely rigid that Violet thought she had hurt her, done something so wrong that Katherine had blown a fuse. But then her body relaxed again and Katherine smiled at her in a dreamy sort of way, like Violet had just done the most amazing thing to her and she was very grateful. Violet liked that moment very much too.

She closed the book, knowing she had to find a Felicity and soon. Maybe, if a doctor didn't work, she should be more daring, more outrageous. She remembered the lesbians she had seen at Aphrodite Rising; the Lambda ones were too boring; the check shirts and dungarees – well, Kathy had been with that group, and she wouldn't do as Felicity; then there were the ones around the stage, with their whips and dog collars. That would certainly turn some heads at the wedding. It was worth a try; *City Limits* might tell her where they met. Violet got into bed feeling a little happier – this was London after all, and if she couldn't find her Felicity here, then she probably didn't exist.

TWELVE

Katherine

Sean and Katherine's mother were sitting on the sofa giggling when she came in from Matt's car. They giggled some more when they saw her.

'What?' Katherine was in no mood for this.

Her mother pointed to a photo album on the floor, Katherine's baby photos.

'Oh, Mum.' Katherine picked it up and closed it. Sean and her mother continued to giggle. Katherine noticed a bottle of gin half empty on the side table.

Sean stood up and staggered over to her. 'You were so cute.' He squeezed her bottom. 'I wish I had known you then.' He leaned his head on her shoulder. 'Your Mum says I mustn't drive home, she says I'm too drunk. She says I'm to stay the night.'

Katherine looked at her mother, who was nodding and grinning.

'Thank you, Mum.' Katherine wanted a shower; she wanted her bed to herself so she could sort her head out. Instead she had Sean, at her mother's insistence, staying the night.

'I need a shower.' She went to her room, collected her towel and pyjamas and then locked herself in the bathroom. She stayed under the hot water for ages, scrubbing herself with soap and then putting on some of her mother's powder. Despite all that, she could still smell Matt on her and was sure Sean would be able to.

'Katherine.' Sean was tapping on the door. 'I need to pee, and your mother's in the downstairs loo. I think she's throwing up.'

She quickly put on her pyjamas and opened the door. Sean half-fell through it.

'I'm sorry babe, if you don't want me to stay, I'll go, really I will. I could drive.'

Katherine took a deep breath. 'No, it's fine. It's just been a long day.' She left Sean to it and climbed into her single bed.

Sean appeared at the door moments later. 'I used your toothbrush, is that OK?'

Katherine shrugged.

'Let's see the dress then.' Sean sat on the edge of the bed.

'I haven't got it.' Katherine was surprised, she hadn't thought Sean would be interested. 'Besides, you're not supposed to see it before the wedding.'

'Oh.' Sean pulled a sad face. 'That is an old wives' tale, and like all old wives' tales, it's a bunch of bull.' He went to the wardrobe and opened it. 'Haven't you got any dresses in here?'

'The skirt I bought for Mum's wedding is there.' Her mother had hung it on the door of the wardrobe.

Sean held it up in front of himself. 'Nice.' He twirled with it in front of the mirror and stopped, facing Katherine. 'What do you think?'

He tried to put it on. 'It's too small.'

'And not your colour.'

'I've always fancied myself in red.'

'Mum's got a red dress, that would fit you.' Katherine was only joking, but Sean stopped his preening.

'Where?'

'In her wardrobe, but you can't . . .'

Sean didn't hear as he had disappeared off in the direction of her mother's room. He came back a moment later with the dress.

'This one?'

'Sean!'

'It's OK, she said I could.' He pulled off his T-shirt and jeans and pulled the dress on over his head. It had a cross-over top with a ruffle along it and a gathered skirt. He was so fair and his skin so smooth, it actually looked quite good on him. He sashayed around the room, flicking the skirt about, then stopped in front of the mirror to admire himself. After eyeing himself from head to toe, he seemed to have a thought, left the room again and was gone longer this time. Katherine lay back on the bed, wondering what on earth he was doing, and whether she should check that her mother was OK. Sean came back with a bundle of clothes.

'Sean, I'm not sure . . .' He wasn't listening, but slipped off his own pants and took a pair of her mother's black lacy panties out of his little pile. He held them up to the light and examined the lace on the front and then sniffed the crotch.

'Sean!' Katherine sat on the bed, shaking her head.

He slid them seductively up his legs, and pulled a pained face as he tugged them up past his waist. Katherine couldn't believe it. Next, he put on a pair of black strappy sandals. They were too small but he teetered around the room in them anyway, stopping in front of the mirror again. He turned one way and then the other, looking at himself.

'Something's missing.' He put his hand on his chin. 'I know.' He left the room again and came back this time with her mother's make-up box.

Katherine shook her head in disbelief.

'You'll have to help me with this.' He held out a bright orange lipstick.

'I don't know the first thing about make-up.'

Sean rubbed the lipstick across his lips, breaking it.

'Oh, here.' Katherine got off the bed and took the lipstick. 'Pucker.'

The colour clashed with the dress and looked awful against his skin, but when she was finished he smiled, delighted. He then picked out some purple eyeshadow, a red blusher and some luminescent green mascara. By the time Katherine had finished, he looked like he had some tropical disease.

Sean looked at himself in the mirror. 'Oh yes!'

Katherine laughed. He looked terrible, but terrible like some of the women she had seen around the Working Mens' Club on a

Friday night, not terrible like he was a man in a dress. If the rest of the squad could see him now, Matt would die laughing.

Katherine stopped smiling. 'You look awful.'

'I look like my Aunt Suzy,' he said, putting his hand on his hip. 'I always thought she was gorgeous.' He puckered his lips and then added, 'In a trashy sort of way.' He pulled his elbows in against his pecs to give himself a cleavage; it wasn't much but it was better than anything Katherine could have managed.

'I wish I had breasts.' He slid his hand inside the top of the dress. He turned to Katherine suddenly. 'I do love you, you know.' He came and sat on the edge of the bed, close to tears. 'I've never felt this way about anyone else before, and when we're married, everything will be all right.'

It sounded to Katherine like a question, a plea almost, but she had no answer to give him. She put her hand on his cheek and he leant his head into it.

'I love you too.' She kissed him on the lips. It felt strange to be kissing someone with lipstick on – Violet had certainly never worn any and it felt a bit like she was kissing her mother. Sean started kissing her back, darting his tongue in and out between her lips. Katherine hadn't meant to start anything, having had quite enough sex for one day, but there was something interesting, not just about the lipstick, but the feel of the thin nylon material of the dress against Sean's skin. He was behaving differently too, as though the dress was making him into someone else. His hands weren't all over her like they usually were; he was letting her do the leading.

She ran her hand down Sean's neck and slid it inside the dress, and heard him draw in his breath. She started kissing him on his neck, then, pushing the shoulders of the dress back, she licked him along his collarbone. Her fingers found his nipples and gently started squeezing them; Sean gave a little groan. She pressed her free hand into his groin, feeling the soft, light material against the hardness. Sean groaned again.

Katherine pushed him backwards on to the bed and lay on top of him, holding his arms above his head, kissing him hard on the mouth, grinding her mouth over his, feeling their teeth touch, sinking her tongue deep into his mouth, kissing him until it hurt. She sat up, straddling him, and ran her fingertips down his outstretched arms. Then she had an idea: she turned around and slowly pulled the dress up his legs, feeling the material slide over the skin. The black lace panties were strained almost to splitting by Sean's erection. Katherine leant forward and blew on it, and as it quivered slightly, he groaned again and tried to sit up, but she pushed him back down. She blew on it again; Sean twisted under her as though trying to get away from her breath. Katherine moved closer and licked it through the panties; Sean squirmed even more, but she held him fast between her knees.

She tucked her fingers under the elastic waistband of the panties and rolled it down slightly so she could just see the tip of his penis. She blew hotly on it and watched it strain against the elastic.

'Oh God, Katherine.' Sean moved his hips from side to side, trying to get out from under her.

Katherine spotted his jeans on the floor and reached over to pick them up without letting Sean go. She went through his pockets and in the back one found a condom – the writing on it was French. She tried to rip the packet open with her fingers and couldn't, so she resorted to her teeth like she had seen Phillipa do. It gave her a wonderful sense of power.

She wasn't sure of the exact technique for putting a condom on, but she wasn't going to let that stop her. She pushed the panties clear of Sean's penis and it sprang to attention. His breathing changed noticeably, faster and shallower. Katherine held the base of his penis and put the condom on like a hat, then rolled it down.

Sean groaned. 'God, Katherine, what are you doing?'

There were little air bubbles under it, so she smoothed it down from the top. Sean was squirming again. She turned her head to look at him.

'Don't you dare come before I'm finished.'

She gave the condom one further smooth down and then got off him. He moved to sit up.

'Stay still.' She pointed her finger at him and he lay down again. She undid her pyjama bottoms and let them fall to the floor;

stepped out of them and climbed back on to Sean, facing his head this time.

Sean was watching her every move, excited and just a little scared – Katherine liked that. He still had the eyeshadow and blusher on, but most of the lipstick was gone, smeared across his face – and hers too, probably. She lifted up one of his hands and put it on her breast under her pyjama top, then took his penis in one hand and started to lower herself on to it, making Sean close his eyes and lean his head back.

'Don't you dare come yet,' she said again.

It was more difficult than she had imagined; Phillipa must have done it often before to make it look so easy. She tried several different angles until she could get it in her. It wasn't very comfortable, but it didn't hurt the way it had their first time. She lifted herself up a little and then down again. Sean was squeezing her breast, his face screwed up.

'Not yet, Sean.' Katherine raised and lowered herself again, and each time it felt better. She put her hands on Sean's shoulders; almost all his penis was inside her now. He was biting his lip.

'Just a bit longer,' Katherine said.

Sean's hips were moving, lifting off the bed, setting up a rhythm. Katherine tried to keep still, so that he could get his penis deeper, but it was difficult. His movements got faster and faster and she knew he was about to lose it. His body went stiff and she could feel his penis jerking inside her.

'Oh momma,' Sean arched his back, then his whole body relaxed.

Katherine climbed off him; his penis made a squelching noise as it slipped out of her. She wiped the back of her hand between her legs and then wiped it on Sean's cheek.

'Go clean that stuff off,' she said. Sean opened his eyes; he looked stunned, amazed, and with make-up on, he looked like a clown.

He sighed and rolled off the bed, holding his penis as he ducked out of the room. Katherine put her pyjama bottoms back on and climbed into bed. She smiled to herself. OK, she hadn't come, hadn't really been close to coming, but she had enjoyed herself.

She curled up into a ball. Sean came back in with a nearly clean face and a limp, condomless penis. He hopped into bed behind Katherine and put his arms around her.

'Katherine, that was amazing.'

'Sh.' She held his hands.

'I've been so worried, but now I know it's going to be all right.' It still sounded like a question, but for the first time in ages Katherine thought that everything *would* be all right.

'Sh,' she said again, and they both fell asleep.

THIRTEEN
Violet

On Thursday morning, Fiona rang.
'She's rung four times already this morning,' she told Violet.
'Who?'
'Who do you think? The woman who is now the love of your life.'
'Alice?'
'Give the girl a prize. Here's her number, ring her before Judy breaks the phone.'

Violet went off to her summer class. She had a half-day, and in the afternoon she set out to look round gyms. They had been told when they enrolled for the course that they needed to find their own work placement and she wanted to get in early and find a good one. She visited a women's gym in Crouch End. The receptionist was snotty and wouldn't take her around or let her look herself. The place was smart but Violet didn't like it. She also went to the YMCA, where it was quiet, but the staff were friendly. The man behind the desk said they had a waiting list the length of his arm for students wanting to work there. He suggested she try The Centre and gave her the number and the address. Violet had no idea what it was 'the centre' for or of, but because she was avoiding going home and avoiding ringing Alice, she went to the address. At first, she couldn't see anything that looked like a gym, but then she found the door. Inside it still didn't look like a gym. There was a reception desk and a cafe. A very effeminate man was sitting at the desk, with blue hair and lots of make-up, pink eyeshadow and green lipstick.

'Can I help, love?' he asked, leaning back in his chair, looking Violet up and down.

'I'm looking for the gym.'

'Of course you are, darling.' With lots of hand-waving, he directed her to it.

It was in the basement along a corridor, and seemed totally empty. Beyond a desk and some papers was the equipment: a few bikes; just a couple of machines; some free weights and mats, not much at all. Violet was about to leave when she heard some voices coming from another room. There were two doors: one to the women's changing, the other to the men's. Violet looked into the women's changing room and found it empty; the voices were coming from the men's. Having grown up with four brothers, she wasn't shy around men, so she pushed the door open a little – and then closed it again quickly.

There were two men in there, one of them kneeling in front of the other and sucking hard on his penis. Violet left the gym quietly and went back upstairs. She sat down in the cafe area, wondering what kind of place this was. There were only a couple of people in there, all men. The two behind the counter were looking into each other's eyes and holding hands.

Violet had never met any gay men before coming to London. She had seen pictures, of course, and even shouted 'faggots' often enough at Jason and James, her twin brothers, but to walk in on them having sex was a little shocking.

'Find the gym, honey?' The man from reception stopped by Violet's table.

'No, well yes.' Violet felt herself start to blush. 'There wasn't anyone there.'

'Oh, that Roger, always skiving off.' He tossed his head. 'I've told him and told him. Oh look, there he is now.'

Violet turned and saw the man who had been standing in the changing room.

'Rodge, you slag, where've you been?' The reception man shouted across the room to him. 'This young lady wanted to see you.'

Violet was getting more and more embarrassed. She just hoped he hadn't see her.

Roger sat down opposite Violet. 'Yes?' he said, looking at her expectantly. Violet explained that she needed work and Roger nodded.

'When can you start?'

'I'm not qualified yet.'

'Young blood, exactly what we need.' Roger smiled at Violet and the man from reception laughed a dirty kind of laugh.

So Violet agreed to start working there, three nights a week, six till nine. She finally got up the courage to ask what kind of 'centre' this was. They laughed at her and explained it was the London Lesbian and Gay Centre. So, it seemed that the man at the YMCA had spotted her for a lesbian when he gave her the address.

Mission accomplished, she headed home where she bumped straight into Julie.

'So –' Julie stood in front of her, '– the wanderer returns.'

'Yeah.' Violet was pleased it was Julie and not Tree or Rainbow, but she would rather it had been no one.

'Rainbow and Tree are very upset.'

'Yeah?'

'They feel you don't respect the house as much as you should.'

'It's a tip.'

'Not the physical house, the house as a unit, living together.'

'Oh.'

'Not showing for the house meeting indicated to them contempt for the process of communication.'

'I was working.'

'And to leave that poetry reading before the end, with Belinda, that is tantamount to treason.' Julie smiled as she said that. 'Personally, I think Belinda is deliciously un-PC.' She giggled.

Violet sighed. 'What can I do?'

'Well,' Julie paused. 'I know they seem like nutcases but it is their house, so play along a little. Write a note saying you're very sorry and suggest another house meeting. By the time we're all free for one evening, they'll have forgotten about it. If that fails, tidy up the place a bit and offer to fix the garden fence. They're too tight to pay for someone to do it.'

Violet wrote the note and spent Friday morning fixing the fence. She also rang Alice and tried to explain that it was a one-off thing and that she didn't want to see her again. Alice cried a lot and said that her horoscope said that they made a perfect match and Violet was denying her own destiny and Alice's. Violet hung up in the end. She had started off feeling guilty and ended up feeling angry.

Violet read in *City Limits* that the place the leather dykes hung out was the New Covent Garden Tavern in south London. It was dark and loud and the women were mostly all in leather but not with the dog collars and leads she had seen at Aphrodite Rising. She was early as usual and settled in a corner table with her beer. Some of the women who arrived looked slightly familiar, but she couldn't tell whether it was because she had seen them before or whether all lesbians were starting to look the same.

They looked a bit scary, most of the women – no dancing, no smiling, just lots of standing around looking at each other. Violet was beginning to wonder if maybe this wasn't the place to find her Felicity, when a woman came and sat at her table.

'Hi,' the woman said, nodding at Violet, who nodded back. 'Not seen you here before.'

'No.'

The woman nodded again and they sat in silence for a while. Violet looked at the woman out of the corner of her eye. She was a light-skinned black woman, thin and strong looking; her hair was cut dangerously short but her face was soft. She had tattoos on her arm.

'Do you like cats?' she asked suddenly out of the silence.

'Yeah.' Violet wasn't sure if it was the right answer. She thought that it might be some lesbian code question and she could be getting herself into trouble.

'Here.' The woman reached into her jacket and pulled out her wallet to show a photo of two kittens. 'They're my babies, Jasper and Carrot.'

The kittens were sweet and Violet smiled.

'Name's Terry.' She held out her hand to shake.

'Violet.'

'So, you want to have sex or are you one of those feminists?'

Violet smiled again; she liked this place. 'Sure,' she said, her heart pounding. She felt nervous. And very excited.

'I don't kiss and none of this safe sex stuff. I hate dental dams.'

'OK.' Violet had no idea what dental dams were, but they sounded painful. 'Where?'

'Can't do it at my place, dog doesn't like it. That's the dog.' She flipped a leaf in her wallet to another photo.

'Nor mine,' Violet said, imagining Tree and Rainbow's faces if they saw Terry.

'Loos?' Terry suggested.

Violet nodded; they both got up and made their way over to the toilets. It felt very odd to Violet; she was wondering what sex would be like without kissing, and what a dental dam was. There was one woman in front of them and they waited in silence. The toilets were painted black and there were only two cubicles. The woman in front of them went in and a few minutes later came out again. Violet and Terry looked at each other and then went in together. Violet felt the sudden urge to laugh, the whole thing too weird to be true. Terry, though, looked very serious.

Once in the cubicle, they stood either side of the toilet bowl and looked at each other, not moving for a moment, then Violet reached out and put her hand on Terry's cheek. Terry pulled her hand away.

'Not the face,' she said.

Violet moved her hand down to one of Terry's breasts, which was small and firm, hard even. Terry just stood there and looked at her. Violet put her other hand out and touched Terry's other breast. She wasn't wearing a bra. Violet circled the nipples with her thumbs. Terry closed her eyes and gritted her teeth. Violet wasn't sure if that was a good sign or not, but decided she would continue until Terry stopped her.

She undid Terry's belt and the fly of her leather trousers, to find men's boxer shorts. Her legs were very skinny; her stomach was flat with well-defined muscles. Violet slid her hand up under Terry's T-shirt and took a nipple between her thumb and first finger, then slid the other hand down into Terry's boxer shorts.

'Wait.' Terry put her hand on Violet's arm and she stopped moving. 'Use this.' Terry reached inside her jacket and produced a large dildo. It was black and rubbery, about ten inches long and a good inch and a half in diameter, one end rounded and the other flat. She took the dildo in her hand and looked at it, then looked at Terry. Violet knew from her housemates that penetration with a dildo was the biggest taboo in the feminist book.

'OK,' she said. She pulled Terry's jeans and boxer shorts down to the floor, exposing her pubic hair.

Violet wasn't too sure how to use the dildo. She gripped the flat end and with her other hand found Terry's slit. She didn't quite believe that the huge dildo would fit into the small hole or that Terry could be wet enough for it to slide in there, but she took a deep breath and pushed the dildo in. Terry gave a little gasp; the dildo stuck, so Violet tried it at a different angle. It slid in further and Terry breathed out hard.

Violet wasn't quite sure what to do next, but she slid the dildo out a little and then back in.

'Yes,' Terry said through gritted teeth.

Violet tried it again; it stuck on something, making Terry gasp again. This couldn't be good for Terry but she wasn't stopping her so Violet continued, moving the dildo faster and pushing it in harder and harder. She kept one hand on Terry's breast, squeezing the nipple between her thumb and first finger, seeing little beads of sweat forming on Terry's top lip. Her breathing was hard and a little ragged. Her eyes were tightly closed and her hands were clenched in fists by her side.

'Harder,' she breathed, just when Violet thought she couldn't push any harder. So she did, ramming the dildo in and out as hard as she could, finding that the action excited her. Terry pushed back against the wall. Violet kept shoving the dildo in and out. She could see that Terry was about to come, her whole body seemed to gather in on itself, more and more tense, and then with an animal-like grunt, she went completely limp, sliding down the wall.

Violet lifted her up, and sat her on the loo seat and slid the dildo out of her, which sent little shivers through Terry's whole body. She just sat there for a moment, eyes closed, then shook her head like a wet dog and pulled up her boxers and jeans.

'Your go now,' she said.

Violet smiled. 'No thanks.'

Terry shrugged. 'You should try it.'

Violet shrugged too. 'Not today.'

Terry wiped the dildo with her hand and put it back in her pocket. 'See you around,' she said, sliding back the lock on the cubicle door.

'Wait.' Violet couldn't just let her walk out. 'Can I see you again?'

'What for?'

'I don't know, a drink maybe.'

Terry looked her up and down. 'I've got a girlfriend.' She reached into her jacket, took out her wallet again and flipped it to a picture of a pretty young blonde woman. 'Doesn't do this stuff.' She patted the dildo in her pocket. She shrugged and left.

Violet stood for a moment, embarrassed and disappointed: she could imagine everyone's faces if she turned up with Terry to the wedding, in her leather jacket and tattoos, but Terry had a girlfriend, so she would have to find someone else. She wondered how she would score this episode in her Felicity notebook; she had hardly touched Terry. The dildo had done all the work and Terry didn't look like she had enjoyed it overly, but it had been interesting if rather brief.

Someone pushed the cubicle; she looked a bit familiar.

'Sorry,' she said, 'I thought . . . I saw her go out and thought. I didn't realise . . .'

'It's OK,' Violet said, 'I was going too.'

The woman stood in her way. 'I know you,' she said accusingly, 'you're Katherine's girlfriend.'

'Katherine?' Violet felt immediate guilt. How could this woman know about her and Katherine, when only Katherine's mother and Miss Phelps knew about it?

'My flatmate.' The woman was standing with her hands on her hips. 'I saw what you did to her.'

Violet realised she was talking about Kathy from Aphrodite Rising, and she was the woman who belonged to the legs – who had walked in on them in the kitchen. The woman closed the cubicle door and locked it; Violet didn't understand what she was doing.

'Do it to me,' the woman said. 'I won't tell Katherine, but it looked so good when you had your fingers in her. Do it to me.' She was taking off her jacket and undoing her trousers. Violet looked at her; she couldn't really believe what was happening here. Her first instincts were to get the hell out of there, but she did need someone to take to the wedding and here was a woman begging her to have sex with her.

'Please.'

'What's your name?' Violet was stalling, trying to think. She didn't need another Alice crying down the phone at her.

'Cynthia. I won't tell Katherine, honest.'

'You won't tell anyone.' It sounded more threatening than Violet had intended, but Cynthia just shook her head.

She wasn't unattractive: light red hair with lots of freckles, cold grey eyes that watched Violet's every move. She was quite drunk . . . Why not? Violet would probably regret it, but hey, she would have to sleep with a few she would regret before she found her Felicity. She slid her hand up under Cynthia's T-shirt, her skin felt clammy. She had on a bra but only a sports one, and Violet pushed that up so Cynthia's breasts were bare. They looked puffy, standing up on Cynthia's body in an odd sort of way. Violet licked each nipple and then blew on them, watching as the nipples contracted in. Cynthia reached out to touch Violet's breasts but Violet pushed her hands out of the way.

Violet spread her fingers out and ran them down from Cynthia's breasts to the top of her knickers. More sad, grey cotton things with a hole under the elastic. Violet put her finger in the hole and pulled; they ripped.

'Hey!' Cynthia said.

Violet put her hand over Cynthia's mouth. She pulled at the knickers until she had ripped the top piece of elastic off and it was only held on by the side seam. She pushed Cynthia's jeans further down and started ripping the leg elastic off. She turned Cynthia around to face the wall so she could get at the back of the knickers. When it was all off she slid her fingers in under the knickers and up into Cynthia. She leaned her hips into Cynthia's bottom and pushed into the cubicle wall. She slid her other hand down the front of the knickers and slid two fingers into Cynthia from the front. She put her mouth next to Cynthia's ear.

'Enjoying it so far?' she whispered. Cynthia nodded but didn't say anything.

''Cause this is what you wanted, isn't it?'

Cynthia nodded again. She looked like she might start crying. Violet felt a bit bad, so she started gently sliding her fingers in and out. Her thumb was resting by Cynthia's anus; she circled that slowly too. Cynthia was breathing heavily now; her cheek was pressed against the wall. Violet could feel the flesh under her fingers changing texture, getting wet and swollen.

'You like that?' she whispered in Cynthia's ear.

'Yes,' Cynthia said faintly.

Violet moved her fingers in faster, smaller movements. Cynthia was panting now, in little gasps. Violet's fingers were starting to ache but she kept them moving. Cynthia's breathing slowed down again; Violet stopped moving her fingers.

'Sorry,' Cynthia said, 'I'm sorry. I've never, you know . . . and Katherine said she hardly ever but you did it . . . I just thought . . .' She moved away so Violet's finger slid out of her and started to pull up her jeans.

'No, wait,' Violet said, realising the woman was trying to talk about coming. 'We can try something else.'

'Sorry.' Cynthia was crying now. 'I've just never . . . and I wanted to. We're supposed to now . . . Before it didn't matter but now everyone's talking like we should, all the time and I just thought . . .'

'Sh.' Violet wiped Cynthia's tears away. 'Maybe a loo's not the best place.' She felt awful. 'Maybe we should try somewhere else.'

'It's not ever going to happen, my mum was like it, so am I.'

Violet kissed her on the cheek, pulled Cynthia close to her.

'I thought with someone I didn't know . . .'

'Sh,' Violet said again. She rubbed her breasts across Cynthia's body slowly and kissed the side of her neck, then put her leg between Cynthia's.

'No, I can't do this.' She pulled Violet away.

Violet stepped back and shrugged: she hadn't started it – though she would have liked to have finished it. 'Maybe another time.'

Cynthia didn't seem to hear her; she was fumbling with the lock on the door. Eventually she got it opened and left quickly. There was a queue of women waiting; they all looked at Violet.

'Anyone else?' Violet asked, but it was just bravado – she was exhausted, all she wanted to do was go home.

A woman in the queue in a black leather cap smiled at Violet. It wasn't until she was nearly at the tube that she realised it was Belinda. It was too late then to go back, and she was too tired.

FOURTEEN
Katherine

She woke early the next morning with Sean's arms around her, got out of bed without waking him and went downstairs. There was some post on the mat, so she took it through to the kitchen and sorted it out while she was waiting for the kettle to boil. There were some wedding replies, one from an aunt of Sean's, another from some cousin of her mother's.

The kettle boiled and she made coffee for her and Sean, smiling as she did it. This is what married life would be like, the two of them together in the mornings. Katherine tucked the other wedding replies under her arm and carried the coffees upstairs. Sean was still asleep so she sat up in bed and opened the rest of the replies.

One of Sean's sister in Australia saying she couldn't come, the next was from Violet. Katherine felt a shiver go through her, like she was sitting in a draught, when she saw Violet's name, but it was worse than that just Violet saying she was coming – she was bringing someone with her. In the space beside her name, written in her straight up and down handwriting, was the name Felicity Hope.

Katherine got out of bed again; she took the reply and her coffee downstairs. She tried sitting in the front room, but all she could see was the beanbag where Violet had pushed her back into the softness of the bag, unzipped her jeans and started going down on her before leaving the last time. Katherine wondered if she would do that to this Felicity Hope.

She went into the kitchen, but there was the big wooden table where her mother had caught them one night. It still had the scorch marks where she had put down the pizzas that had burnt while they made love for the first time. She bet Felicity Hope wouldn't burn pizzas.

Out in the back garden, she pictured how she and Violet had lain on a rug laughing about the awfulness of the wine that Katherine's mother had left for them, and wondering if it would kill the little bush they had drenched with it. The bush was still there, and Katherine imagined she could even still see a patch of flattened grass from the rug.

She stood with her coffee in one hand and the wedding reply in the other and found that she was crying. Violet had only been in London three weeks and already she had found someone else, someone with a silly, prissy name: Felicity bloody Hope. Katherine could just see her, little and blonde with big breasts and a high tight bottom. She could see her holding on to Violet's arm coming into the church, looking around with disdain at the smallness of it, the flowers, the other guests. Then, while Katherine is walking down the aisle, they are whispering and giggling together, Violet and Felicity Hope. Making fun of Katherine: her hair, her dress, her shoes even; the fact she has no father to give her away. Tears were falling in her coffee and on to the reply card; Katherine sat down on the back step.

Everything had been perfect at last, and now Violet had gone and spoilt it. Her mother was right – Violet was a bad influence on her and she had done the best thing by ending it with her. Even if at first she had missed her so badly that it sometimes felt like a bit of her body had been amputated.

She should have listened to her mother and not invited her, but she had no idea Violet would say yes, and that she would want to bring someone, some Felicity Hope, with her. Nor had she realised she would feel quite as badly about the whole thing. But now that Katherine had invited her and Violet was coming along with her

Felicity bloody Hope, she couldn't stop her and would just have pull herself together. She would have to show Violet just how over her she was, how happy and normal she was; she would show her what a wonderful person Sean was and how right they are for each other. How bloody perfect they were for each other.

Katherine heard someone come into the kitchen and wiped her eyes. It was Sean, fully dressed.

'You OK, babe?' He sat down beside her.

'Yes.' Katherine put the reply in her pyjama pocket.

'You've been crying.'

Katherine leaned her head on his shoulder. 'It's just because I'm so happy.'

Sean stroked her head. 'Me too.'

He started kissing her, softly at first but then his tongue got pushier and he tried to get his hand inside her pyjama top.

'No, Sean.' She pushed him gently away. 'I've got college and you've got to go.'

He looked a bit sulky but he left and kissed her again as she waved him off from the front door. 'I love you,' he said, and he ran out to his car.

Katherine had a long shower, just letting the water run over her body, feeling it soothe her, calm her. Until her mother banged on the door and told her not to use all the hot water.

The rest of the week was college and training, then more training. She saw Sean every night, as well as Phillipa and Matt, who seemed to be keeping a polite distance which suited Katherine just fine. Katherine claimed too much work to go out drinking with them after training, and exhaustion on Saturday after a particularly strenuous training session. Mr Williams was gearing them up for their next big meet and because Katherine was missing a Saturday training for her mother's wedding, he seemed to be picking on her more than usual. She hadn't been able to match her Paris times in training, but then she didn't dare try to use Phillipa to race against. In fact, she was trying to forget about Phillipa – and Violet too – and that seemed to make her swim more slowly. She just hoped the German would be there as competition for her in Munich – their next international.

On Sunday evening, after another hard training session, Sean and Brian came round for dinner. Katherine was in the kitchen helping her mother with the full roast dinner, the men were in the front room talking.

'I'm so happy,' Katherine's mother said, putting the lids on the peas and carrots, before squeezing Katherine's hand. 'I always felt bad that you didn't have a father, and I know it's a bit late, but I hope you'll be able to see Brian as your father.'

Katherine was stirring the gravy. She saw Brian as her mother's awkward, goofy, rather comical boyfriend. There was nothing remotely father-like about him.

'So, we were wondering . . .'

Katherine had noticed that her mother was talking in the 'we' all the time now, and not meaning her and Katherine, but her and Brian. She was starting to find it annoying.

'. . . if you would like him to give you away.'

Katherine stopped her stirring. She had thought about this problem – of having no one to give her away – and had decided that she and Sean would walk up the aisle together. As a child, she had fantasised about her wedding and imagined her father, some shadowy figure who looked a bit like Paul Newman, walking beside her down the aisle. She had not imagined being given away by a tall, thin, balding man with beer-bottle-bottom glasses.

'Actually, Sean and I are going to walk down the aisle together.'

'Oh.' Her mother sounded a little upset.

'We've talked about it to the minister and he thinks it's a really good idea. I mean the idea of being "given away" is so archaic – this is the 80s after all.'

Her mother didn't look convinced. 'The offer is there if you want it.'

The dinner was nice, and Brian told them all about his collection of rare and first edition comics. Sean seemed genuinely interested; Katherine thought they were both to old for comics, but it sounded like you could make money if you knew what you were looking for. Her mother was pretty quiet; Katherine worried that she had upset her. She tried to think of other ways to involve Brian in the ceremony. An image came to her of him as a bridesmaid, in a little tutu with a basket, skipping down the aisle in front of them, tossing rose petals. Katherine smiled to herself. Then she pictured him as a pageboy in bow tie and too short trousers, pulling the pigtails of a bridesmaid and laughing his toothy, goofy laugh.

'What's so funny?' Her mother had been watching her.

'Nothing.' Katherine felt herself start to blush and looked at Sean for help, but he was grilling Brian about Spiderman and Judge Dredd.

'Oh,' her mother said knowingly, obviously imagining she was thinking about Sean and sex, and Katherine didn't try to correct that impression. She diverted her from further questions by asking about the flowers for *her* wedding. She knew her mother was worried about them, along with her shoes, the food, and the pub.

'Oh, aren't I being silly, worrying so.'

Brian put one hand on hers and lifted her chin with his other hand. 'It will be perfect, whatever happens, for me it will be perfect, because I'm marrying my angel.' He kissed the tip of her nose.

Katherine could see the tears in her mother's eyes and felt close to them herself. She felt bad about all the uncharitable things she had ever thought about him. He obviously loved her mother very much and made her very happy, and for Katherine that was such a relief after years of living through one failed relationship after another.

Brian stayed the night for the first time, and so did Sean. Katherine couldn't concentrate enough to have sex though. She found herself straining to hear any sound coming out of her mother's bedroom: the idea that they might be having sex in the next room was unimaginable. She couldn't bear the thought and yet she couldn't stop trying to hear what was going on.

Sean started to get impatient. 'She told me he was well hung,' he said, out of nothing.

'I don't want to know.' Katherine didn't believe it.

'OK.' Sean lay on his back and stared at the ceiling.

Katherine couldn't bear it. 'When did she say that?'

'I thought you didn't want to know.'

'Oh, Sean, don't be a pain. When?'

'When you were out with Phillipa.'

So, he hadn't been told that Matt was there as well.

'I don't believe you,' said Katherine.

'She said they had amazing sex, that he was so gentle.'

Katherine tried to picture it, but all she could get was bony arms and legs pinning her mother to the bed, like a spider.

'I think she was hinting.'

'What at?' Katherine had an image of Sean and her mother having sex: she was on top riding him like a horse, he was having trouble breathing.

'Me being gentle.' He snuggled into her and squeezed her breast.

'Sorry Sean, I'm just not in the mood.' She turned over and pretended to sleep. Sean turned away too and after some fidgeting he fell asleep – Katherine could hear his breathing, shallow and regular. She lay very still and tried to hear if there were noises coming from her mother's room. She thought she could hear low voices and then silence. She got up and went to the bathroom; the light was on in her mother's room. Katherine sat on the toilet in the dark for a while. She could hear voices again, a little louder, short bursts of words and then silence. She couldn't make out what was being said, though, so she got off the toilet and stood in the hallway. She knew she shouldn't be there, and would be mortified if she was caught eavesdropping, but she needed to know what they were saying.

Then she heard her mother's voice, stern and hard, saying something about being naughty. Brian replied, high-pitched and whining, but nothing Katherine could catch. Then there was another sound that Katherine couldn't work out; it sounded like a slap, but thinner. It was a shocking sort of sound; Katherine felt her heart race. It sounded again and again and then there was someone crying, pleading, and another thin slap. Katherine put her hand out to the door handle; something very wrong was going on in there, someone was hitting someone. So much for her mother going on about how gentle Brian was. There was some more low voices and then a louder slap and a cry of pain.

Katherine threw open the door. There on the bed, tied hand and foot, was Brian. His top half was covered in leather, with no holes for his eyes or nose, just one for his mouth. His bottom half was naked except for something around the base of his penis. That was shocking enough, but far more shocking than that was Katherine's mother. She was standing beside the bed, dressed in thigh-length leather boots, long leather gloves, and a red underwear set that was crotchless and left the nipples uncovered. She had a whip in one hand, raised above her head, ready to bring it down on Brian's naked bottom half. Katherine could see some welts where she had already hit him.

'Katherine,' her mother said.

Katherine shut the door and raced downstairs. She was stunned, completely stunned. Of all the possible scenarios she had imagined for her mother, and there were a few, she had never, ever imagined it would be like that. She stood in the kitchen, holding on to the table, wondering what she should be thinking, hovering between laughing and crying, holding the table tight, rocking backwards and forwards. The kitchen light came on; Katherine put a hand over her eyes. No wonder they always stayed at Brian's place – he probably had a proper dungeon set up there, chains from the ceiling . . . she giggled.

'Katherine?' She turned around; her mother was standing in front of her. She had put on her dressing gown, but still wore her boots and gloves. She looked upset, though not angry or embarrassed.

Katherine thought she was going to start laughing again.

'I'm sorry,' they both said at the same time.

Katherine did laugh then.

'I don't see what's funny.' Her mother sounded hurt.

Sean chose that moment to come bursting into the kitchen in just his underpants and socks. Katherine took one look at him and laughed even harder; her mother saw him and started to laugh too.

'What?' Sean asked, putting his hands in front of his pants as if he was naked, which made Katherine laugh even harder. She had to sit down, she was laughing so hard, tears streaming down her face. Her mother sat down too and then stood up again.

'I'd better go and see to Brian.'

Katherine nearly fell off her chair for laughing. Her mother went back upstairs and Sean stood and watched Katherine, waiting for her to calm down. She rested her head on the table.

'What?' Sean asked finally, after Katherine had stopped laughing.

'You don't want to know, believe me, you don't.' She was suddenly very tired. 'Come on, let's go back to bed.'

FIFTEEN
Violet

In her book, she wrote:

6. 14 Sept. New Covent Garden Tavern, Terry, loos. 6/10
Unsuitable because has a girlfriend.
7. 14 Sept. New Covent Garden Tavern, Cynthia, loos. 2/10
Unsuitable because . . .

That was another difficult one. Because she left in tears? Because she couldn't come? Violet left a gap there, she would go back to it later.

Friday was her first evening at the gym and she went in straight from college. It was pretty quiet, she just had to sit at the desk and check people's membership cards. Roger was there too, but he mostly stayed out of the way. It was largely men who came in, chatting and gossiping; the few women got on with their workouts and left. Violet did notice a few looks from them, but they didn't actually try and engage her in conversation, for which she was quite grateful.

'Tomorrow night,' Roger said as she was leaving, 'wear shorts and a vest – those trackie bottoms are just awful.'

SWEET VIOLET

Violet was a bit annoyed, but she didn't say anything. He went about in tight Lycra shorts and a skimpy vest, so presumably what they were selling was sex appeal. Violet couldn't see herself in that role, though she knew she was OK-looking. With her hair cut short, she looked just like her brother, and nothing stuck out of her swimsuit where it shouldn't.

That was part of the reason why she picked women up so easily, because she looked OK. Katherine had said she had nice eyes, but she couldn't see it. Katherine – why did it always come back to Katherine? It was only three weeks to the wedding and she still hadn't found a Felicity.

She stopped for a drink in the cafe, still avoiding spending too much time at home. She noticed some women in leather going upstairs.

'The SM lot,' said Mark, her camp colleague, shivering dramatically.

Violet wondered if this lot were the dog collar and whips crowd she had seen at Aphrodite Rising: that would be good at the wedding, maybe she should check them out.

She looked on the noticeboard and saw which room they were meeting in. She went back to the bar and had another beer to fortify herself. She wasn't dressed for it, but then she didn't own anything that would dress her for it.

She went up the stairs and stopped outside the door; she could hear voices inside. She took a deep breath and opened the door. Ten or twelve heads turned and stared at her; all talking stopped.

'Hi,' Violet said, her voice high and squeaky.

Still no one said anything; the women looked at her suspiciously. They were all in black: leather, denim, some lace even, but it was all black. Most had various metal adornments, piercing, handcuffs, chains and clamps. In her blue jeans and anorak, she felt almost naked.

A big shaven-haired woman with a pierced eyebrow seemed to be leading the group. 'This is an SM meeting,' she said threateningly.

'That's why I'm here.' Violet tried to sound firm.

'Well.' The woman clearly didn't believe her. 'We do like people to arrive on time.'

'I was working, sorry.' Violet suppressed a smile and sat down near the door.

The big woman was called Gwendolyn and was demonstrating a new sex toy. It was in an old-fashioned box and appeared to give electric shocks through an electrode. The woman she was demonstrating on was called Debs; she was small and blonde with spiky hair – perhaps the effect of the electrodes.

The demonstration was almost over and Violet thought it was rather tame. Gwendolyn suggest some other places to apply the electrode and the women giggled like a roomful of schoolgirls. After she had finished, there was tea and biscuits, the women mingled a bit and they tried out the electrode on each other. Violet stayed in her seat and watched them. Debs came over to her; she was wearing leather chaps, black of course, with only a G-string under them, and a leather waistcoat with nothing under it. She looked artificially brown.

'You into SM then?' she asked as though she didn't believe it.

Violet nodded.

'You a top or bottom?'

Violet worried that it was a trick question and that she was going to be found out as a fraud. 'What do you think?' she asked, hoping to sound cool.

Debs looked her up and down, then took Violet's hand and examined her nails. 'I'd say a top,' she concluded.

Violet smiled, looking at Debs's own nails, which were long with black nail polish. 'That would make you a bottom, then.'

Debs smiled too. 'Only the best.' She bent forward to pick a piece of fluff off Violet's jacket, giving her a close-up view of her cleavage. 'So what are you into? Whips, cuffs, watersports?'

Violet wasn't sure if swimming counted as a watersport; she somehow doubted it. Before she had a chance to show herself up, though, Gwendolyn called Debs away. Violet watched Debs's bottom as she walked away. Now she could take *that* to the wedding, no problems.

The other women were whispering and giggling. Violet thought

SWEET VIOLET

they were probably talking about her – time for her to leave. As much as she would like to take Debs to the wedding, Debs and Gwendolyn were probably an item and there was no way she was going to mess with Gwendolyn. She headed for the door; Debs came over and stopped her.

'Don't go.' She put her hand on Violet's arm. Even through the material of her jacket, Violet could feel that touch like it was the electrode Gwendolyn had been using earlier. She didn't leave.

'All these tired old SMers, look at them,' Debs whispered in her ear. Violet felt suddenly very hot.

'That's Pickles there.' She pointed out a woman nearly as scary looking as Gwendolyn, with short, bleached blonde hair and a permanent sneer, in a kilt with safety pins through it and more safety pins in her ears and nose. She had a woman on a dog chain kneeling in front of her and she was resting one booted foot on her.

'And that's Jennifer.' The woman on her knees. 'She works in a bank, the assistant manager or something. And they are Jacky and Jill.' She nodded her head towards two women in matching leather trousers and jackets, deep in discussion about handcuffs.

'Police issue,' one was saying. 'Light, strong and hardly leaves a bruise.'

'Oh, nice.' The other touched the said cuff with reverence.

'They're hardware girls,' Debs whispered. 'But they don't like to use the stuff too much in case it gets dirty.'

'And that is Faye.' She directed Violet to a sad-looking woman in black jeans and a T-shirt. 'She was Pickles's bottom until Jennifer came along. Hopefully someone will take pity on her tonight and whip that lard-arse of hers until it bleeds.'

Violet tried not to look too shocked by all this.

'So, you want to come back to mine then?' Debs asked her.

Violet was shocked then. 'I thought you and Gwendolyn . . .' She looked over and Gwendolyn had a woman across her knee and was demonstrating her toy on the woman's bare bottom.

'I think Gwendolyn has other things planned for tonight.' Debs didn't look the least bit upset about it.

Violet smiled. 'Let's go then.' She was going to thoroughly

enjoy this; Debs was perfect for the wedding, very pretty and totally outrageous. On the way out of the building, Debs popped into the loos and came out wearing jeans, and a jacket over her waistcoat. Mark saw them leave together and shook his head at Violet. 'You be careful,' he whispered at her.

Violet laughed. 'You're just jealous.' She waited for some camp reply but he didn't say anything, just shook his head and looked worried.

They got the tube to Highgate and then walked for what seemed like miles down a very steep hill until they came to a big estate.

'It was built by the Victorians for single women coming to London to work,' said Debs, 'now it's full of lesbians. Great, isn't it?'

The flat was on the fourth floor and had a lovely view, but it was tiny. Just a bedsit with a microscopic kitchen and the bathroom across the hall. It had low ceilings and was painted black which made it seem even smaller, and there was a futon folded up as a sofa. Violet had learnt a lot about furniture, working for Judy and Fiona – she'd never heard of futons before that. On the ceiling above the futon were mirrors and some big hooks with chains dangling off them.

Debs took some handcuffs out of her bag and tossed them on the futon together with a dog collar and chain, then some things that looked like D-clamps but smaller. 'Take your pick,' she said, and she slid her jacket off seductively.

Violet went over to her and undid the zip of her waistcoat; she pushed it off Debs's shoulders and admired her breasts. They were round and high and tanned. Violet brushed her thumbs over them, Debs arched her back slightly.

'What's your safe word then?' Debs asked.

Violet had no idea what she was talking about; she said the first word that came into her head. 'Felicity.'

Debs looked at her strangely. 'OK,' she said as though it wasn't really. 'Mine is "star".'

'OK.' Violet wanted to get started; she pushed the palm of her hand into Debs's breast. Debs picked up the handcuffs and handed them to her. Violet put them around each of Debs's wrists; the click as they locked into place gave Violet goosebumps. She then hung them over one of the ceiling hooks so Debs's arms were above her head, her feet barely touching the ground.

Violet ran her hands down Debs's body, which was the same unnatural brown all over and felt almost leathery to the touch. She was smaller than Violet had thought; so small that Violet could almost get her hands right round Debs's waist. She licked each nipple and watched the cold air do its stuff. Then she undid Debs's jeans and pulled them down, revealing the black G-string. Violet threw up a silent thank you, to whatever god or goddess ruled over lesbian underwear, that not all wore grey cotton knickers. Debs had kicked off her shoes so Violet pulled the jeans right off. Noting that there was no tan-line, she ran her fingers around the elastic of the G-string, following it to where it disappeared up between Debs's cheeks. She gripped Debs's bare bottom in one hand, held the back of her head with the other and kissed her, hard and fast. Debs responded, their tongues tangling and their mouths grinding into one another's.

Violet pinched Debs's nipple between her thumb and forefinger; Debs seemed to like that, her breathing was harder. 'Use the clamp,' she whispered.

Violet picked it up off the futon; she unwound it a little and then carefully wound it up over Debs's nipple, thankful that she had taken woodwork at school and not sewing. Debs drew in a sharp breath and Violet stopped winding.

'Tighter,' Debs gasped. Violet wasn't sure it was good for her but she did as she was told. 'Oh God.' Debs closed her eyes. 'The other one.'

Violet put the other clamp on but didn't do it up as tightly. She wasn't sure what to do next. Debs seemed to be enjoying herself, and Violet found that it was quite a turn-on having someone completely at her mercy, even though she didn't know what else to do with her.

Debs had a lovely body, small and compact, the G-string sitting in a perfect triangle like some artificial pubic hair. Violet slipped her hand down inside it and then pulled it out again – it seemed

Debs didn't have any pubic hair. She pulled off the G-string and there was Debs, completely naked, not a hair on her body.

Debs was watching her. 'You like that?' she asked.

Violet nodded, she ran her fingers over the shaved skin and let her middle finger slip inside Debs. She was in for another surprise; Debs had a stud in there, pierced through one side of her labia. She drew in a sharp breath as Violet's finger touched it. Violet was fascinated; it felt so strange, a hard cold piece of metal in amongst the soft warm wet flesh. As she ran her thumb over it and watched Debs throw her head back, she imagined how much it must have hurt to have it done, and felt all the muscles inside her contract protectively.

She knelt down in front of Debs and rubbed her cheek over the naked mound, gripped both cheeks of Debs bottom and ran her tongue over the skin, feeling it turn to goosebumps. She slid her tongue into Debs and felt the shock of the metal against it, rolled it around with her tongue and then sucked the stud into her mouth and pushed it back out again, as Debs groaned. She flicked the head of the stud with her tongue and slid her fingers in past it.

Debs was breathing hard now, her body swaying slightly. Violet dug her fingers hard into Debs's bottom, trying to keep it still.

Debs started to pant. 'Oh God.'

Violet flicked her tongue harder against the stud and pushed her fingers deeper, adding her thumbs. Debs seemed to be opening up to her fingers.

'Harder,' she panted. Her legs were starting to twitch and her feet were pressing into the floor. She clamped her thighs around Violet's head. Violet could barely breathe but she kept her tongue going and dug her fingers deeper into Debs, who was very close to coming now, Violet could feel it, she was so wet and soft. Violet took the stud into her mouth again and pulled it with her teeth as hard as she dared.

'Oh God!' Debs whole body convulsed, legs, stomach, groin, and she let out a short scream.

Violet gently let go of the stud, pulled her head back and rested it against Debs's stomach. She felt the muscles around her fingers tighten and then release; she pulled them out slowly and Debs shuddered again. She lifted the handcuffs off the hook and laid Debs down on the futon. She realised she didn't have the key to unlock the cuffs but she took off the nipple clamps. One of the nipples was red and swollen, and she kissed it, then kissed Debs on the forehead and pulled the cover over her.

'Very touching,' a voice behind her said.

She swung round. It was Gwendolyn, sitting on a chair, her electrode box on her lap. 'Not bad for an amateur.' She put the box on the floor. 'I'd have used a dildo myself, don't like all those bodily fluids, but different strokes, eh?' She laughed. 'Haven't even taken your jacket off – I like that, though I usually put a lab coat on, in case of blood.'

Violet didn't know whether to be scared, angry or embarrassed. 'How long have you been there?' she demanded, determined not to show she was scared.

'Long enough. I thought I'd come in and finish up, but you don't need it, do you?' She stood up and took a step towards Violet, who stepped out of her way, wondering if it was just her size that made her seem so threatening. Gwendolyn knelt beside Debs.

'OK there, matey.' She squeezed her breast. Debs nodded. 'Have to use your safe word?' Debs shook her head. 'Early days yet, she'll learn.' Debs didn't respond.

'So.' Gwendolyn turned back to Violet. The shaved head and pierced eyebrow certainly added to her scariness. 'Want to watch a pro at work then?' She pulled Debs up by the handcuffs without looking at her and reached for her electrode box. Violet thought she saw real fear in Debs's eyes.

'No thanks,' she said. She tried to catch Debs's eye, to see if she was all right.

'Don't worry about her, she loves it. Don't you, matey?' She pulled Debs to her knees in front of Violet.

'Don't you, matey?' she asked again, more roughly, when Debs didn't answer.

'Yes,' Debs said, and she looked at the floor.

'If you want to come with me . . .' Violet offered, kneeling beside Debs.

Gwendolyn laughed. 'One orgasm and she thinks you'll run away with her,' she said to Debs. She pulled the handcuff chain again. 'Go put your collar on.'

Debs got up, buckled the collar around her neck, handed the lead to Gwendolyn and knelt in front of her.

'Good girl.' Gwendolyn patted her head. Debs looked up at her with such total devotion and gratitude in her eyes that Violet couldn't stand it, or understand it.

'I have to go.' She made for the door.

'Come next week and you can have Faye – needs a lot of work but I'm sure you'd enjoy that. I made a start on her tonight – boy can that girl scream.'

Violet left without answering, ran down the stairs and out into the night. She had enjoyed having that amount of control over Debs; she had to admit that. But to inflict serious pain on someone, even if that was what they wanted . . . she didn't think she could do that. She walked up the hill to the tube station. It was a pity really, because Debs was perfect otherwise.

When she got home she wrote in her book:

8. 22 Sept. Debs, her flat. 9/10. Unsuitable because big scary SM girlfriend. Big pity, perfect otherwise.

SIXTEEN

Katherine

It was Saturday morning and Katherine's alarm was going. She turned it off, thinking that it was time for training, and then she remembered it was her mother's wedding. Things had been a little odd between them since Katherine had caught her in the act. Katherine had tried to say that it was OK, and that she was sorry: firstly for going into the room, even though she thought Brian was hurting her mother, but also for laughing. Katherine thought that might be what was really upsetting her mother – not so much the discovery but that Katherine had laughed. Her mother seemed too embarrassed to talk about it and Katherine hadn't seen Brian since; he had sneaked off some time during the night. She was worried that she wouldn't be able to keep a straight face when she saw him today.

The wedding was at ten. Before that, Katherine had to get her mother up and dressed and down to the hairdresser; check out the pub; collect the flowers and then get herself ready. She climbed out of bed, went downstairs and put the kettle on. She also made some toast, although she wasn't hungry and didn't think her mother would be either, but it was a big day and they both needed to keep their strength up. She put everything on a tray and took it up to her mother's room. She knocked before she went in; Brian wasn't there but she wasn't taking any chances.

'Mum?'

'Yes,' her mother called sleepily.

'Morning.' Katherine put the tray down and sat on the edge of the bed.

'What's the time?'

'Seven.'

'I've got to get up, why didn't you call me earlier?' She started to get out of bed.

'No, Mum, there's loads of time, just relax and have some breakfast, enjoy the peace while you can.'

Her mother didn't look convinced, but she lay down again. 'You're a good kid really.'

They drank their coffees and both ate a piece of toast.

'In a month, this will be you,' said her mother.

'I want champagne and strawberries for my breakfast.' Her wedding was at the much more civilised hour of two o'clock. Her mother's had been arranged on such short notice that ten was the latest they could get.

While her mother showered, Katherine laid out her mother's outfit: a powder blue suit with a white, high-necked blouse to go under it. Katherine had been there when she bought it. Normally she only ever wore black or navy blue, so to see her in such a light colour was a bit of a shock. It made her look older, more like someone's mother, although Katherine didn't tell her that. She wasn't that old, thirty-eight, having had Katherine when she was twenty – not shockingly young, but unmarried. The fact that she was unmarried and meant to keep the baby had caused a huge split in the family. Katherine had never met her grandparents or her uncle; there was one aunt who sent Christmas cards, but she lived in Canada, so she wasn't coming to the wedding.

Katherine drove her mother to the hairdresser's, then went on to the florist to pick up the flowers, then back to the hairdresser's. The flowers were pretty, little blue forget-me-nots in among lots of white flowers. There was a chain of flowers for her mother's hair, buttonholes for the men and some little arrangements for the tables in the pub.

The same people were doing the flowers for Katherine's wedding and the woman wanted to chat about those. Katherine had wanted red flowers, but that had been watered down to pink. She didn't know why anyone asked her opinion about anything to do with her wedding, because they then spent their time arguing her out of it. The woman wanted to do the church too, but Katherine thought that was too much, and too expensive. She tried not to think about how much it was costing – Sean's parents were helping, but still she didn't know how her mother was going to pay it all off.

By the time Katherine got back to the hairdresser's, her mother had been made to look like some cruel parody of Barbra Streisand. Her hair was brown and naturally frizzy; she normally tied it back off her face in a ponytail. The hairdresser had fluffed it out to ridiculous proportions until it looked like she'd had a nasty shock. Her mother took one look at the expression on Katherine's face and burst into tears. Katherine managed to persuade the hairdresser to flatten it down somewhat, and then to persuade her mother that it looked great. In the end it did look great, with the flowers through it.

They stopped on the way home to drop off the flowers at the pub where the reception was being held. Katherine could easily have done it by herself, but her mother insisted on coming too, to check up on everything. There were two women sitting in the room, dirty aprons on, smoking over the uncovered food. The food itself looked a little tired even at that early hour, and there didn't seem to be much of it. Her mother looked like she was going to cry again, so Katherine showed her the cake, which was beautiful. It had three tiers, all decorated in white and blue, and as for the figures on the top, the woman wore a powder blue suit, not a wedding dress. Someone had painted glasses on the man so it even looked a little like Brian. Her mother did cry at that, but in a happy sort of way.

Back at their house, there was a mad panic to get dressed. One of her mother's friends, a loud, round woman called Betty, was there to help with her mother's make-up and things, so Katherine had time for a quick shower and to get herself ready. She put on her new skirt and looked at herself in the mirror. She never felt comfortable in skirts, as she hated the way her legs stuck out the bottom of them, and felt too tall and thin. Betty tried to persuade Katherine to put on some make-up, but Katherine declined, especially after she saw what had been done to her mother – green eyeshadow plastered over her lids.

At 9.45, the car arrived to take them to the town hall, a big black car with light blue ribbons tied to the front. The sight of it nearly had Katherine's mother in tears again.

'Everyone's been so nice,' she said as they got in the car, and dabbed some of her mascara off. They got caught in the Saturday morning traffic, and seemed to spend ages crawling along with people looking in the window. Katherine's mother was panicking and Betty kept saying, 'Fashionably late,' which Katherine didn't think was very helpful.

The actual ceremony seemed totally unreal, like a scene from a soap opera. It was over in no time at all; they were hurried in by some officious man in a security guard's uniform and then hurried back out again. The registrar said something about it being a serious undertaking and that it was illegal to marry anyone for convenience, so they could stay in the country. Katherine looked around at the people gathered there and thought they did look a rather odd bunch, but she still didn't think that was any call for being so rude. They signed the book: her mother and Brian, Brian's best man with wild hair and a squint, and Katherine, as her mother's witness. Sean was there at the back of the room, in an Armani suit, looking a bit out of place among the guests. Brian looked serious and almost presentable and Katherine didn't once feel the urge to laugh at him.

Her mother cried through most of the ceremony, undoing the work Betty had done on her make-up. Katherine cried too, mostly because her mother was, but also because, even though she knew she wasn't losing her, it felt like she was.

Afterwards they had photos in the town hall gardens, a sad patch of grass with a few trees. They had to wait for the wedding party before them to finish and for her mother and Betty to come back from the toilet after fixing their make-up. The sun came out for a moment, but it was so windy that the women in hats couldn't keep them on. Someone had brought a bottle of champagne, but no glasses, so it was being passed round and people were drinking straight from the bottle.

Sean came over to Katherine, took out a tissue and offered it to her.

Katherine took it. 'It's silly, I know.'

'No it's not. I'll probably cry at our wedding, and I know my mother will.'

'That's only because she hates me.'

'She doesn't hate you,' he said, rather unconvincingly.

The photos seemed to take forever; first Brian and her mother, then Katherine was called over, and after that it was every possible combination of friends and family. Katherine's mother held tight to her hand all through the photos – as other people came in and out, the two of them stood there holding hands, like the still eye of a hurricane.

Then the photos were over and everyone piled into cars to go to the pub. Katherine went with Sean in his car.

'You look gorgeous,' Sean said, and he kissed her, holding her breast through her shirt. 'When you stand in the light, you can see right through that blouse.' Katherine crossed her arms over her chest.

'Don't worry, no one else noticed.' Katherine didn't believe him; she wished she had brought her cardigan, or better still, was in her jeans.

'You have a lovely body, I don't know what you're worried about.' He ran his hand up her leg, lifting the skirt up to her thigh. Katherine pushed it back down again.

'Spoilsport.'

They were one of the first cars there. The food didn't look so bad with the flowers arranged between the plates and the smoking women gone. There was a man pouring champagne at the bar and Sean went to get two glasses. The room started to fill with people and someone put on music.

Katherine's mother and Brian arrived and people cheered and toasted them, then there were speeches. Brian's best man made a mercifully short speech about their old days together as bachelors;

Brian got up on a chair and said what a lucky man he was to have found his soulmate, and to get the daughter he always wanted in to the bargain. Katherine blushed and Sean squeezed her shoulder.

There was some more mingling: lots of people Katherine hardly knew, telling her how lovely her mother looked. She did too, despite the hair and Betty's make-up, she had a radiant glow about her. People started eating and the food wasn't that bad.

'I hope we're not using these people for our wedding,' Sean said after spitting some sausage roll into a napkin. 'My parents would die.'

'I don't know, I quite like it here.' Katherine was teasing, but Sean looked at her in horror. She imagined Sean's parents putting on surgical gloves before touching anything, and wearing masks against contact with the unhygienic masses. It was completely unfair on them, but the image of it made Katherine laugh.

No one seemed to notice there wasn't much food, mainly because they were all drinking so much, Katherine included. Although Mr Williams's alcohol ban was in place, because of the Munich competition the next weekend, Katherine thought that she had a reasonable excuse – it's not every day your mother gets married.

By the time the cake was cut, she was feeling a little giddy. There were some more speeches, impromptu ones. Betty got up, very drunk, and said again and again what a great friend Katherine's mother was and how much she loved her. Brian finally managed to get her to sit down by offering her more champagne. Then they pushed the tables back and started dancing. Katherine sat in a corner; she hated dancing and especially hated her mother's dancing, which involved spreading her arms wide and shaking her breasts at people. She had taken off her suit jacket, the blouse was completely see-through and her dark blue bra was clearly visible under it. When she shook, her breasts wobbled backwards and forwards, and every now and then she had to lift up her bra to get them back in. Katherine just wanted to die.

Then suddenly her mother stopped dancing; she stood still in the middle of the dance floor and stared at the door. No one else seemed to have noticed and they carried on dancing around her, but Katherine looked over to the door. A man had come in; he was tall and thin with fuzzy blond hair and a beard. He was wearing a dark suit that looked like it only came out for wedding and funerals – and more funerals at that.

Katherine's mother took a step towards him and then stopped; he took a step towards her. It was like they were the only two people in the room. They both looked surprised and shocked, pleased and sad, all at the same time. Katherine had a feeling in the pit of her stomach, like something very important was about to happen, but it could just be that she'd had too much champagne. Sean was talking to someone's daughter about how he won his medal at the European Championships, so Katherine left him to it and made her way over to her mother, who was off the dance floor now and standing in front of the man. They shook hands quite formally and her mother suddenly hugged the man, pulling him tight to her and crying again. She looked around the room, searching for someone, and when she saw Katherine, she waved her over urgently. Katherine approached them slowly. It was her father, she just knew it was, he looked just like her, the hair, the height, even the eyes.

Katherine felt all sorts of things in the slow walk towards them: excitement, nervousness, resentment, anger – but the over-riding feeling was one of disappointment. Here he was, this rather sad-looking man, clearly not rich or famous or clever. Not a secret agent or a sportsman; or a nuclear scientist – well, he could be that, but the nerdy type, not the 'world-changing-discovery' type. All her childhood fantasies blown out the window at one look. Katherine tried to arrange her face so that she could appear surprised, not disappointed, when her mother introduced them.

'I don't believe it,' her mother was saying. 'When I sent the invitation . . .' She saw Katherine and grabbed her arm. 'Katherine, you'll never guess who this is.' Fortunately, she didn't leave her a chance to guess. 'I want you to meet my brother, Teddy.'

Relief flooded through Katherine – her uncle, not her father. Her mother let go of her arm and took Teddy's. 'Come on, I want to you meet Brian.' She whisked him off in the direction of the bar. He smiled at Katherine and gave her a friendly wave and a little shrug; Katherine smiled back and turned quickly away. She suddenly wanted to cry again: she had lost her mother and now it felt like she had lost her father. Even if he had been disappointing, he would have been better than nothing.

She went outside and stood in the car park, hoping the fresh air would clear her head. She had drunk too much and was probably going to throw up. There were people wandering past, in their Saturday clothes, doing normal Saturday things. Katherine felt they were all staring at her, in her see-through blouse and silly skirt. She sat down on the ground next to Sean's car, making a note to herself not to be sick on the car, because that would really upset Sean.

Out of nowhere, Sean arrived and sat down beside her. 'Our wedding's not going to be like this.'

'We're having pink flowers.'

'No, I mean the nasty wine, the crap music, the odd people.'

Katherine knew what he meant, but she felt a little protective of her mother and her friends. 'Just your family, they'll be the odd ones.'

Sean had the grace to smile. 'There's odd and then there's odd. Who was that man who just came in?'

'That's my uncle.' Katherine tried to say it normally, but her voice quivered on the word 'uncle'.

Sean looked at her for an explanation.

'I thought he was my father.' She started crying and Sean put his arm around her. 'I thought I didn't care about my father and then I saw him, and thought he was and then he wasn't . . .' She couldn't get any more words out.

'It's OK.' Sean kissed her forehead. 'You've got Brian now.'

She looked up at him, ready to be angry with him for not understanding, but she saw that he was joking. She thumped him anyway, harder than she meant to.

'Aagh!' Sean grabbed her hands and held them to stop her doing it again. She struggled against him and then stopped as a thought occurred to her.

'Did you want to have sex with that girl you were talking to?'

'No,' Sean said defensively and too quickly.

'I'm not accusing you.' Katherine tried to explain. 'I just want to understand things.'

'What things?' Sean still sounded wary.

'You know, the differences, between men and women.'

'Oh.' He seemed to relax a little.

'I mean, do you look at someone and want to have sex with them?'

Sean nodded. 'Don't you?'

'No.' Katherine didn't.

'Not even me?' He looked disappointed.

She thought about it for a moment. 'Not really. I don't think women are like that.' But even as she said it, she knew that it wasn't true. She had seen the look in Violet's eyes often enough and even in Phillipa's eyes the other evening. Maybe it just wasn't true of lesbians, but even as Katherine was taking comfort in that as some small proof that she wasn't a lesbian, she remembered catching a fleeting sight of it in her mother's eyes the other night, when she had caught her in the act of whipping Brian.

'You do want to have sex with me, though?' Sean was looking worried.

'Of course,' she said, hoping he didn't mean right then and there in the car park.

'I want to give you an orgasm,' Sean whispered into her ear. Katherine started to blush. 'I'll do anything you like, even you know . . . with my tongue.' He made it sound quite disgusting.

'Thank you.' Katherine didn't know quite what else to say.

'Is that what, you know . . . you and Violet did?'

Katherine didn't really want to talk about Violet and certainly not to Sean, but he was sitting looking at her, his eyes wide with expectation. 'Sometimes,' she said. 'And sometimes we used cucumbers.' It wasn't true, but Sean's eyes opened even wider. 'And sometimes we strapped on dildos and went to the park and fucked gay men up the arse with them.'

Sean's mouth dropped open and then he closed it again, realising she was winding him up.

'I think that's most men's fantasy,' he said, trying to cover up his embarrassment.

'Being fucked with a dildo?'

'No, watching two women, you know . . . do it.'

Katherine thought of her evening with Matt and Phillipa – it hadn't been quite like that.

As if Sean was reading her mind he said, 'Matt says he's done it.' Katherine felt herself start to blush. 'But he's such a liar. He reckons Phillipa's a lesbian and gets him to pick up girls so that she can sleep with them.'

Katherine stopped blushing; Sean carried on talking but Katherine wasn't listening to him. She remembered the exchange she had heard as she was leaving Phillipa's place. It had seemed a little strange at the time that Phillipa was thanking Matt. If what Sean said was true that meant . . . Katherine tried to sort out what exactly it did mean. So many things and most of them contradictory sprang to mind: apparently, Phillipa fancied her more than she had ever realised . . . But if Matt had told Sean so much, how long before he revealed Katherine's involvement?

Sean was still talking, shaking his head. 'He's such a liar.'

Feeling sick again, Katherine leaned her forehead against the cool glass of the car window.

'I'll take you home.' Sean looked worried, but Katherine wasn't sure if it was about her or the fact that she might throw up on his car.

'No.' The party was going back to the house after the pub; she couldn't face a house full of people. 'Let's go to yours.'

They never went to Sean's: his parents were always there, and although she knew Sean wasn't ashamed of her, he was always awkward with her around them. The first time she had gone there, Sean had called to collect her and made her change out of her jeans and put on a skirt. She had been furious with him, until she got there and they were all dressed up for dinner: Sean's father in a black jacket, his mother in a long blue dress, both with perfect manners and polite conversation. Katherine was too terrified even to eat, for fear that she might do something wrong. She felt so very out of place, and would have felt even more so if she had been in her jeans.

'We can't,' he said now.

SWEET VIOLET

'Aren't they away at Ascot or something?'

'Badminton, but we can't.'

'They hate me.'

'No they don't, they just . . . you know.'

'No, I don't know. You always say that and I never know.'

'Well OK, it's me they hate.' Then he stopped and thought about it. 'That's not exactly fair, they're just disappointed in me.'

'For marrying me?' Katherine had never heard him talk like that about his parents.

'No, before I even met you. Forever probably.'

'But your swimming.'

'Oh, but I don't win, and I can't ride, and I'm too young to marry, and while they think you're lovely, if very young, they don't think you're right for me.'

'Oh.' Katherine didn't know whether to defend herself or leave it; she felt angry on his behalf. 'I'm too common.'

'No.' Sean shook his head.

'Because I have no father?'

'No. My father said it's because you're a better swimmer than me and that I will come to resent it.'

'That's stupid.' Katherine laughed, but Sean was serious.

'If it's any consolation, they don't like Matt for the same reason.'

'What, they want you to hang out with Patrick and Ian just because you're a better swimmer than they are?' Katherine couldn't believe it.

Sean shrugged. 'Something like that.'

'That's really stupid.'

'They're probably right, they usually are.' Sean looked really depressed. Katherine hugged him. 'Sometimes I hate Matt, he always beats me.' Sean turned away, like he was looking for something to punch. 'And it's not just swimming, he's better at everything: tennis, basketball, golf, even with girls.' He turned back to Katherine. 'Except you, you're the one girl he didn't beat me too.'

Katherine felt a wave of nausea.

'Come on.' Sean seemed suddenly happier, as he unlocked the car.

'Where to?'

'Mine, let's go have sex on my parents' bed.'

'Hang on.' Katherine ran back inside, finding Brian not her mother. She kissed him on the cheek. 'Happy wedding! Tell Mum I'm with Sean, I won't be late.'

Sean was waiting for her with the roof of the car down. They drove through Coventry and out into the green belt. Sean's parents lived in a huge house behind a huge double gate and semi-circular drive. He slid the car to a halt in front of the house and jumped out of the car. Katherine expected there to be a butler to open the door and a line of servants to greet them. There wasn't of course, just Sean with his key and an alarm system that you needed an engineering degree to understand.

Katherine followed Sean in, although it no longer seemed like such a good idea. The house was so perfectly tidy that she barely dared breathe for fear of upsetting something. She stayed in the hallway while Sean disappeared off and came back with a bottle of wine and glasses. Katherine shook her head; she'd had quite enough to drink already. Sean led her up the stairs; everywhere there was cream carpet and pastel shades, it was always like being in a really posh hotel. They turned right at the top of the stairs and passed several doors before getting to Sean's enormous room at the end of the hall, with its big windows overlooking the back garden. There was nothing in the room to suggest that Sean lived there, except for his England blazer hanging on the wardrobe door.

Sean pulled her into his arms. 'So?'

'So,' Katherine said, 'not your parents' room then?'

Sean cleared his throat a little nervously. 'No, I don't think so.'

Katherine laughed. 'Looks fine to me.' But it seemed different tonight, more special – and somehow more formal.

There was a new, crisp, plain-blue cover on his large double-bed; Katherine sat on the edge of it and bounced. 'It feels like we're in a hotel tonight.'

'No room service.' He put the bottle of wine and glasses on the floor. He took off his jacket and hung it up, then knelt on the floor and took off Katherine's shoes. She lay back on the bed and closed her eyes.

'This is going to be for you,' he said as he ran his hand slowly up her leg.

She didn't quite understand what he meant, and she was so tired all of a sudden that she couldn't have kept her eyes open if she had wanted to. She felt his hands running softly over her thighs, then he pulled at her knickers and she lifted her bottom to help him take them off her. She felt the warmth of his breath up her legs and in her pubic hair, then the wetness of his tongue. She was distracted for a moment, worrying about when she last washed, but relaxed again when she remembered her shower that morning. She felt light and fuzzy, like cotton wool, and her body was warm and so relaxed she could barely feel the bed under her. She sighed. Sean's tongue was warming and comforting somehow, she felt safe and snug and so very tired.

She woke some time later under the cover; Sean curled up beside her. It was still light outside but getting darker, and there was the sound of a car in the driveway. She looked at her watch, it was seven. She gently shook Sean.

'Sean, I think your parents are home.' She had never seen anyone wake up so quickly – he was out of the bed and the room before Katherine had time to sit up. He came back in again, reached under the covers for Katherine's knickers, gave them to her and left the room, carefully closing the door. Katherine put her knickers on and smoothed down her hair. Sean had an en suite bathroom where she washed her hands and face. She had an awful headache from the drink. She stood in the bedroom, not sure whether she should stay there or go downstairs. In the end, she decided to go downstairs – she was Sean's fiancée after all, it wasn't a crime to be there. She straightened the bed cover before she left, though, because the room looked improper somehow with it rumpled.

Sean was in the hall talking to his father when she appeared at the top of the stairs. They both stopped and looked at her.

'Hello,' Katherine said as normally as she could, smiling. Sean's father looked at her and then at Sean. She couldn't be sure, but she thought she saw him smile. Then Sean's mother came out of the lounge and saw them looking up at Katherine; she didn't say anything, just turned and went back into the lounge. Sean nodded his head towards the front door and they left. They both started laughing once they were safely in the car and out of the driveway.

SEVENTEEN

Violet

It was past midnight and the noise from downstairs had been going on for hours. Violet hadn't realised a ritual would be so loud: singing and chanting, stomping and drum banging. She had to be up at seven for a big move, and if she didn't get some sleep soon she was going to turn into a zombie.

She pulled on her jeans and went downstairs; she wasn't going to ask them to be quiet, but a hot drink might counteract the noise. They were using both the front rooms – Violet could see flickering lights under the doors as she hurried past to the kitchen. She put the kettle on and surveyed the mess: there were dirty plates piled everywhere and bits of foods in various containers all over the place. She wasn't going to clean up after them. They might think she was inconsiderate for not turning up to poxy house meetings, but at least she did her own dishes, and didn't keep them awake half the night.

They had asked if she wanted to join them – well, Rainbow had asked, while Tree stood behind her, glaring at Violet, daring her to refuse.

'We're celebrating the Goddess in all of us,' Rainbow had said. 'It's such good fun – we light candles and raise energy and send it out into the world to do good.'

'Like destroying the patriarchy,' Tree had snarled.

'We take our clothes off and wash each other and rub ourselves down with oils and then we become snakes and slither around, licking each other with our tongues.

That had tempted Violet, but the idea of having to spend time in the same room as Tree, naked, put her right off. She knew she had made the right decision when she saw them all arriving in their tie-dyed scarves and baggy vests. She had retreated to her room, too tired to go out looking for Felicity.

The lounge door opened and closed. Violet hoped it was someone going upstairs to the loo, but she heard footsteps coming towards the kitchen. She looked around for somewhere to hide, but there wasn't anywhere except under the table and she didn't know when the floor had last been cleaned so she wasn't going to risk it.

A tall slim woman waltzed into the kitchen, completely naked and shining with oil. She didn't notice Violet and stood picking at the leftover food. The kettle started to boil and Violet took it off the hob, the woman turned around.

'Oh, hello, didn't see you there.' She continued to pick at the food, completely unselfconscious of her nudity. 'I broke the circle,' she said, giggling. 'The incense was getting up my nose and everybody had sort of paired off.' She cocked her head to one side and looked Violet up and down. 'So, who are you?'

'Violet.' She held out her hand and then drew it back, unsure of the etiquette when meeting a naked woman for the first time.

'I'm Ellen, and you're the reason I'm left out. You were supposed to be the twelfth woman.'

'Sorry,' Violet said, trying to decide where to look. The woman had lovely eyes so she looked there. 'No one told me.'

'Didn't fancy slithering like a snake amongst a coven of naked women?' She moved her body to demonstrate her point, her arms above her head.

'No.' Violet's gaze had dropped to Ellen's breasts which were rising and falling as she moved.

'More of a one-to-one wombmoon.' She pronounced 'woman' like the others did, as a combination of 'womb' and 'moon', because – as Rainbow had tried to explain to Violet at length –

they didn't want to have anything to do with men, not even in the sense of being a 'wo-MAN'.

'Maybe.' She pulled her eyes away from Ellen's breasts, but they drifted down to her long, slim legs and then back up to the perfect triangle of sandy pubic hair, still waving itself in front of her. She returned her eyes to Ellen's face and noticed a wicked smile there.

She was so close now that Violet could smell her, a faint woodsmoke smell. 'I can see the Goddess in your eyes.' She said like a chant. 'I can see her in your eyes.' She rubbed her body against Violet's. 'You have gorgeous eyes.' She rubbed her cheek against Violet's. 'Let's be snakes together.'

Violet tried to imagine this woman at Katherine's wedding. She realised she was getting pretty desperate here, but there were only two weeks to go. She thought it could be fun, going in with this tall beautiful woman in tie-dyed headscarf and Indian pants, smelling like a log fire and slithering like snakes.

Violet put her hands on Ellen's waist; her skin was soft and slippery.

'Take your top off.' Ellen tugged at the T-shirt in which Violet had been trying to sleep. But Violet didn't want the others coming out and catching them, and she was very uncomfortable about anyone seeing her even half-naked.

The lounge door opened and shut again. Ellen stopped tugging and looked guiltily over her shoulder, but whoever it was went upstairs to the toilet.

'Come up to my room,' Violet said, and they snaked past the lounge and up past the toilet into Violet's bedroom.

Ellen fell on the bed giggling; she writhed around a bit doing her snake impersonation. Violet watched her; she had a lovely body.

'Come on in,' she said to Violet. 'The snake-pit's warm.'

Violet knelt beside her and ran her hand down the length of Ellen's body, along her leg and to her foot.

'That's not what snakes do.' She pulled Violet's T-shirt out of her jeans and pushed it up. 'Snakes do this.' She rubbed her bare skin across Violet's. It was an amazing feeling. Violet had only ever touched other women's skin with her hand, and to feel it with her whole body was just bliss – she wondered why she had never thought about it before. Actually, she knew why she hadn't – because it involved taking her clothes off. Violet took a deep breath and pulled her T-shirt off over her head.

'That's better.' Ellen rubbed her oiled breasts backwards and forwards across Violet's. Violet could feel her nipples grow erect as Ellen's brushed past hers, she was in heaven. She had thought she knew pretty much all there was to know about making love to a woman, even though she was young, and up until now she hadn't seen much to change her opinion about that – a dildo here and some handcuffs there, but nothing like this. Nothing as mind-blowingly simple as the feel of another woman's nipples rubbing past hers.

'And these.' Ellen was tugging at her jeans. Violet wasn't so sure about that, as she didn't have any knickers on. Bare breasts were one thing, but exposed bits were quite another.

'Later,' she said, leaning over Ellen and kissing her softly on the lips. Ellen didn't really respond. Violet tried kissing her hard, but Ellen pushed her away.

'It's better to do it side by side.' Violet didn't understand. 'You were on top then, that infers a power imbalance. We should stay side by side and then things are equal.' She said it as if it was the most obvious thing in the world and as if Violet was rather stupid not to know it.

'Oh.' She wasn't going to argue: she wanted to have sex with the woman and would do it any way Ellen wanted, within normal limits of course.

She lay down beside Ellen and tried to kiss her that way. It was more difficult as their noses seemed to keep getting in the way, but Ellen responded now, letting her lips soften, snaking her tongue around Violet's.

'Now, isn't that better?' She sounded like a smug schoolteacher.

Violet ignored it and pulled her in closer, pressing her leg up between Ellen's. She worried for a moment that the oil on Ellen's body would stain her jeans, but as Ellen started grinding her pelvis into Violet's, she soon forgot about it.

Violet reached around and grasped Ellen's naked bottom. It was perfectly formed: small, firm and fitting into Violet's hand like it was made for it. Their nipples touched every now and again and it seemed to send sparks through Violet's whole body. Ellen was moving quite frantically now, her body writhing as she ground it against Violet's. Violet moved one hand off Ellen's bottom and slid it between their two bodies, knowing Ellen would be wet and near to orgasm. She longed to get her fingers in there and feel the soft flesh expand around them, or better still get her tongue in and taste it. She wanted to see Ellen writhe for real.

Her finger found the wet opening in the pubic hair, but before she could slide them in there, Ellen was pushing her away.

'No!' she said angrily, sitting up.

'What?' Violet had no idea what she had done wrong.

'No penetration.' Ellen turned and looked at her.

'Oh.' Violet didn't understand; how else were you supposed to have sex?

'That's what men do, they violate our space. We wombmoon have to create our own alternative ways of making love.' She was lecturing.

'Oh,' Violet said again. She couldn't think of alternative ways.

'We were doing fine as we were. Or here.' She took Violet's hand and pressed the back of it between her legs, then she started rubbing herself against it, lifting her bottom off the bed and pushing her pelvis forward. 'That's good too.'

Violet felt like she was in some sort of class being tutored – not two women having sex any more, but teacher and pupil – she didn't like it. Nor was she particularly keen on having Ellen rub herself against her hand; it might have felt good to Ellen, but it did nothing for her. She wondered if it would be rude to pick up a book and start reading. She didn't think Ellen would notice as she had her head thrown back and her eyes closed. Ellen rubbed for what seemed like an eternity and then with the slightest shudder came. She flopped down on the bed.

'That's how Bedouin women give birth in the desert,' she said, smiling. 'I was sending the energy I raised to them, to help fight their terrible oppression.'

Violet was pleased her energy had gone somewhere useful. She wiped the back of her hand on the sheet.

'Now it's your turn.' Ellen shook out her shoulders as if she was preparing for a marathon swim.

'Actually,' Violet said, 'I've got a headache.' It was the oldest cliché in the book but she was too tired to think of anything else.

'Sex is the best thing for headaches, releases all that built-up energy.'

'I'm very tired, I have to get up at seven for work.'

Ellen was starting to look a little hurt. 'It has to be reciprocated, otherwise there's a power imbalance.'

Violet was wondering in whose favour. 'Maybe tomorrow.'

'Oh yes, we're going up to the Women's Pond before we go back to Greenham.' She smiled her wicked smile and Violet had visions of sex outdoors. She had never done that before, except with Katherine in her back garden. She remembered about the wedding and suddenly she wasn't so annoyed with Ellen.

'That would be great.'

Ellen left the room and Violet got under the covers; it was 2 a.m. and she really was tired. She heard Julie meet Ellen on the stairs.

'We wondered where you'd got to,' Julie said, and then she whispered, 'You haven't been with Violet have you? She's so un-PC.'

'Well, how are these women supposed to learn unless we teach them?'

Violet rolled over and went to sleep.

In the morning, Judy and Fiona came to collect her. 'Alice called again,' Fiona said, as soon as Violet got into the van.

'Oh.' She had forgotten about her.

'Wanted to know why you weren't answering her calls.'

'I did, I told her it was over.'

'Judy told her you had broken both your arms.'

'What?' Violet looked over at Judy, but she was concentrating on driving.

'Alice said she would call round with flowers.'

'She doesn't know where I live.'

'She does now.' Judy laughed.

'Sorry,' Fiona said.

Violet had visions of the wild-eyed Alice sitting in the front room of the house, Tree and Rainbow listening with horror to what had happened, then sending down a decree excommunicating her from the lesbian community.

'I'm going to have to move.'

'Don't be so melodramatic. When she starts her next book, she'll forget about you.'

'Book? I thought you said she was a doctor.'

Judy looked at Fiona accusingly; Fiona shrugged. 'Well she is. I never said medical doctor; Violet just assumed. She's got her PhD, she even showed me her thesis, it was on some medieval nun who wrote chants.'

Judy shook her head.

Today they were moving two women from quite close to Violet's house out to Walthamstow. Violet couldn't understand why anyone would want to live there. She spent most of her time looking over her shoulder worried that she would bump into her aunt, whom she hadn't even called since she moved out.

After they had finished, they dropped Violet home, where there wasn't any sign of Alice but there were voices coming from the front room. Violet sneaked upstairs and got changed, then went into the kitchen to see if there was any food. It was still piled high with dishes; it made her want to scream.

She was almost out of the front door when Tree appeared from the lounge.

'Violet, we need to talk.' She sounded just like Violet's father.

'Sorry, have to go.' Violet ducked out of the door and pulled it shut behind her. As she passed the bay window at the front of the house, she saw a huge pair of eyes staring out. She ran for the gate and all the way to the tube station.

City Limits said that the Women's Pond was a 'must' place to go for lesbians, but unfortunately its directions were, as usual, less than useless. Violet roamed Hampstead Heath for nearly an hour before she saw some women who looked like lesbians turning down a little path that she hadn't noticed before. She followed them and saw a big sign proclaiming LADIES BATHING POND and a long list of rules and regulations. Violet only read as far as NO MEN ALLOWED and decided she liked the place. It still didn't prepare her for what greeted her when she reached the bottom of the path. It was enough to throw off all worries about Alice and anger at *City Limits* for leading her on such a wild-goose chase. There in front of her was a sea of women, mostly topless, some even completely naked, lying around on a gentle sloping lawn with a pond at the bottom of it.

She scanned the crowd for Ellen, couldn't see her, and started to pick her way between the women.

'Violet.' She heard someone call her name. She looked around and saw Julie waving, with Ellen beside her. She worked her way over to them.

'I was just about to go for a swim.' Ellen jumped up as she approached. 'You want to come?'

Violet got the impression she was trying to avoid having to introduce her to everyone there, the other women were looking at her with more than a casual interest. It suited Violet fine; she didn't want to have to make small talk to a bunch of strange women. Strange because she hadn't met them before, but strange too because she had heard them the night before making the weirdest noises. Also she was hot from her wandering. 'OK, but I haven't got a swimsuit.'

'Don't worry, they won't let you go in naked but you can just leave your underwear on.' Violet had no intention of taking it off.

Ellen had been naked, but was pulling her underwear back on. More sad, grey cotton things, Violet noticed. She looked around; most of the women had sad, grey cotton things on. She remembered Debs and sighed.

'You coming?' Ellen was standing and about to leave.

Violet walked with her back across the lawn of women to the little dock area where you got into the water. Violet was aware that they were getting a lot of looks as they passed; she assumed they were mostly directed at Ellen's long legs.

'Oh I hate that,' Ellen said once they were clear of the lawn.

'What?' Violet felt another lecture coming on.

'The way they are looking at you, they're no better than men.'

Violet didn't say anything; she went into the changing room and took off her jeans and T-shirt. She had on black Marks and Spencer's sports underwear. It could pass as a bikini, but Violet was intensely aware that it wasn't and felt exposed in it. When she emerged, Ellen was already in the water; she joined the queue of women waiting to get in. She didn't understand why there was a queue, until she saw that there was only one ladder for getting in and a big sign saying NO DIVING. The woman on the ladder was up to her waist in the water, squealing.

'No screaming.' The burly lifeguard shouted at her. 'And you, you have to put a top on.' She directed this to someone behind Violet. Then she turned to someone in the water and shouted at them not to make so much noise. So much for Utopia.

Finally it was Violet's turn, and she soon realised why the woman had been squealing – it was freezing. She got in quickly and discovered that not only was it cold, it was none too clean either, with leaves and algae floating on the surface and who knew what in its murky depths. Violet didn't dare put her head under; she would have to swim breaststroke. Ellen was waiting for her near the raft in the middle of the pond, she waved and Violet swam over to her.

'That woman's a fascist,' she said of the lifeguard.

Violet thought that was a bit strong but didn't say anything. As they swam together to the far end of the pond, Violet realised it was the first time she had been swimming since coming to London. It was lovely too, very quiet despite the number of women there, the ones in the water talking almost in whispers if at all. The pond was surrounded by trees, the sky reflected in the water and there were even a few ducks swimming around the edges.

'This is so beautiful,' she whispered to Ellen. 'It's hard to believe we're in London.'

'You should come to Greenham.' Ellen caught hold of one of the buoys secured about the pond and floated her legs out behind her. 'It's like this, but without the pond. We sing around the campfire at night and chant, and raise energy to send the Americans home. And during the day we make pots or weave or write poetry.' Violet had heard some of that poetry, and she hoped their pots were better.

'Or we have meetings to sort out personal issues, the whole group, because we know that the personal is political and if we express how we feel then we can build a more open world,' Ellen continued. 'It's so great. We're making our own alternative society, and doesn't it freak out the men in power? You should come down.' She reached over the buoy and took Violet's hand. 'It would do you good, to see that there is another way.'

It sounded like Violet's idea of hell.

She pulled Ellen towards her across the buoy and kissed her, then pushed the heel of her hand into Ellen's breast, feeling the nipple through the thin, now transparent material. She wondered what it would be like to have sex in the water, both bodies weightless. She moved around the buoy and put one arm around Ellen and held on to the buoy with her other. She felt Ellen's legs against hers, their stomachs touching, their breasts. She kissed Ellen on the lips; their mouths warm in contrast to the water, but soft like it. She slid her tongue deep into Ellen's mouth and wondered if that is what it would feel like inside her fanny. She had the idea she could lie Ellen backwards across the buoy and pull off her sad, grey knickers and spread her legs. She would sink her tongue quickly inside her before she could stop her and Ellen would writhe like a water snake.

Violet's fantasy and the kiss were broken by a lifeguard bellowing through the loud hailer.

'The two women at the end of the pond, stop that kissing at once!'

Ellen pushed Violet away. 'Hide,' she said, and dived under the water.

Violet wasn't going to risk catching anything from the water, so she swam back towards the knot of women around the raft.

'You can't hide from me,' the lifeguard was shouting. 'I can see you.'

Violet reached the edge of the raft and hung off it; the women on it were looking at her.

SWEET VIOLET

'Come out at once,' the lifeguard shouted.

'Stay there.' Violet looked up and saw a woman in a pink bathing suit and a flowery bathing cap. It was Belinda. She slipped into the water beside Violet. 'Here.' She took off her cap and handed it to Violet, who pulled it on.

'I'd offer you my suit too, but I don't think yours would fit me.' She laughed.

'Thank you,' Violet said again.

'No problem.' She smiled at Violet. Again, Violet noticed what a lovely smile it was. Belinda swam off, very slowly and sedately, keeping her head carefully above the water. She reached the out ladder, climbed up and disappeared into the changing room.

'OK.' The lifeguard was sounding more and more annoyed. 'I want everyone out of the water. I want to know who that was, kissing.' The women around the raft sighed. Having seen Ellen get out and walk safely past the lifeguard, Violet swam over to the ladder, hoping no one would tell on her. She climbed out.

'Was it you?' The guard demanded of the woman in front of her.

'No, it bloody wasn't.'

She didn't even ask Violet, just let her walk on past. Finding Belinda wrapped in a towel in the changing rooms, Violet thanked her for the cap.

'There is a price to pay for all Utopias,' Belinda said quite solemnly. 'And that lifeguard is the one for the pond.' She smiled and took the cap. 'It suited you.'

Violet picked up her jeans and T-shirt and made her way back over to Ellen.

'You made it,' Ellen giggled when she saw Violet. 'I thought we were done for.' Ellen had taken her underwear off again and was sitting down. The guard was still making everyone get out of the water, but some women were staying in as a protest, so she sent one of the other lifeguards to get the park security man.

'Should we go?' Violet sat down beside Ellen.

'No, there's no way she can prove it was us.' She lay down and stretched out. Violet sat and watched her; she reached out and ran her hand over Ellen's stomach.

'You have a lovely body,' she whispered in her ear.

Ellen sat up abruptly. 'All women's bodies are beautiful,' she said angrily.

'I know . . .' Violet stared, but Ellen wasn't listening.

'Just because mine happens to conform to some male stereotype of what a woman should look like doesn't mean mine is more beautiful than anyone else's.'

'I didn't say it was.' Violet was once again baffled by Ellen's response to what she thought was a perfectly innocent comment.

'I'm sick of being objectified, by men, but especially by women who are subjected to the same objectification themselves and still insist on dumping it on other women. I can't help the way my body is, I wear clothes that cover it as much as possible so it doesn't oppress other women, but sometimes I just have to take them off and walk naked on this earth. My fear of oppressing them is now oppressing me and it's women like you who perpetuate that oppression and stop me fulfilling my full potential as a wombmoon.'

Violet thought that was it and would have said something but nothing sprang to mind.

Ellen hadn't quite finished though: 'It's women like you who are stopping all women reaching their full potential and the overthrowing of the patriarchy.'

Violet was aware that everyone around them was staring; she knew too that Ellen wouldn't be coming to the wedding with her. 'So.' She decided attack was the best form of defence: 'Sex is out of the question then?'

Ellen gave her a filthy look, collected up her clothes and stomped off, followed by her friends.

'Oo-er!' a woman in front of Violet said as she watched Ellen go. 'I bet she was a goer.'

Violet smiled at the woman who looked familiar.

'Hi.' She held out her hand. 'Name's Hazel. Great here, isn't it?'

Violet remembered now. 'We've met,' she said. The woman looked her over and Violet added, 'At Aphrodite Rising.'

SWEET VIOLET

'Oh.' Hazel looked suddenly deflated. 'Not a good night – my Val went off with that new woman, Sue.'

Violet didn't know what to say. Hazel looked at the grass for a moment, lost in thought, then seemed to pull herself together.

'Still, life goes on, eh?' She reached into her bag and pulled out a leaflet. 'We've got a dance tonight, actually.' She thrust the leaflet into Violet's hand. 'Do come.' It sounded more like a desperate plea than a casual invitation.

Violet looked at the piece of paper. She had just lost Ellen as a wedding guest, but maybe she would find someone there. 'OK,' she said as she stood up.

'Oh, thank you.' Hazel took her hand and squeezed it. 'It will be awfully fun, you'll see.'

Violet went back to the changing room, took off her wet underwear and pulled on her jeans and T-shirt. She thought Belinda might still be there but she wasn't. After the wedding, Violet would have to track her down and thank her properly.

Back home, the house was silent; there was a note for her but she ignored it. She went up to her room and got out her book. In it she wrote:

9. 29 Sept. Ellen, My room. 4/10.
Unsuitable because can't take a compliment.

She went and had a bath.

EIGHTEEN
Katherine

They were on a coach again, heading for the airport this time, to get a plane to Munich. It felt just like the Paris trip, with Mr Williams delivering the same speech about alcohol and sex, even though there was no one new and they had all heard it before. Katherine felt very different though, partly because she was wearing her England uniform for the first time. It was a very silly thing, with a pleated skirt in the most staticky nylon she had ever worn, a blouse with a daft scarf that had to be tied just so, and a blazer that was much too warm. She wanted to wear it with pride, because she was very proud to be representing her country, but she was finding it difficult with the skirt clinging round her legs and the scarf half-choking her.

Also, so much seemed to have happened since Paris – she wasn't the shy newcomer any more. She was still nervous, not about the hotel or the pool this time but about the swimming. It helped that she knew they all had single rooms, in the old Olympic Village, so she wouldn't have to share with Phillipa. The squad was smaller, whittled down to sixteen; almost certainly the sixteen who would be going to the European Champs and hopefully the Olympics.

She sat next to Sean on the coach. Mr Williams hadn't split up the sexes yet; he obviously thought the journey to the airport was too short for anyone to get up to anything. The flying time to

SWEET VIOLET

Munich wasn't long enough either, but they were not being allowed to sit together on that. Katherine was getting thoroughly sick of it all, if they were adult enough to be able to swim for their country, surely they were adult enough to be trusted to refrain from sex when they were told to.

Kathering looked over at Phillipa and Matt sitting opposite them, giggling and whispering to each other. Well, some of them were adult enough. She tried not to think that they were talking about her. She decided the best form of defence was attack.

'So, when did you sleep with Phillipa?' she asked Sean. He looked a little shocked – the question must have seemed to come out of nowhere.

'Well, I . . .' He looked worried. 'How did you know?'

Katherine tried to remember how she did know – from some of the things he had said, but mostly from something Phillipa had said too, though she couldn't quite place what.

'Oh, I just do.' She hoped he wouldn't press her on it.

He didn't. 'Before I met you, well . . .' He stopped to think about it. 'Actually, I think it was the first meet you came to, the one in Oxford.'

'Was Matt there?'

'No!' Sean said angrily. 'I can do some things by myself.'

Katherine laughed. 'I meant, was he at the meet?'

'Oh.' Sean was embarrassed. 'Yes, but he was off chasing some Dutch girl.'

'The one with the big breasts?' Katherine remembered her.

'Yes.'

'Did he catch her?'

'He says he did. In the women's showers, he said, but you know him . . .'

Katherine did know him, and she remembered finding him coming out of the changing room, a little flushed and very pleased with himself. Katherine had just thought he had been trying to steal a peep.

'Is there anyone he hasn't slept with?' Katherine had meant it as a joke, but regretted it as soon as the words were out of her mouth. 'Apart from me,' she added hastily, hoping Sean hadn't noticed. He hadn't, of course. She supposed that, in the strictest sense of the word, she hadn't had sex with him, as he hadn't actually penetrated her with his penis. But she knew that Sean wouldn't accept this as a line of defence and nor could she honestly offer it as one.

Sean shrugged and looked a bit annoyed. 'Do you want to?'

'No.' Katherine said, probably too fast. 'He's much too sure of himself.'

'And I'm not.' It didn't seem like she could say anything right.

'No,' she tried. 'and that's why I'm marrying you.'

Sean smiled at long last and put his arm around her. Matt and Phillipa were still giggling; Katherine couldn't stand it.

'So, was she any good?' She knew that Sean might get annoyed with her again, but she wanted them to feel that they were being talked about, to see how they liked it.

Sean wasn't annoyed. 'Well,' he said, 'it was a bit weird, she just took control. I didn't have to do anything.'

'I thought you liked that,' Katherine teased him.

'But it was like I wasn't even there, like she was thinking about someone else entirely.'

'Oh.' Katherine didn't know what to make of that.

'Afterwards, it was like it hadn't happened at all, I can't explain it.'

They travelled the rest of the journey in silence, Katherine wondering if what Sean had said made her more or less sure that Phillipa was a lesbian. But then, thought Katherine, maybe Phillipa was a bisexual. That would probably make more sense. They checked in at the airport and then hung around in the departure lounge waiting for their flight.

There was a journalist there, going over to Munich on the same flight to cover the meet. He was a rather shabby-looking man, in an old suit with fraying cuffs with a terrible orange tie. His hair was grey and frizzy and he looked like he needed a shave. He wanted to interview Katherine and made a beeline for her as soon as she came into the lounge, hovering around her, making her nervous. She asked Mr Williams if it was all right, as she had no idea about these things. He shrugged. 'Just don't say anything stupid.'

Katherine didn't know if she would be able to say anything sensible. They went and found some seats out of the way; the journalist put a small tape recorder down between them. He seemed as nervous as Katherine, not at all what she had expected from a reporter – she thought they would be smarter, better dressed and well, younger.

He started off with some pretty easy questions about how often she went to training and where she went to college, only he said 'school', like he thought she was still at secondary school, and she had to correct him. Then he asked if she had a boyfriend, which she thought was beside the point, but she blushed and said that, actually, she was engaged. He looked surprised and said he thought she was a little young for that. She got really annoyed with him then, but tried not to show it; luckily their flight was called and she had to go. He seemed very disappointed.

'We can sit together on the plane and finish this,' he said.

Katherine couldn't think of anything worse; he was starting to give her the creeps. 'No.' She stood up. 'I have to join the others, Mr Williams is very strict like that.' She hurried away and found Sean.

'Hide me from that man!'

'Who?'

'The journalist, he's so sleazy.' Katherine turned around and the journalist was staring at her. She giggled. 'Oh God, look, he's staring.' Sean seemed put out that the man wanted to talk to Katherine and not him, but when he turned to look, the journalist had disappeared.

As soon as they were in the air, though, the man was back, asking if they could continue. Katherine was sitting next to Claire, and had to grab her arm to stop her giving up her seat to him. 'I don't feel well, I get airsick.' she pulled the airsick bag out of the pocket in front of her seat and stuck her nose in it as if that was proof. 'Sorry.' She smiled weakly at him and then stayed like that until he had gone away.

'You should try these wrist bands, they really help,' Claire offered.

He was waiting for her as they got off the plane, but Mr Williams was yelling at them all to hurry up, and they and their luggage were whisked away through a side exit on to a waiting coach for the Olympic Village. Katherine remembered seeing it on sports documentaries about the 1972 Munich Games; everyone saying how modern it was – and all things modern were good, according to her mother.

It was dark when they got there but it all looked rather sad and tired now, peeling paint and endless miles of ugly concrete. They were assigned their rooms and sent straight to bed, the women in one block, the men in another, separated by the dining hall and a large pond. Katherine caught a glimpse of the Irish squad and thought she saw the German tank, which meant she would have some tough opposition and could prove her win wasn't a one-off. There were to be some swimmers from the Eastern Bloc countries there, who hadn't been in Paris, so it would be good to see how she swam against them. Katherine wondered where they were staying: she had heard their chaperones kept them on pretty short leads and didn't let them mix with the other swimmers.

The rooms were tiny, just big enough for a single bed, a built-in wardrobe and a tiny desk. They were freezing cold too, colder than it was outside. Katherine went to the bathroom at the end of the corridor and quickly cleaned her teeth. Back in her room, she wished she was sharing with someone, as it felt cold and lonely there by herself.

She climbed into bed; they had an early start tomorrow, and already it was 10.30 p.m. She tried her mother's breathing again, slowly in and out in a continuous figure of eight. It relaxed her but she still didn't feel sleepy. She thought about setting up a fantasy, but didn't dare. Even though she was alone in the room, it felt too dangerous.

Eventually she did get off to sleep, only to have disturbing dreams about being chased by a man not unlike the journalist. She had just turned to face him and find out who he was, when she was woken by banging on her door. At first she thought it was the man, trying to shoot her, and then she realised it was Mrs Jenkins with her wake-up call. She showered quickly and then packed her bag for the day, before putting on her uniform going down to the dining hall.

Phillipa was the only one there from their squad; she waved and beckoned Katherine over.

'Come and sit with me, unless you're not talking to me.'

'No, of course.' Katherine wasn't quite sure what to say to her. She went and queued for her breakfast and then sat down next to Phillipa.

'So, are you angry with me?' Phillipa asked.

'No, not at all.' Just embarrassed, confused and self-conscious.

'If it's about what happened at my place, forget it.'

'Forget it!' That sort of thing might happen to Phillipa every day, so that she could forget it, but it certainly didn't happen to Katherine and she didn't think she could forget it just like that.

'Oh, so don't forget it then, but it's no big deal and I promise I won't tell anyone – and so does Matt, I made him swear to it.'

'OK.' It made Katherine feel a little better.

'Hey, look.' Phillipa spotted the tank coming in. They watched her get her breakfast and then look around for somewhere to sit. Katherine tried to hide but Phillipa waved and called her over.

'Hello,' she said as she sat down next to Katherine. 'I am Annette and you are Katherine and Phillipa.' She shook each of their hands, holding Katherine's for a second longer than necessary.

'You are swimming well?' she asked Katherine.

Katherine nodded.

'Good, then I am looking forward to our races together.' She tucked into her breakfast and didn't say anything else, while Phillipa and Katherine looked at each other. Annette was so unnecessarily po-faced that Katherine had to bite her lip to stop herself laughing. Matt and Sean arrived, then Mr Williams came in and hurried everyone along as it was time for their warm-up.

When they got to the pool, the Dutch team were still in there – although it was England's turn – because the East German team had started late before them. Mr Williams did a lot of shouting that didn't make a blind bit of difference. When they got in the water, they only had twenty minutes. Katherine tried to use it to focus and relax. She was starting to believe that different water in different pools liked or disliked her. Sometimes she could just cut through it like it wasn't there at all, like it was actually helping her, and sometimes it felt like she had to fight it every stroke. She tried to get a feel of the water; this pool felt fairly neutral. If Katherine treated it nicely, it might just be nice to her.

Today she wasn't swimming breaststroke; instead she was in the 200-metre freestyle. Mr Williams had decided it was time to concentrate on her stronger strokes. It meant she had one race early in the morning and then two close together in the afternoon. If she went to the Olympics, she would probably only do the freestyle races — although because it was over a week and not just one weekend, she would have more time to recover between races and might also do the butterfly.

Katherine's stomach tightened into a knot every time she thought about the Olympics, and if she did well in Munich, she was almost certain to go. She wanted to go more than anything she had ever wanted in her life, and she was so close to it.

Her first heat was the butterfly. She got off to a good start and easily won; though it wasn't a very good time. Mr Williams was too busy shouting at Claire about her backstroke, and Katherine wasn't even sure he had noticed the result.

The creepy journalist was there and wanted to continue the interview. Katherine said she wasn't allowed to while they were racing, but he had checked her schedule and knew she had a long gap. There wasn't anyone around who could help her, so she went and had a long shower and spent ages getting changed, hoping he would give up and go and interview someone else.

When she came out, he was there waiting, still in his old suit — now so crumpled that he must have slept in it. The more Katherine saw him, the more convinced she was that he wasn't a journalist at all, but something more sinister, like a private eye or a hit man. She had no idea why anyone would be after her but he just didn't feel right.

They went and sat outside one of the side doors. He had suggested they go for a walk, but Katherine wanted to be some-

SWEET VIOLET

where she could get help if she needed it. Not that there was anyone around: the pool building was as grey and ugly as the accommodation in the Olympic Village, with the same abandoned feel to it.

He asked her some more innocent enough questions and Katherine gave him short answers, about college and school, and then he said: 'Your parents must be very proud of you.'

Katherine noticed then that he didn't have his little tape recorder with him, nor was he taking notes.

'My mother is,' she said warily. 'Are you supposed to be taking notes?'

'Ah.' He looked around as if he had just realised that himself. 'Photographic memory.' He tapped his head. 'And your father?' He continued as if nothing was wrong.

'I haven't got a father. Listen, I'm not happy about this.'

'Everyone has a father,' he said, ignoring her protest.

'He left before I was born.' She stood up. 'I've got to go and prepare for my next race.' She still had two hours but she couldn't handle this any more, so she headed back inside.

'I'm sure he would be proud,' the journalist called after her.

Katherine stopped in the doorway and looked back at him. The sun was shining, which seemed to give everything a clean, sharp edge, everything except the journalist; he looked as if he was out of focus. Katherine went in and shut the door; it was all too weird.

She watched some races. Claire came third in her backstroke, just missing a place in the final once again, and cried. Phillipa was through to the butterfly final, Sean just missed out on a place in his butterfly, and Matt scraped a place in the breaststroke.

They had a team meeting at lunch. The competition was tougher here than in Paris with more of the Eastern Bloc countries. Mr Williams shouted a lot and Katherine started to feel nervous about her freestyle. She wanted to get in the pool again to see if the water was for or against her, but she knew that the next time she would be in there was when she dived off the blocks in her 100-metre race and it would be too late then. Not that she thought she could change the water's mind if it took against her; it's not as if she could give it flowers or anything. A picture came to her of her kneeling beside the pool, offering rose petals to the water as a peace offering.

She noticed that the journalist was still hanging round: each time she looked in his direction, he was staring at her. She wanted to ask Mr Williams to tell him to go away, but he was too busy with his shouting, so she wondered if Sean would do it for her. She sidled over to him. She usually didn't spend much time with him at meets, as he put her off. At first he was annoyed about it, and then he realised it wasn't anything personal, as she stayed away from most of the team, so he got used to it.

'That journalist is hanging around again,' she whispered to him. 'I think he's following me.' She realised she sounded a little paranoid.

'Where?' Sean looked around. Katherine pointed behind her.

'I don't see him.'

Katherine turned around and he had gone. 'I don't think he's a journalist at all.'

Sean looked at her sideways. 'What then?'

'I don't know.' Katherine was starting to feel silly. 'A private eye or something; he didn't even have a notebook.'

'No notebook, well . . .' Sean was making fun of her. Mr Williams had noticed they weren't paying attention and shouted at them. When Katherine looked back for the journalist she couldn't see him.

After lunch it was the freestyle races. Katherine was in the second heat; Annette, the German girl, had won the first. There were two Russians in Katherine's; they looked a bit scary, both with close-cropped hair and bulging muscles. Katherine knew she was just projecting all her prejudices, but the way they were staring straight ahead, expressionless, they looked like robots.

Katherine climbed on to the blocks and looked into the water. 'Please' she begged it silently. 'Please be nice to me.' They were on their marks and then off. Katherine was in lane three, with one of the Russians either side, churning up the water all around her. At the turn they were both still with her, one even slightly ahead. She tried to up her stroke rate but couldn't seem to get a grip and she could feel them getting away. Then a picture of Violet came to her, laughing with her Felicity, a tanned woman in leather, with spiky blonde hair. That gave her the kick she needed. She found the strength to surge forward between the Russians, clear of their messy water, and touch the wall first.

Phillipa was in the next heat and Katherine stayed to watch. She had an easy race, just one Russian and an East German, the latter a skinny little thing with long bony arms and legs. At the turn Phillipa was nearly half a length in front. As she watched the race, Katherine felt like she was being watched and turned to see the journalist staring at her from the stands. Katherine was aware that she was only in her swimsuit, and dripping wet at that; she suddenly felt cold. She ran off to the changing rooms.

She had a shower and was putting on a dry swimsuit when Phillipa came in, not looking too happy.

'That squirt.' She threw her towel on the floor.

'What?'

'That piddly little East German beat me.'

'But you were well ahead.'

'Came up on me in the last twenty. God I hate that, she can't be more than sixteen.'

'Actually seventeen.' Annette had come into the changing room. 'And even skinnier than you, Katherine.' She laughed. 'She is very good, yes?'

Phillipa sat slumped on the bench.

'Us old ones, we are finishing our careers.' Annette went over to Phillipa. 'They are just starting, we should help them.'

'You still made the final?' Katherine asked Phillipa.

'Yes.' She looked close to tears. 'But what's the use, you'll all just beat me.'

Katherine hadn't realised winning was so important to Phillipa, who normally seemed so relaxed about the whole thing.

Annette didn't seem to notice that Phillipa was upset. 'Two hundred next, Katherine, we are in the same heat. I hope to beat you.' She turned to leave.

Katherine didn't know whether to laugh or be angry, she wondered if it was just the fact that Annette was speaking a foreign language that made her sound so strange. She rather thought it wasn't.

'The squirt is my cousin, so be nice,' Annette said as she left.

'Her cousin?' Phillipa snorted. 'More like her little lover.'

Katherine didn't know about that, but they were so physically different – and from opposite sides of Germany – that she felt they couldn't be related.

'At least we know the squirt's not on steroids,' Phillipa said and laughed, but it sounded a bit flat.

'I'd better go,' Katherine said.

'I hope you beat the bitch.'

Katherine wasn't really looking forward to the 200 meteres.

'Pace yourself,' Mr Williams shouted at her repeatedly.

She was out in lane two, being a newcomer and not having very good posted times yet. Annette was in lane four and the squirt was in three.

'Katherine, this is my cousin Claudia.' Annette introduced them while they were waiting to get on the blocks. 'I hope to beat you both.' She smiled and then snapped on her goggles. Katherine smiled at Claudia who smiled shyly back.

'Hello.' She held out her hand and Katherine took it.

Then they were on the blocks. Katherine looked into the water and tried to concentrate, but she caught a movement out of the corner of her eye – it was the journalist. The gun went, but it took her a moment to react and the others were hitting the water as she left the blocks.

She cursed herself and the journalist: what the hell did he want? Why couldn't he leave her alone? Claudia was half a body length in front of her; she had to concentrate. She pulled back some of the difference, so on the first turn they were level and Annette slightly ahead. She kept up with them to the second turn, but they got away a bit on her for the third. The last fifty, and she knew Annette could finish strongly, Claudia too if her 100 was anything to go by, but so could Katherine and only two of them would go through. She conjured up a picture of Violet, this time Felicity wasn't small and blonde but tall and slim, dressed in scarves, dancing like a snake. They were laughing still, at Katherine on her

SWEET VIOLET

wedding day. She used the image to spur her on to the end and touched just after Claudia, but before Annette.

It was a very fast time, a new East German record, and Katherine's time was equal to the British record. After they had climbed out of the pool, Annette came over and congratulated Katherine. She hugged Claudia too, until the chaperone stepped in and whisked Claudia away to wherever they were changing – they didn't share a room with the other swimmers.

Annette ran off to the changing rooms. Katherine wondered if she was upset and was starting to follow her when she heard Mr Williams shout her name. She turned and saw him bearing down on her, looking like thunder, with the journalist hanging round behind him.

'What the hell was that?' he demanded. 'You lost nearly two-fifths.' He shook his stopwatch at her as if to prove it.

'I qualified.' Katherine tried not to sound sulky.

'You bloody qualified, you could have had a British bloody record. If it had been the final, would you be saying "I got a silver"?' He asked it as if it was the most stupid question in the world. 'What the hell were you doing?'

Katherine saw the journalist hovering behind Mr Williams. 'It's him,' she said, pointing at the journalist. 'He's been following me.' She hadn't wanted it to, but it came out as a whine.

'So bloody what? You're a public figure, people will follow you.'

'But he . . .' She knew she sounded like a spoilt child. 'He gives me the creeps.'

'I don't care if he gives you herpes. It's no excuse for not concentrating.' He came up close to her and jabbed his big finger on her collarbone. 'Concentration, concentration, concentration!' He shouted into her face and then stormed off.

As Katherine stood there trying not to cry, the journalist came towards her. 'Go away!' she yelled at him.

'I just . . .'

'Piss off and leave me alone.' She ran to the changing rooms.

NINETEEN
Violet

Violet had a bath and changed into some clean jeans and a T-shirt ready for the dance that Hazel had told her about. She sneaked downstairs, where it was quiet and dark. She didn't want to eat in the house, although she was very hungry, because she didn't want to risk getting caught by irate flatmates – or catching anything from the filthy kitchen. She grabbed the note addressed to her and left, stuffing it in her pocket with the Lambda leaflet about the dance – where she hoped there would be some food. The address was Shepherd's Bush, so she headed for the tube, having worked out that she would need to change at King's Cross. Once she was underway, she took out the note:

'Dear Violet –' She heard it in Tree's voice although it was Rainbow's curly writing

> Alice came to us today in great distress, having been told you had two broken arms. She was shocked and horrified to learn that it was a lie, that it was in fact far from the truth. She was distraught to find that you had not been faithful to her, even as recently as this afternoon with one of our dear friends who you upset greatly, but that is another matter altogether. She was upset too that you hadn't even discussed what level of commitment your relationship was going to have, nor the

political and personal ramifications that non-monogamy might have on such a relationship. She is a wonderful woman – both Tree and I have read her thesis on Hidergard of Brennan and found it both enlightening and moving in a way most academic tests fail to be. We feel you have treated her very badly and demand that you attend a house meeting to defend your actions.

It was signed Tree and Rainbow.

Violet screwed it up and tossed it on the floor of the tube, put her foot on it and ground it into the wooden slats. She had thought she was so smart – coming to London, getting a flat, a job, and sleeping with so many women, and now here she was, single still, no Felicity to take to the wedding, and about to be thrown out of her flat. She did feel bad about Alice – she should never had left her like that – but she had never said anything about a relationship, monogamous or otherwise, and even if she had, it was none of Rainbow and Tree's business.

She took the Lambda leaflet out again; maybe she would find someone there. She noticed some writing on the back and turned if over. In neat script was written: 'Flatmate wanted, immediate move' and a phone number. Violet couldn't understand why she hadn't seen it before, or how it came to be on the back of the leaflet. She turned the leaflet over and then back again quickly to check that it was still there, but it was.

She got off the tube at Shepherd's Bush and walked out of the station, past the phones. Outside, she stopped and looked at the leaflet again, went back to the phones and dialled the number on the back. It was Saturday night, so she doubted if anyone would be home.

The phone rang twice. 'Hello,' said a familiar voice.

'You're looking for a flatmate?'

'Oh yes.' The voice sounded surprised.

'I found your number on the back of a flyer, I didn't know if . . .'

'Come round tomorrow, say twelve, we can have brunch.' She gave Violet the address and hung up.

Violet stood there for a moment, feeling so much better. She knew she couldn't expect to turn up and just get the room, but she was suddenly hopeful. She set off for the dance thinking that maybe she would find her Felicity after all.

It was 8.45 when she got there, she'd had enough of being one of the first to arrive. The dance was in an old building: 'Rochester Hall' was engraved in the stone over the entrance way. She climbed the wide steps and pushed the door open. At first she couldn't see anyone there, and then she noticed two women sitting behind a table off to the left beside an open door.

Violet thought she recognised them, but it was hard to tell because they were kissing very passionately. It took a moment for them to realise she was there and untangle themselves. It was the two women who had been with Hazel the night she had met her in Aphrodite Rising.

'Oh, hello.' The one who Violet thought was Hazel's ex. There was something in her tone that Violet didn't like, but couldn't quite place. She paid her money and went through the open door, into the main hall. There were tables covered in white paper, some bare floor and then a stage with a disc jockey playing records. The hall was nearly empty, but there were two women dancing – at least Violet supposed they were both women, this being a lesbian do. One had a yellow sequin dress with a ruffle round the bottom of it, a spray of blonde hair and ridiculously high heels. The other had a man's suit and tie and cropped grey hair. They were waltzing expertly around the dance floor, seemingly completely oblivious to everything about them.

There were a few other women sitting eating, in groups of two or four. Then Violet heard some laughing and a large group of women emerged from a side room, carrying plates and talking loudly. They settled at a table in the middle of the hall, next to the dance floor.

Apart from the dancing couple, most of the women were in chinos with shirts, a lot had waistcoats in various bright and loud patterns, some had bow ties. Most had the flicked-back hairstyle Violet had noticed at Aphrodite, even when they had short hair. They were all white.

Some women came in behind Violet and paused beside her for a moment, then they saw who they were looking for and with lots of waving and kissing went over to join them. Violet decided she couldn't stand in the doorway all night and headed across the hall to the side room for food, feeling very hungry.

There were more white covered tables in there, laid out with food, salads mostly, some cheese and cold meats – limp, pathetic-looking things. There was French bread and of course hummus. Violet helped herself and went to the table where two women were pouring glasses of wine.

'White or red?' one of them asked. It was Hazel. 'Violet!' She looked very pleased to see her, and came out from behind the table. 'I wasn't sure you'd come.' Violet noticed the other woman looking at her closely.

Hazel took her arm and led her back into the main hall, then paraded her right across the room before sitting her down at a table on the far side.

'So.' She sat down opposite Violet and looked at her rather nervously. 'How are you?'

'Fine,' Violet said. 'Hungry.' She wanted to eat, but felt she couldn't with Hazel looking at her so intensely.

'Go on, dig in. I made the hummus.' She looked at Violet's plate. 'You haven't got any.' She stood up and went back to the kitchen area and came back with some on a plate. 'It's very good.'

Violet tried to smile, but as she looked at the salad, she noticed little brown things like flies.

'Listen,' Hazel started, as Violet poked one of the brown things with her plastic fork. 'I've gone and done a rather silly thing.' It was a sultana. Violet pushed it to the side of her plate.

'A jolly silly thing, really.'

Violet looked up at her.

'I told you that Val had gone off with that Sue.'

Violet nodded, wondering what that had to do with her and why anyone in their right mind would put sultanas in a salad.

'Well.' Hazel took a deep breath. 'They're both here tonight.'

Violet picked up a piece of bread, hoping there was nothing odd about it.

'I sort of told them and everyone else that you were coming and I told them, well actually I didn't tell them, they just assumed . . .'

Violet took a bite of the bread.

'. . . that you were my girlfriend.'

Violet breathed in at the wrong moment and a piece of the bread went down her throat; she coughed and the offending lump flew across the table and landed between them. Both of them sat and looked at it for a moment, as a wet patch started to form on the paper around it. Violet wanted to laugh, but she thought that would be rude, and was aware of women at the next table staring at them.

'If you don't want to, I quite understand.' Violet looked at Hazel: she was good-looking in a boyish kind of way, with short, bleached blonde hair, black-rimmed glasses, big without being fat. Violet tried to imagine her at the wedding. An image came to her of Hazel in full riding gear, with jodhpurs, hat and crop, saying, 'Jolly good show, this.'

Violet started to laugh. 'I'm sorry,' she managed between giggles, pointing to the lump of bread.

Hazel sat for a moment and then she laughed too. Violet put her hand over Hazel's, there wasn't anyone else in the room who looked remotely like a Felicity possibility. 'So, how long have we been seeing each other?' she asked.

Hazel looked very relieved. 'Just one week.'

Violet pushed aside the food; she wasn't going to risk any more. 'Care to dance?' she asked Hazel. There were other women up dancing now, and the butch–femme couple had retired to hold court at their table, like some king and queen of the lesbian world.

Hazel was a good teacher and after a while Violet felt she almost had the waltz and sort of knew what she was supposed to be doing with the foxtrot. It was nice to be led around the dance floor, pressed into Hazel's ample bosom. She was very funny, telling wicked stories about the other women there.

The older couple were called Toni and Maria, and Violet didn't get any prizes for guessing who was who. They had been together for thirty years. To Violet, who couldn't usually manage more than one night, that seemed impossible.

'They call each other Mr and Mrs,' Hazel said and laughed. Violet didn't think it was funny; it was what her parents called each other.

Maria had a good figure for fifty, but her face was a mass of lines and wrinkles, accentuated by a thick layer of make-up.

'They want Lambda to do a fund-raiser for her to have a facelift.'

Violet looked at Hazel to see if she was joking.

'True, we had to turn them down. They nearly left because of it and that would have been a shame because they are far and away the most entertaining people we have.'

Some other butch–femme couples had now arrived, but none of them were as glamorous as Toni and Maria.

Violet and Hazel sat down for a rest and someone came over from the head table saying that Maria would like to dance with Violet. Violet shook her head but Hazel said she should. 'As new blood, it's expected of you.'

'New blood', Violet was starting to hate that phrase.

Maria clutched her to her breast and whirled her around the floor, even though Violet was supposed to be leading. She smelt of wine, lipstick and too much perfume and she talked the whole time, making it difficult for Violet to concentrate on counting her steps.

'Twenty-nine years we've been together and the things I've had to put up with.' She sighed. 'The other women he sees, even brings them home sometimes.' She pulled Violet closer. 'It's nice to dance with a young, firm thing.' She clutched Violet's bottom. 'Slaps me around sometimes.' She sniffed delicately, Violet tried to move her bottom out of reach. 'Can't bear seeing me have a good time.' Violet caught a glimpse of Toni, as they whirled past, looking daggers at them.

Fortunately the music ended and Violet excused herself, saying that she needed a pee. Hazel was in the kitchen tidying up; Sue and Val were in there too, snogging in the corner rather than helping. Hazel looked miserable and Violet took her hand.

'Come on, we can show them a thing or two.' She leant Hazel up against the wall and started kissing her. Hazel was a bit tentative at first and kept looking over Violet's shoulder to see if Val was noticing. Violet pinched her nipple through her waistcoat to get her attention.

It might just have been to show Val but Violet didn't see why they couldn't enjoy it too. She ran her tongue along Hazel's lips and across her teeth, until she opened her mouth a little and let Violet slide her tongue inside. Violet ran her hands down Hazel's side and around to her bottom, pushing her pelvis into Hazel's. They might as well make it look convincing. Hazel was kissing her properly now, their tongues circling each other as she pressed back at Violet's pelvis. Suddenly Violet was very hot: she wanted to undo Hazel's waistcoat and shirt, pull off her own T-shirt and rub her breasts across Hazel's like she had done with Ellen. She imagined handcuffing Hazel to a bed somewhere and licking her till she begged her to stop, or even using a dildo on her like she had done with Terry. She gripped Hazel's bottom harder, wishing they could leave the dreary hall and be alone somewhere together.

'Let's go,' Violet whispered in her ear.

'No.' Hazel was breathing hard, but looking over to Val and Sue who were still kissing. 'I have to lock up.'

'Let Val do it.'

'I am the group secretary.'

Violet started to undo Hazel's waistcoat, which got her attention away from Val for a second. She finished with the waistcoat and started on the shirt. 'Stop me any time you like,' she said. Under the shirt a black lacy bra. Violet kissed her exposed neck, and repeated, 'any time you like.'

'We can't do it here.' Hazel had her eyes closed and her head back against the wall.

'No?' She couldn't see why not. Val and Sue were still kissing but with one eye on what Violet and Hazel were doing now. 'Come on.' She took Hazel by the hand and led her out through the main hall to the entrance.

'I really can't leave,' Hazel said again.

'You're not.' She led her through the door to the left and out to the cloakroom; there was a woman sitting in there looking very bored.

'It's our shift now,' Violet said, opening the door for her to leave.

'But I've only just come on.' She looked at Violet and then Hazel, shrugged and left. 'OK then.'

They went in and Violet shut the door. The room was tiny, about three feet wide and six feet long, with the hatch in the middle of it, a chair and the rail of coats.

Violet backed Hazel into the coats. 'What if . . .' she started to ask, but she shut up when Violet kissed her again. Violet took up undoing the buttons where she had left off; Hazel tugged at her T-shirt and Violet let her pull it off over her head. She pushed Hazel's shirt and waistcoat off down her arms and then struggled to undo her bra. She hadn't had much practice at it and it took her a moment. Hazel pulled Violet's sports bra over her breasts and up to her neck, but Violet wouldn't let her take it all the way off.

Hazel cupped one of Violet's breasts in her hand. 'Very nice,' she said as she ran her thumb over the nipple. Hazel's breasts were large and pale with veins showing through the skin, their nipples were pale too and huge. Violet bent her head down and took one in her mouth.

'Oh, sweet Jesus.' Hazel closed her eyes.

They started kissing again, rubbing their breasts across each other's. Violet undid Hazel's belt and trouser button, and as the coat they were leaning against began slipping off its hanger, Hazel slid with it, rather gracefully, to the floor. They didn't stop kissing all the time, while Violet continued with Hazel's trousers, getting the zip undone and pushing them down to her hips.

'What if . . .?' Hazel whispered breathlessly, but Violet pushed her back and pulled her trousers further off. Hazel was now half-lying, half-sitting on one coat with the others hanging over her. Violet was kneeling in front of her, her back against the wall, the hatch above her head. She took one nipple in her mouth again and rubbed the other with her thumb, ran her free hand down over Hazel's stomach and slid it into her knickers. They were black lace too and Violet rejoiced silently.

She rested the heel of her hand on Hazel's mound and let her index finger slip into the wet slit. She reached around with her thumb and found the fleshy button at the top.

Hazel arched her back and let out a sighed breath. She was very wet and Violet moved her fingers in and out and her thumb in a circle. No matter how many times she did this and with how many women, Violet never stopped being amazed by the effect it had on them and her. The feel of the skin under her fingers changing texture, the skin on the body too, as she rubbed. The way the women moved their bodies, arched their backs, threw their heads back – and the noises they made, whatever noises they were, grunts or groans or screams as they built up to an orgasm – and then the great letting go. And what amazed her most of all was that she was the cause of all this.

Violet watched Hazel's face. She had that worried, concentrated look that Katherine used to get just before she came, and Violet moved her fingers faster and sucked the nipple tighter.

'Oh yes.' Hazel arched her back more, pushing the nipple further into Violet's mouth.

'Yes,' she said again, more urgently. Violet rubbed harder and faster, sinking her fingers deeper into Hazel. Hazel was moving her hips now, setting up a wild rhythm of her own. 'Yes, yes, yes.'

Just then Violet heard footsteps. Hazel must have heard them too, as her eyes flew open and she reached up to grab a coat to cover herself. One fell down on her head, but leaving her body bare. Violet didn't know whether to stop or go on: Hazel was so close to coming, it seemed a pity to waste it. The footsteps stopped just the other side of the wall behind Violet. She reached up and pulled another coat down to cover Hazel properly and as she did, her fingers slid out of Hazel and the movement sent her into an orgasm. Violet could see her body convulsing under the coats.

Violet tugged her bra back into place, stood up and turned around.

'I hope that's not mine.' It was Toni, holding out her cloakroom ticket. Violet took it and hunted along the rail for the matching ticket, stepping carefully for fear of treading on Hazel. She found Toni's black trenchcoat and a fur stole that had to belong to Maria, and handed them over. Toni took them, turned and left without saying another word.

Underneath the coats, Violet could see Hazel still shaking. When she pulled the coat off from over her head, she was laughing. 'Oh god, Toni of all people.'

Violet hunted around for her T-shirt and put it on. Hazel found her shirt and waistcoat but not her bra, and then Violet saw it sticking out of the pocket of one of the coats.

'Imagine trying to explain that.' Hazel was laughing so hard there were tears in her eyes.

They had just made themselves decent when Val arrived.

'We need you to . . .' She stopped when she saw their dishevelled state.

'Yes?' Hazel asked cheerfully.

'It's just . . . Oh don't bother.' She ran off, obviously upset.

'Wait.' Hazel ran after her.

Violet sighed, it looked like she had lost yet another possible Felicity. She hung the coats up. The one Hazel had been lying on smelt distinctly of sex. She pressed her nose into it, hoping the owner appreciated it.

She looked at her watch: midnight, time for Cinderella to go home. She walked to the main door and out into the night. It was raining lightly, perfect for her mood. She stood at the top of the steps in shelter and watched the people out in the world. A couple came out of a restaurant with a newspaper over their heads. They stopped at the pedestrian crossing and kissed, then ran across the road and out of sight.

She sighed again. She just knew the last tube would have gone, she didn't have any idea about buses, and then there was the wedding, the weekend after next. It looked like she would just have to go alone, sit there in the church and put on a brave face while Katherine got married to some chinless swimmer.

She walked down the steps into the rain.

'Violet.' She heard someone call her name. 'Where are you going?' It was Hazel, running after her.

'I thought . . .'

'I was giving her the keys. Come on.' She took Violet's arm and turned her around.

'Where to?' Violet didn't really want to go back inside.

'My place?'

'OK.' Violet didn't think she had a 'my place' any more to go back to.

'My car's here.' Hazel's car was a dark green sports car, low to the ground and very fast. Hazel drove it casually with one hand on the wheel and the other on the back of the seat behind Violet's head. They drove along some sort of motorway and then passed Euston Station. Violet tried to keep track of where they were, but Hazel ducked in and out of backstreets and then came to a sudden stop outside a very grand house in a leafy street. Hazel jumped out and came around to open Violet's door, like some gallant gentleman.

'The lock's busted, I keep meaning to get it fixed.'

They walked up the steps; Hazel unlocked the front door and ushered Violet in. She flicked on the hall light, which was a large chandelier.

'My grandmother's,' Hazel said when she saw Violet looking at it. 'Horrid old thing.' The hallway was like Hazel's waistcoat, all red and gold flocked wallpaper. Hazel led the way through the dining room into the kitchen, all oak panels and a huge red fridge from which she got a bottle of champagne and two glasses. She headed up the stairs and motioned Violet to follow her.

'Is this all yours?' Violet asked, trying not to sound too overawed.

'Yep, Grandmother left it to me, not my taste, but can't be arsed to redo it.'

Violet assumed they were heading for the bedroom, but they passed two before Hazel knocked open a door with her foot and led Violet into the bathroom. It wasn't like any bathroom Violet had ever seen before. It was all black and white with the biggest bath Violet had ever laid eyes on, sunk into the floor like a swimming pool.

Hazel started running the bath and then opened the champagne and poured out two glasses. Violet stood by the door, again trying not to look awestruck. It was clear that they were going to do it in the bath. Violet had never done that before but she thought it would be fun. She had never had champagne before either – two firsts in one night. She was worried, though, about having to take off all her clothes to get into the bath.

Hazel already had her waistcoat off. She handed Violet a glass, but when Violet took a sip, some bubbles went up her nose and she coughed. Hazel laughed. She tried again. It was really bitter, whereas she had thought it would be sweet. Hazel must have seen.

'There's beer in the fridge if you prefer.'

Violet didn't really want anything to drink. Hazel had been plying her with drink all night, but Violet didn't need to drink to get in the mood, and she didn't like being drunk anyway, preferring to stay sober and in control.

Hazel was unbuttoning her shirt, looking at Violet as she did it. She wasn't slim like Ellen, but in the lacy underwear she looked gorgeous. Violet was surprised to find how attracted she was to larger women. She remembered her night with Grace and Peaches and smiled.

Hazel had taken off her trousers and was unhooking her bra. She tossed it to one side and then slid off her kinickers.

'Well,' she asked Violet, 'you going to get in with your clothes on?'

Violet took off her T-shirt and hung it on the towel rail, with Hazel watching her every move. She slipped off her shoes and then her socks and trousers, folding them and putting them with her T-shirt. She was stalling and Hazel knew it too. She took a deep breath and then pulled her bra off over her head, which just left her knickers.

'Do you want me to turn my back?' Hazel was teasing her, but when she did look away Violet found it easier and quickly pulled them off and kicked them out of the way. Hazel turned back around and Violet felt herself start to blush.

'You're just perfect, come on.' Hazel slipped into the bath and Violet quickly followed her. She turned off a tap and pushed a button that started bubbles going.

'Bubbly in the bubbles.' She raised her glass to Violet and then drank it down in one.

Violet moved in close beside her and they kissed. She found the bubbles a bit distracting – the way they moved the water around her body, like there was a third person in there with them. She could taste the champagne on Hazel's lips and feel their skin slide together as they moved.

'You know what I'd like?' Hazel said, breaking off the kiss.

'What?' Violet lifted her breast out of the water and licked the nipple.

'It's a bit kinky.'

Violet sucked the nipple into her mouth. She could do kinky: she had done handcuffs and dildos, she had done three in a bed. She had been out on the scene, and didn't think there was anything much that would shock her. She was wrong.

'You've heard of watersports.'

'Yes.' She had heard, but she wasn't sure what they were. Not swimming – the bath wasn't that big.

'I want you to pee on me.'

Violet let go of Hazel's nipple. 'Pee?'

'Yes.'

Violet stood up.

'It's not that weird, it's actually really sexy.'

Violet wondered if Hazel had peed in the bath already, and she got out quickly.

'And shitting.' Hazel was standing up in the bath now. 'That's even better, someone crouched over you, straining, shit dripping on to your body.'

Violet felt suddenly very cold and grabbed her clothes.

'It's not that weird.' Hazel said again. 'Lots of people do it.'

Not her though. Violet headed for the door.

'No Violet, don't go. I won't make you if you don't want to, but it is really nice.'

Violet was in the hallway, pulling on her clothes.

'Feeling it squeeze through your fingers.'

At the front door, getting her shoes on.

'Having it smeared across your face.'

Out into the street, wondering where the fuck she was.

TWENTY

Katherine

The changing rooms were empty, except for Annette packing her bags.

'It has been very nice to meet you, Katherine,' she said in that odd way of hers.

'Yes.' Katherine wasn't sure what else to say, still a bit shaky after her confrontation with the journalist. She wondered how that was going to look in print.

She started to get out of her swimsuit, trying to decide whether to have a shower or not. She noticed Annette hadn't left and was standing looking at her. She covered herself with her towel.

'Sorry,' Annette said, though she didn't sound it. 'I didn't mean to make you shy.' Katherine smiled at her use of words. 'I think you are very beautiful.' She said it in such a straightforward way that Katherine found she couldn't deny it like she normally would.

Annette stood there continuing to look at her. Katherine felt very strange. Other people had told her she was beautiful: her mother, but that didn't count, as all mothers think their daughters are beautiful; Violet had said it too, and although she had sort of believed Violet, she thought it was a phase, just like their relationship was a phase. Sean said it as well, but he had to, because he was her fiancé and that's the sort of thing fiancés had to say. So here for the first time, someone had said Katherine was beautiful and she believed them.

Katherine lowered the towel again. Maybe it was just that she was feeling unsettled by the journalist and Mr Williams shouting at her, but she felt drawn to this woman. Annette put down her bag and came towards her. For the first time, Katherine noticed that she had lovely eyes, green and sparkling, wide cheekbones and sandy, curly hair. She wasn't at all like a tank, just a little short and well built. She stopped in front of Katherine and rached out her hand, running it lightly over the top of Katherine's arm. Katherine felt her nipples contract; Annette noticed and smiled. She took another step closer so their bodies were nearly touching and rubbed her cheek against Katherine's. It was such a light touch, almost no touch at all, but Katherine felt it all through her body and found herself breathing harder. Annette turned her head so their lips brushed, and Katherine could feel Annette's breath against her skin.

She stood there naked except for her towel in her hand and she was aware only of those lips, millimetres from her own. She suddenly wanted Annette to kiss her, wanted it more than she remembered wanting anything else in her life. She put her arms around Annette and pulled her in closer, pressed her lips into Annette's and felt their incredible softness and warmth against her own. Annette responded instantly, opening her mouth slightly and letting Katherine's tongue seek out hers, soft and wet. It was the longest kiss Katherine had ever had, perfect and complete in itself, not leading to anything, not coming from anything, just a kiss in that moment, of that moment. Katherine was aware only of the kiss, their tongues, lips and teeth and Annette's clothed body pressed hard against her naked one.

It would have gone on even longer if not for the sound of footsteps coming closer. Annette pushed Katherine gently away, towards the showers, and she went in and turned on the water. She heard urgent whispering in German and then:

'Katherine, I'm sorry. I have to go.' Her voice sounded a little strange, but it was hard to tell over the noise the shower was making. Katherine had a quick wash. The water was only lukewarm and smelt of chlorine as though it came from the pool. When she came out, Annette was gone and so was Katherine's bag with all her clothes. In its place was a plastic bag full of someone else's clothes.

Katherine looked around the changing room, but there wasn't anywhere else her bag could be. If this was someone's idea of a joke, it was a pretty sick one. Katherine sat down beside the plastic bag, which was from a German supermarket by the look of the writing on it. It must have been Annette who had switched the bags, but Katherine didn't understand — first she kisses her and then she steals her clothes, that was pretty weird.

She looked inside the bag and found a pair of sad-looking polyester pants and a white cotton shirt. She held them up to her. They looked a little small but they would cover her better than a wet towel. She put them on. The trousers were too short and caught around her crotch, especially without knickers, and the shirt was too tight across her chest, but she was decent, if not fashionable.

She walked out of the changing rooms wondering how she was going to explain her missing uniform. As soon as she was out of the door, two burly men grabbed her and a woman started yelling at her in German. She struggled against the men and looked around for help. The stadium was empty. She shouted for help but her words just echoed around the empty space along with the German woman's. The woman stopped shouting when she heard Katherine. She looked a little familiar. She raised her hand and Katherine thought she was going to slap her, but instead she slapped one of the men. She shouted at him in German and then turned back to Katherine and said something in German to her.

Katherine had done three months of German at school and forgotten most of it. She remembered enough to understand the woman was asking her a question. The woman repeated herself.

'I don't understand.' Katherine said in English, but then she realised she did understand.

'Where is she?'

Katherine recognised the woman now; it was Claudia's chaperone.

'I don't know,' Katherine said, wondering if she meant Claudia or Annette – although it didn't matter, because she didn't know where either of them were.

The woman swore in German; it was funny how Katherine remembered that bit of her lessons. Someone came running over, shouting and waving his arms. It was the journalist. He launched himself at the men holding Katherine, and managed to get one punch in before the man swung at him and sent him crashing to the floor.

Mrs Jenkins appeared behind him with Mr Williams on her heels, shouting and waving his arms too, but keeping out of the reach of the men who were holding Katherine. Mrs Jenkins disappeared and then came back with some men in uniforms. They shouted and the German woman shouted and Mr Williams continued to shout, then someone blew a whistle and everyone shut up. Katherine pulled herself free of the men and crossed her arms.

One of the men in uniform started ordering people about: the East Germans were escorted into the changing room; Mrs Jenkins and Mr Williams were shooed outside; and the prostrate journalist was seen to. After they were all sorted out, he turned to Katherine and asked her something in German.

'I don't understand German.'

'Then you are not Claudia Schwartz?'

'No.'

'Where did you get her clothes then?'

'Someone stole mine and left these.'

'And who could that have been?

Katherine was starting to see what had happened here. 'I don't know, I was in the shower.' She shook her wet hair at him as proof.

'I see.' He sighed. 'Your name?' He took out a notebook. Katherine gave him her name and the room number she was staying in at the Village.

'You had better go now.'

Katherine hurried out of the stadium and found Mr Williams and Sean waiting for her.

'What on earth . . .' Mr Williams started at her but stopped when Sean stepped past him and gave Katherine a hug.

'Are you all right?'

Katherine felt suddenly close to tears.

'Get on the coach,' Mr Williams ordered.

'I'm fine.' Katherine leaned her head on Sean's shoulder.

'Now!' Mr Williams shouted.

All the others had been waiting and were curious, but Katherine wasn't ready to try and explain anything to anyone. She had to get it sorted out in her own head, so she sat in the seat next to Sean, closed her eyes and pretended to go to sleep.

First there was the kiss. Katherine could almost feel it again, it had been, so . . . She couldn't quite find the right word for it . . . soft, she supposed, complete somehow. Katherine had to admit to herself that she had initiated it. All Annette had done was say she was beautiful, and rub her cheek against Katherine's; it was Katherine who had started the kiss. After that, it would seem, Claudia had arrived and Annette had helped her to snatch Katherine's uniform and sneak past her chaperone. Katherine felt pleased and excited to have helped in her defection.

The one thing that worried her – and she felt bad for worrying about it when so many other much more important things were going on here – was whether Annette had meant the kiss, or if it was just some kind of decoy to distract Katherine.

Sean put his hand on her thigh and she jumped. She had forgotten he was sitting beside her, for which she immediately felt guilty.

'Sorry.' Sean took his hand away.

'No, no.' Katherine took it and held it in hers. 'I'm just a bit edgy, that's all.'

'I'm not surprised. Did they hurt you?'

Katherine looked at her wrists, which were a little chafed. 'Not really.'

Sean kissed her wrists.

Katherine closed her eyes again, she had heard so many stories about the Eastern Bloc athletes, about the things that were done to them to make them such good competitors. Being taken away from their families at five or six to go to special schools, the drugs they were supposed to be given, even the girls being made pregnant and then given abortions to make them stronger. Every now and then, one of them would defect and these awful stories would come out. You hardly ever heard of them after that – they didn't seem to compete as well away from their own countries, which just made people believe the tales of drug-taking even more.

Katherine had always felt pleased when she heard someone had defected, as though it confirmed how awful the Communist countries were. But sometimes – when she heard Mr Williams complaining about not having enough money to fly to Paris or buy new uniforms, and she saw how hard some swimmers worked to earn enough money to pay their own way to meets, and the good swimmers who dropped out because they couldn't afford to take time off for training – she did wonder if special schools and government funding would be better.

Back at the Olympic Village, there were more police. They were searching the rooms: everyone was lined up and had to go to their room with a policeman, and the whole place was buzzing with excitement. Katherine tried to look for Annette, but she wasn't allowed out of the dining hall and couldn't see her anywhere there.

The same policeman who had questioned her at the pool, questioned her again. Katherine was still wearing Claudia's clothes and he went with her to her room, searched it and then waited outside while she changed. Without her bag, she had only two swimsuits and one change of clothes. She couldn't say she was sorry to have lost her uniform though – Claudia was welcome to it.

The policeman took the clothes, delicately folded them into a plastic bag and sealed it. Katherine wondered what they would do with them. As she had been wearing the trousers with no knickers on underneath, she had visions of tracker dogs sniffing the crotch and then chasing her down the street.

The policeman made careful notes of what she told him. She decided not to mention that Annette had been there, just saying that the changing room was empty and she had been in the shower. She wasn't sure if the policeman believed her or not, but she got the impression he didn't really want to find Claudia and was just going through the motions.

Dinner was late but no one seemed to mind. The hall seemed noisier than usual, with lots of people looking over at Katherine or wanting to ask her questions. Mr Williams called her over and sat her down; he looked at her very seriously.

'Are you all right?' He seemed genuinely concerned and Katherine found that touching, if a little unsettling – she wasn't sure it suited him. She nodded.

'Because if you don't want to swim tomorrow . . .'

'No,' Katherine said quickly. It had never occurred to her not to swim.

'I'd have had to kill you.'

Katherine laughed, that was more like it. 'Of course I'll swim.' It occurred to her then that Claudia wouldn't be swimming and neither would Annette, most probably. That meant she had a better chance of winning but she immediately felt guilty for thinking that.

'And if you know who helped the East German girl –' he spoke sternly and Katherine shook her head, maybe too emphatically '– don't you dare tell anyone.' Katherine smiled. 'Now let's get Steve to have a look at you.'

The physio was just finishing with Sean and let him stay while he looked Katherine over.

'I've never been at a meet where someone's defected before.' Sean was very excited.

'Oh they were always doing it in my day.' Steve had swum in the 70s. 'And you should have heard some of their stories.' Katherine listened while Steve detailed some of the more extreme tales that she had already heard, but she wished he would just shut up and massage her.

After he had finished with her, she went up to her room, even though there was still half an hour till lights out. She wanted to get away from everyone asking her questions. She got her toothbrush and went and cleaned her teeth. When she got back to her room she noticed her bag on her bed. She didn't remember leaving it there; then she realised it was the bag that had been stolen. She looked inside; everything was there, her uniform neatly folded, her swimsuits washed and dried and her towel.

She sat on the bed, then got up and ran to the door to see if she could see anyone in the corridor, but it was empty. She went and sat on the bed again and looked through her things to see if there was a note or anything, but there wasn't. She wanted to see Annette to tell her that it was OK, that she hadn't told the police about her being in the changing rooms. And she wanted to see Annette to get some kind of explanation about the defection – like was Claudia really her cousin? But most of all, she wanted to see Annette to find out whether she had meant that kiss.

Katherine sat on the bed and realised that she wanted very much for Annette to have meant it, because *she* had. She took a deep breath. Yes, she had meant the kiss, and what was worse, she wanted more than just a kiss, she wanted to hold Annette naked, she wanted to run her tongue over Annette's skin and watch the goosebumps rise. She wanted to sink her fingers deep inside Annette and watch her face while she came.

Katherine couldn't believe it, she had all these feelings for someone she hardly knew, a woman. Feelings like she'd had for Violet when they were together, feelings she thought were childish and that she should have grown out of. Feelings that she had never had for Sean. Katherine lay down on the bed and cried.

There was a gentle tapping on the door. Katherine sat up and wiped her eyes. She hoped it was Annette and then hoped it wasn't. She thought it might be Sean and then dreaded it being him. She crossed the floor and opened the door. It was Annette.

'I came to explain,' she said, as Katherine let her in.

'No, don't.' Katherine held up her hand.

'I would have asked, only . . .' Annette started.

'I don't mind.' Katherine interrupted her. She was scared Annette was going to say that the kiss meant nothing. She was intensely aware of Annette's body close to her own.

'You have been crying?' Annette noticed the tears; she wiped one off Katherine's cheek. 'Why?'

Annette was looking right into her eyes and Katherine knew

she couldn't lie. 'Because you kissed me and I thought I wouldn't see you again.'

'Oh, Katherine.' Annette put her hand behind Katherine's head. They stayed like that for a moment, looking into each other's eyes, as though they were both too scared to start kissing, scared where it might lead. Katherine could feel the tension of the waiting right through her body. She closed her eyes and leant her head back into Annette's hand, felt Annette's cheek brush hers, felt her breath on her neck. She turned her head and their lips met, soft and warm. They started kissing, more urgently than before. Little kisses, faster and harder, tongues darting and teeth touching, until they were both breathing hard. Katherine held on to Annette's waist, slid her hand down to her bottom and pulled her closer.

Annette's free hand caressed Katherine's neck, moving slower than their tongues and lips. She ran it down over Katherine's breasts. Katherine felt a shiver run right though her body and arched her back to push her breast harder into Annette's hand. Annette started tugging at Katherine's T-shirt, pulling it up out of her jeans. Katherine unbuttoned Annette's shirt, both still kissing all the while. Katherine pushed Annette's shirt back off her shoulders. Her breasts were small and firm and Katherine squeezed a nipple. Annette broke off the kiss for a moment while she pulled Katherine's T-shirt off her, then they were back in it, kissing and holding each other's breasts, kneading and pinching each other's nipples.

Annette broke the kiss off again and pushed her away slightly. She looked Katherine over and then bent her head down and rubbed her cheek over first one nipple and then the other. Katherine felt like her body was on fire – the slightest touch felt like a knife, a brand, but she wanted more. She wanted every bit of her body to be touching every bit of Annette's.

Annette started to undo Katherine's jeans, kneeling on the floor in front of her. Katherine pulled her to her feet and tried to undo her trousers, but she couldn't get the top button undone. Annette helped her and they both struggled out of their trousers. Katherine managed to slip off her shoes but Annette had to sit down on the bed to untie hers.

Katherine knelt on the bed behind Annette and ran her hands over her back, feeling the ribs and muscles with her fingertips. She licked a line from her shoulder to her neck, then Annette turned her head so that their lips met and they started kissing. Katherine rubbed her breasts over Annette's back. Annette turned more and pushed Katherine down on the bed, then lay on top of her, one thigh between her legs.

'You are so beautiful,' she whispered in Katherine's ear. Katherine held Annette's bottom, pressing her thigh up between Annette's, pushing her pelvis into Annette's.

'You make me so hot,' Annette breathed.

They kissed again, hard and fast, both breathless, their bodies pushing into each other. Annette ran her hand over Katherine's thigh and then slipped it between their legs, sliding two fingers up into Katherine. She threw her head back. Annette's fingers felt like ice inside her and she pushed her hips up, wanting them deeper, harder. She slid her fingers inside Annette, who was so wet, the skin inside felt like satin. She found Annette's clitoris with her thumb and started rubbing it, making her groan. Both their bodies were covered in a sheen of sweat that glowed under the hard light of the room.

Annette slid her fingers deeper, brushing them over Katherine's clitoris, backwards and forwards. The feeling was so intense, it was almost unbearable, yet every time Annette moved her fingers, Katherine wanted them deeper, harder. She pushed her hips up off the bed and Annette pushed down harder. Her whole body seemed to be throbbing, beating like a drum, faster and faster.

Katherine still had her fingers inside Annette and, though it was hard to concentrate, she kept rubbing Annette's clitoris with her thumb, trying to get a rhythm going. They were both now moving their hands and bodies faster and faster until there was almost no movement at all, just a wild vibration. Katherine felt that vibration building up inside her body, getting stronger and faster like a tuning fork reaching its harmonic until it seemed to explode around her. She felt her body convulse, the muscle around Annette's fingers contract and then relax again, and all the tension in her body drain out. A moment later, Annette let out a grunted sigh, and her body shook slightly and Katherine's fingers were squeezed, inside Annette.

They rolled together and lay there for a moment, just holding each other. Katherine wanted to say so much to Annette, but she didn't know how to start or what words to use, and she didn't want to spoil the moment either. This relationship – or whatever it was – wasn't going anywhere and never could. She would just have to settle for knowing that while it had been, it had been perfect. Annette gently untangled herself from Katherine and sat up.

'I have to go.'

'I know.' Katherine sat up too.

'They will think I have been caught by the East Germans.' She smiled at Katherine and brushed some hair off Katherine's face. 'I wish I could have known you better.'

Katherine tried to smile, but she wasn't sure her face was working properly.

Annette got off the bed and started to dress. Katherine watched her; she wanted to tell her to stay, not to go, to come back to England with her, but she knew that Annette couldn't and wouldn't. Instead, she just lay there and watched her dress, then tried to smile as Annette kissed her on the forehead.

'Goodbye, Katherine,' she said, and she let herself out.

Katherine pulled the covers over her head and drifted off to sleep.

TWENTY-ONE
Violet

It took Violet till six to get home. The sun was coming up, the birds were singing, it was a beautiful day but she wasn't in the mood for it. She hadn't been that far from home but she had turned the wrong way out of Hazel's street and ended up going miles out of her way, without enough money for a cab. She was tired, cold and hungry, and for once she was pleased to be home – until she saw her bag sitting by the front door, packed.

She ran up the stairs and threw open her bedroom door. There was someone in the bed. She turned on the light and a pair of huge, scared eyes stared out at her.

'Violet.' a voice simpered. It was Alice.

Violet ran back down the stairs, grabbed her backpack and slammed the front door shut behind her. She went to the twenty-four hour bagel shop on the High Street and bought two cream cheese bagels and a large coffee with loads of sugar. Then she went to the little park behind the Shopping City and found a bench in the sun, like the homeless person that she was.

She had until midday before she was due to see the flat – the whole morning. She ate the bagels and drank the coffee. She wasn't going back to her aunt's house, no way, no how – she would rather sleep on the street. She watched the early morning joggers go by, then the dog walkers. She plotted terrible revenge on Tree and Rainbow, imagining ordering a side of beef to be delivered there by big burly men, or getting the council round to condemn the place as unfit for human habitation. She remembered the pint of milk she had hidden in the fireplace, and hoped they hadn't found it and that the smell of it going off would drive them out of the house for good.

From about nine o'clock, she noticed people going into a building opposite with towels and bags. It took her a while to realise it was a swimming pool, then she went across. Her bag was only a little bigger than most and no one gave her a second look. She found a locker, showered and spent the next two hours doing lengths.

It was perfect. Gliding through the water, she was able to forget about the house, forget her hopeless search for Felicity, just concentrate on getting her body through the water. When she had swum everything out of her system, she showered again, washing her hair, and changed. She couldn't leave her bag there, but at least she was clean and relaxed.

She caught the 41 bus along West Green Road and then walked a little way to the address the woman had given her. She looked about for somewhere to hide her bag – she couldn't go in with it, as it would show up her desperation. She stowed it in the hedge just inside the gate. It was exactly twelve when she rang the doorbell, which played the tune of 'Three Blind Mice'. Violet smiled. She heard someone come down the stairs, the keys in the door, then the door opened and there stood a very familiar person. It was Belinda.

'Oh, hello.'

'Hello.' Belinda didn't bat an eye.

'I didn't know it was you.'

'Come up, I've got coffee and doughnuts, but you look like you could use some scrambled eggs. Mind the cats.' Two large grey and white cats sat at the top of the stairs and blinked at her. One ran away as she approached, while the other rolled on to its back and demanded that she stroke it. 'That's Vincent,' Belinda said.

It was as if she was expecting her – not just a prospective

flatmate, but *her*, Violet. The flat was clean and bright, painted in light yellows and blues and with darker blues and yellows here and there. She showed Violet round; the room on offer was small but bright.

Belinda sat her down in the small kitchen at a dinky two-person table and poured her some coffee, then set about making the scrambled eggs. She talked as she cooked. 'I like the place kept tidy, but I'm not obsessive about it.' After the kitchen in the other house, this one looked like a 50s ad for some miracle cleaning product. 'I'm very quiet, I don't have a TV and I don't like to be disturbed when I'm writing, which I do in my room.' Violet had seen the portable typewriter in there. 'The rent is £50 per month, not including bills, and you have to write down your phone calls.' She turned back to Violet and smiled. 'It's yours if you want it.'

Violet tried not to look too surprised or pleased. 'Just like that?' she asked. 'You don't even know my star sign.' She was only half-joking.

'I'd say Gemini with Virgo rising.'

Violet was amazed; she didn't know anything about the rising bit, but she was a Gemini. 'How did you know?'

'A lucky guess.'

She served up the eggs. They were delicious and exactly what Violet needed. They ate in silence, then Belinda said, 'When do you want to move?'

Violet finished the last of her egg. 'How about now?'

'OK.' Belinda smiled and her whole face lit up. 'You'd better go and get your bag then.' She handed Violet some keys. 'These are yours.'

It wasn't until Violet was down the stairs that she realised Belinda had said 'bag' – not 'bags' or 'things', but 'bag' singular. She wondered if Belinda had seen her hide it. She retrieved it from the hedge and then walked around the block with it so as not to make it too obvious if Belinda didn't already know. It was a lovely area: there was a park close by and an Indian restaurant, a fish and chip shop and a corner store – everything a girl could want. Violet went in and bought some milk, just for the joy of being able to take it into the house openly.

SWEET VIOLET

When she got back, Belinda was in her room with the door closed, tapping away on her typewriter. Violet felt a little rush of excitement at living with a real writer – it was going to be great. She went into her new room, which was light blue with a small double bed and a window that looked over the back garden. Violet opened the window and the smell of roses greeted her.

She unpacked her bag, putting her clothes in the blue dresser painted with little flowers, and hanging her trousers up in the matching wardrobe. When she was finished, she lay on the bed. Above the bedhead was an old-fashioned photo of a woman who looked a bit like Belinda. On the wall opposite the door were three small photos of Belinda standing in the desert in various poses.

She fell asleep and woke later in the afternoon to the sound of Belinda still typing, and with one of the cats curled up at the foot of her bed. She had a shower and did the dishes, then went out to the shop and bought some things for dinner. She baked potatoes and cooked up ratatouille to go with them.

Belinda emerged from her room, stretching and yawning, about seven. 'You're an angel,' she said as she tucked into the food.

Waking on Monday morning, Violet knew exactly where she was and it felt totally like home. Belinda set off for work early and left some coffee in the pot for her; Violet did the dishes from the night before and went off to college. This became their pattern: on the nights when Violet worked in the gym, Belinda would cook dinner; and on the other nights, Violet would cook. Belinda spent at least two hours in her room typing each night.

She had only two weeks left to find a Felicity to take to the wedding, but Violet found that she couldn't be bothered going out looking for her. All she wanted to do was to stay home, curled up on the blue sofa with the cats, reading a book and listening to Belinda type.

There were photos of Katherine in all the papers – 'the new British swimming sensation', they were calling her. Violet looked hard at the photos to see if she could spot any difference in her appearance, but could only tell that she looked happy about her medals.

College, meanwhile, was dull, the lectures mostly on things Violet already knew. Garth sat beside her in most of them and kept her entertained with a running commentary on who was sleeping with whom, and who said what about whom. Where he collected all this gossip, she had no idea, but she loved it. He was after one of the black men on the course – rampantly heterosexual, and only went out with black women, but Garth loved a challenge. He gave Violet daily updates.

At the gym she now wore shorts and a vest. Roger nodded his approval before ducking into the loos with some muscle Mary. The women who came in seemed to like her outfit too, and more started coming along. Roger had her showing them how to use the equipment, and she started to enjoy herself.

On Saturday she had a job with Judy and Fiona, moving a couple from Walthamstow to Dalston. They had the biggest double bed Violet had ever seen, and Judy shook her head at it. 'Don't like the look of that,' Fiona muttered as they loaded it into the van.

It was a beautiful day and when she got home, Belinda was sitting in the garden.

'Let's go to the pond.'

They drove there in Belinda's 2CV and found a place down by the water.

'So, the wedding's next weekend?'

Violet was surprised, as she didn't remember telling Belinda about it, but she nodded. 'Have you found anyone to go with?'

'No.'

Belinda was in her bright pink bathing suit with a big floppy straw hat. Her eyes were cornflower blue and her lashes so pale, you had to look closely to see she had any. She was wearing glasses. 'My eyesight is perfect,' she had told Violet. 'But I feel more the part when I've got them on. I think I write better with them.'

'Coming for a swim?' she asked now, sweeping off her hat and putting on her funny bathing cap, the one that had saved Violet getting barred from the pond for life.

'OK.' Violet had brought her swimsuit this time. They picked their way through the throng of reclining women and lowered themselves into the cold water. Belinda swam her bobbing breaststroke, her head held high out of the water, and Violet swam beside her.

'I'm reading tonight.' Belinda said out of nothing.

'Oh.' Violet was disappointed, having imagined another night in, listening to Belinda typing.

'You can come if you like.'

Violet remembered the last reading she went to at Holborn House and pulled a face.

Belinda saw. 'No, this one should be nice. No rampant feminists, I can be as un-PC as I like.'

'OK then, if you promise Tree and Rainbow won't be there.' They swam on some more, and Violet thought it would be nice to hear her read again, to see other people's reactions to her reading, people who might appreciate it. Then it occurred to Violet that she hadn't even thought about whether she would meet anyone there who could be her Felicity for the wedding. A week ago, that would have been her first and only thought.

They swam around the pond a couple of times, and Belinda waved to several women she knew. In her bright bathing cap, she looked like some sort of water nymph. They got out of the pond and went back to their place on the lawn to dry off. It was so peaceful, with a few clouds floating by in the sky, the sound of women swimming in the pond, the smell of freshly mown grass. Once again, Violet felt she had found heaven, a very different heaven to Aphrodite Rising, but heaven all the same.

The reading was in a cafe near Covent Garden. Belinda was very nervous, and had changed several times before deciding on a light blue dress and smallish straw hat with matching blue flowers. Everyone else was more casually dressed. Belinda was reading in the second half of the programme. She sat through the first half clutching a glass of white wine in her hands and listening intently to the other readers. Violet didn't like most of it. One woman read a funny story about children playing in a boat on a canal and nearly drowning. Two men read rather dreary poems and then a woman sang some songs.

At the interval, Belinda disappeared off to the loos. Violet watched the people milling about, getting drinks and chatting. Most of them were much older than Violet, and Belinda was probably the youngest reader. There were a couple of women who might have been lesbians but no one came over to talk to her. Belinda came back, looking a little pale.

'Are you all right?'

She nodded.

The reading started again, another man and more boring poems, then one with an unlikely story about gangsters that went on forever, then it was Belinda. She stood up at the mike and cleared her throat, then someone adjusted the height for her.

'Can you hear me?' she asked timidly, and the people said they could. She read her bingo poem, 'Two Fat Ladies', and everyone laughed and clapped when she finished it. Then she read a poem about seeing two women kissing in the Women's Pond. Violet felt herself start to blush. She looked around to see if anyone had noticed, but they were all watching Belinda, smiling and nodding. Belinda looked up at the end of the poem, straight at Violet. Violet blushed harder, even though it had been a nice poem, saying how natural and beautiful a kiss could be. She had never had anyone write anything about her before, and she was embarrassed that Belinda had seen the kiss. Everyone clapped at the end and Violet felt oddly proud.

The last poem that Belinda read was called 'Hats'. Violet laughed at the title, because she knew Belinda loved hats – the flat was full of them, and she was always wearing one. The poem started off describing all the hats she had and what they were for. Violet could picture them, and where they were in the flat. Then Belinda read:

> And in a box in my wardrobe
> There's a hat bought for a wedding
> I may never be invited to . . .

Violet felt her heart beat faster.

> So it sits on the shelf, just like me
> Waiting to find its Felicity.'

Everyone clapped like mad and called for more, but Belinda was off the stage and back in her seat, flatly refusing.

The last item was the woman singing again, but Violet didn't really hear her, just sat next to Belinda, intensely aware of her presence, looking at Belinda's hands folded neatly in her lap – lovely hands, long fingers, neat nails. Violet found herself wondering what it would be like to hold those hands, the hands that had tapped out the poems on the typewriter. She wondered what it would be like to run her hands up those arms and hold those shoulders while she kissed those lips.

The singer finished and everyone was clapping again and getting out of their chairs, walking around, talking to each other. Violet and Belinda just sat there side by side. Some people came up to Belinda and said how much they liked her poems, and she thanked them. One of the men who had read sat down next to Belinda and started talking about metre and rhythm. Violet wished he would go away. Belinda smiled and nodded but didn't say much, and eventually he left.

Belinda turned to Violet then. 'Did you like them?' she asked shyly, as though what Violet thought really mattered to her.

'Oh yes,' Violet said and she started to blush again. She couldn't think of the right words to tell her how much she liked them.

Belinda smiled. 'I should have warned you, about the pond one.'

'And "The Hat"? Would you really come to the wedding?'

It was Belinda's turn to blush. 'I wasn't fishing for an invitation.'

'But would you?'

Belinda looked shy again. 'If I can wear the hat.'

Violet laughed. 'Only if it's raining.'

'OK.' Belinda held out her hand to shake on it. 'It's a deal.'

They went for dinner in a little Italian restaurant nearby. Belinda ordered her food and Violet had the same – she had never had Italian food that wasn't pizza.

'How did you know about Felicity?' Violet asked as they were waiting for their starters.

'What do you mean?'

'That I had put the name Felicity Hope on the wedding reply, as my partner.

'I didn't.'

'But in the poem, you said something about finding Felicity.'

'I didn't mean a person with that name.'

'What?'

'Felicity means happiness, intense happiness. You said your "partner" was called Felicity?'

'Felicity Hope.'

'That's very clever.'

'I wasn't trying to be clever.'

'You don't have to try.' Belinda put her hand over Violet's and smiled so sweetly at her that Violet thought she was going to melt. It was the nicest thing anyone had ever said to her. Unfortunately, the waiter brought their starters then and Belinda took her hand away.

'It's quite some name to live up to,' Belinda said, tucking into the antipasto. 'Hello, I'm Felicity,' she said, trying it out. 'Felicity Hope.' She giggled, and Violet did too, suddenly relieved, like a huge weight had lifted from her shoulders. For the first time in a while, she thought that things might turn out all right after all.

On the tube home, Violet tried to work out how she could arrange it so that she could kiss Belinda. She felt suddenly shy and awkward. She was almost certain that Belinda wouldn't mind, might even like it, but she didn't want to blow it, there was too much at stake here. They got off at Turnpike Lane and walked along the road. It was a beautiful evening.

Belinda was carrying her hat in one hand and her shoes in the other. 'It's the last day of summer tomorrow,' she said, sighing.

Violet laughed; it was so warm that it felt like the summer would go on forever. Belinda was quite serious, though.

Violet unlocked the door and let Belinda go in first. As she followed her up the stairs, she thought about catching her and kissing her there, like she had done to Angela, but that didn't seem right somehow. She made them some coffee and they sat together on the sofa. Violet imagined reaching her arms up as if she was stretching and then putting them round behind Belinda on the back of the sofa, like some adolescent boy, but Belinda stood up and yawned. 'Good night then,' she said. 'And thank you for coming along tonight – it's a bit lonely by yourself.'

Violet stayed on the sofa with the cats, not nearly ready for bed. She had never felt quite like this before, so uncertain, shy and excited all at the same time. Even with Katherine, she had just gone for it, so sure of herself, so certain that Katherine would respond. Now, despite all the women she had slept with – or at least had sex with, it had never gone as far as sleep – Violet was at a complete loss as to how to start. She finished her coffee and went to bed. Maybe by the morning she would have come up with a plan.

She hadn't of course, nor the next morning, nor the next. The weather turned suddenly cold; she went to college, worked at the gym, came home, sat on the sofa with one or other of the cats, listening to Belinda typing, all the time on tenterhooks. Each time she saw Belinda, she wondered if then was the right moment to try and kiss her, but it never was. She thought she was going to explode from the tension and bits of her would be found all over London. Some days it made her extremely happy, gave her boundless energy, some days she could barely get out of bed. She thought about Belinda most of the time, wondered what it would be like, that first kiss – soft and gentle, or passionate, tearing each other's clothes off like she had done with Hazel.

Violet began to regret all the other women she had slept with; those encounters seemed sordid now, unclean, as though they had made her unworthy of Belinda. By Friday she was ready to throw the whole thing away, she couldn't imagine sitting beside Belinda for the long trip to the wedding in Coventry without going mad.

They left the flat at four o'clock and drove around the north

Circular and on to the M1. By the time they reached the Watford Gap Services, Violet thought she was going to be sick.

'Can we stop here?' she asked.

Belinda looked at her, worried. 'Are you all right? You've been very quiet.'

Violet had been going over all the things she could say. Belinda pulled the car into a parking space and started to get out of the car, but Violet stayed where she was.

'Violet?' Belinda stopped, half in the car and half out.

'You know, Belinda . . .' Violet started. It felt like the hardest thing she had ever had to do. She stared out of the front window, watching an Asian family in saris go into the services.

'What?' Belinda asked, when Violet paused for too long.

'I really fancy you.' Violet said, and then she regretted it – it sounded so silly, so childish. Belinda didn't say anything for a moment. Violet looked at her; she was smiling, trying not to laugh. Violet didn't know if that was a good thing or a bad thing.

'Oh Violet.' Belinda kissed her lightly on the lips. 'That's so sweet.' Violet still wasn't sure if that meant they were on or not. She put her hand on the back of Belinda's head and kissed her back, softly at first and then harder, their lips squashed together, their tongues tentatively touching. Violet found that she was shaking.

Belinda broke off the kiss and laughed. 'We can't do this here.' She looked around at the people passing them on the way in and out of the services. She took Violet's hand and squeezed it. 'We'll have to wait.'

They drove on to Coventry, Violet's whole body buzzing in anticipation.

TWENTY-TWO

Katherine

Katherine woke feeling oddly calm; showered, dressed in her uniform and went downstairs for breakfast. She felt like she was floating, quite serene and untouchable. She sat next to Sean and kissed him on the cheek, feeling no guilt about the night before. Annette was gone, off somewhere safe with Claudia, she hoped, and last night was, well, last night. Today was a new day, the sun was shining and she had three finals to win.

In the pool at the warm-up, the water was definitely on her side. It buoyed her up and pushed her along faster and faster, until Mr Williams shouted at her not to wear herself out. Katherine felt like she had all the energy in the world flowing through her, that she could do anything.

The journalist was there, with a bandage on his head from the fracas. She waved and went over to ask how he was. He had spent the night in hospital, but was fine. In fact, since he had shaved and his hair was tidy, his suit was uncreased and he had a new tie on, he looked like a decent, respectable human being.

Katherine sensed he wanted to tell her something, but Mr Williams called her away for a team talk. She and Phillipa had butterfly first, then Sean was in the men's race and Matt in the breaststroke. Ian had qualified for the backstroke after someone had been disqualified. Sean and Matt were both in the men's freestyle 100 metres and Patrick had qualified in the 200, then there were the relays. Mr Williams shouted at them for a bit, not saying anything he hadn't said a hundred times before. Katherine wondered why he bothered, since no one listened after the first three or four times, but she guessed it made him feel better.

In their butterfly race there were two empty lanes, Annette's and Claudia's. It seemed wrong to go ahead without them, disloyal somehow, but as Katherine hit the water after the gun went off, she realised it wasn't disloyal at all, she was going to swim for them. The water was still being nice to her, and she turned first. On the second fifty, she slipped a little and felt the French swimmer, who had won the silver at Paris, overtake her; Phillipa was close too. She kicked harder and pulled the French girl back, touching just ahead of her. One of the Russians came in for the bronze, leaving Phillipa fuming in fourth.

Katherine had a long gap now. She accepted her medal from the German official, then went to get changed. She noticed a lot of police about, but none seemed interested in her. She went and sat in the competitor area and watched some of the races. Sean picked up a bronze in his butterfly and Matt did the same in the breaststroke. She noticed the journalist hanging around and went over to him.

'Do you want to finish the interview?' she asked.

'Actually, no.' He seemed so normal today, not the least bit creepy or sleazy. Katherine wondered if he had changed or if she had.

'I wanted to say goodbye.'

Katherine was surprised and for some reason disappointed. 'Oh,' she said; and then when it looked like he was going to leave, she added, 'I wanted to thank you, for yesterday. Jumping in like that, it was very brave.'

He touched his bandage gingerly. 'Much good it did.' He laughed. He was actually quite good-looking when he laughed.

'It was the thought that counted,' Katherine said as she held out her hand. He shook it and then held it for a moment, smiling down at it, then turned quickly and walked away. Katherine couldn't swear to it, but she thought she saw tears in his eyes.

Lunch came and went and then there were the freestyle races, again in the 100 there were two empty lanes. Katherine wanted to put in a good time despite not having Annette to swim against, so when the gun went, she put her head down and swam as hard as she could. On the turn, only one of the Russians was anywhere near her, but she lost her in the last fifty metres and finished half a length in front. Mr Williams was jumping up and down: she had set a new British record, and she hadn't even had to use Violet to spur her on.

She didn't have much time before the 200 metres, so she changed into a dry swimsuit and let Steve massage her shoulders. Thankfully, he hardly said a word, so she could just lie and relax. There would be only one free lane in the 200 metres. Katherine was looking forward to it: she knew she should feel tired after the 100 metre swim, but she still had that calm, invincible feeling she had woken with.

Back on the blocks again, Katherine felt totally focused, one hundred per cent concentrated. She was off with the gun and flying — swimming faster than she had ever swum. She was ahead on the first turn and even further on the second. But she could feel herself slowing up to the third turn and in the last fifty she was struggling. It felt like the water had turned against her, and she fought it with all her strength, kicking and pulling herself through it until she reached the wall, just ahead of one of the Russians.

She didn't have the strength left to get herself out of the pool. Mr Williams came over and pulled her out.

'What did I say?' he demanded. She didn't understand the question. 'Pace yourself.' He answered it for her. 'Bloody pace yourself.' She nodded.

He helped her over to the bench and sat her down.

'Are you all right?' he asked.

She nodded again.

'Then pull yourself together, you've still got the relay.' He walked off.

Katherine had not exactly forgotten about the imminent relay, but now the thought returned like a punch in the stomach. She didn't know if she could walk to the changing rooms, let alone swim another 100 metres. She needed to get back to that calm place, so she tried some of her mother's breathing. That slowed down her heart rate, stopped her arms and legs shaking, but she still felt totally spent. She closed her eyes and an image of Annette came to her, smiling at her, telling her she could do it, do it for her. Katherine stood up and shook out her arms and her legs. She could do it, she was strong and calm, though she knew now that she wasn't invincible. It was only one more race and she would find the energy from somewhere to swim it.

The East German team had pulled out, but the Russians were still in, as well as the Irish and French. The West Germans had a replacement for Annette, but they weren't the threat that they would have been with her. Katherine watched the others swim their 100 metres, then it was her turn and she was off. The water seemed to have forgiven her and it let her pass through cleanly. They were in third at the start of her leg, and she pulled back the German at the turn and caught the Russian just before the end, sneaking past her into the lead, touching the wall first.

She was too exhausted to be as excited as everyone else was. She sat on the bench and watched the men's race. They came in third and, against the Russians and the East Germans, that was as good as they were ever going to do. By the time they came to the freestyle medal ceremony, Katherine could barely stand up. She climbed to the top podium and smiled and waved for the 100 metres, then she did it again for the 200 and one final time for the relay. There were a lot of photographers there and everyone seemed to want to take her photo, so she smiled and held up her medals.

The relay ceremony was nice – Phillipa hugged her, Claire cried and Beverly laughed. As they posed for more photos, Katherine noticed that Phillipa had done her hair and even put on some lipstick. She leaned forward while they were having their photos taken, to show some cleavage, then laughed when she saw Katherine looking.

'I'm nearly finished as a swimmer,' she said. 'I've got to think about my future.'

'As a page-three girl,' Katherine teased her.

'If they pay enough.' She sounded as if she was only half-joking.

Then it was on to the coach to the airport, on to the plane and then another coach back to Coventry. Katherine slept a lot of the way, and when Sean dropped her home, she barely had the energy to thank him, let alone kiss him. Her mother was in with Brian, of course. They had recorded all her races and she had to sit there with them as they replayed them. She saw how close she was to being beaten in the 200 final, and had to put up with Brian telling her how she should have swum the race. But more than that, she saw the two empty lanes and wondered how Claudia and Annette were and if she would ever see them again.

She was on the main news that night and in all the papers, mostly with the photo of the relay team and Phillipa showing off her cleavage. There was a little about Claudia's defection: she had been granted asylum in West Germany and then she and her mother were going to America to start a new life there. Annette was mentioned briefly and it seemed she was going with them as Claudia's coach.

In the week that followed, she had calls from the TV, radio and newspapers, wanting interviews; and from sportswear companies, wanting to sponser her. She left all that to her mother and Mr Williams. She tried to get on with her college work and get ready for the wedding, which was suddenly only two weeks away. She had final dress fittings and hair appointments to make, the florist to check up on and the caterers. At the last minute, they wanted to know what vegetables she wanted, what wine. She couldn't have cared less, but they demanded answers. The car hire company couldn't get the car they had wanted and tried to sell them something more expensive and not as nice, so they dropped all that and decided to go in Sean's car instead. The hotel found they had double-booked the room for the reception and wanted to change the day, but Katherine screamed down the phone at them until they found her another room.

She was sure the day was going to be a disaster, and Sean was useless – whenever she asked what he thought about anything, he said, 'Whatever you want, it's your day.' Like it was nothing to do with him. She was sure that his parents were going to be horrified with what she had organised, and in her worst moments, she imagined them refusing to pay their half and landing it all on her mother. She was a nervous wreck before long and ready to call the whole thing off.

'Come on,' Sean said on the Friday of the weekend before the wedding. 'Let's go away for a few days.'

They had swimming training on the Sunday afternoon and Katherine had an essay due in on Monday.

'We can't.'

'Why not? Bring your homework with you, we'll come back Sunday morning.'

Katherine thought about it. The alternative was to spend Saturday night watching the video of her races again and listening to Brian telling her how he onced boxed for Nottingham County.

'OK, where?'

They drove to North Wales and checked into a hotel near Snowdon. It was 8.30 when they got there.

'Sorry, you have missed dinner,' the woman informed them when they asked. 'It's 7.30 to 8, the chef's gone home, and anyway, you have to book the night before.'

Sean managed to persuade her to make them sandwiches and they went up to their room, giggling. He had brought a bottle of whisky and some chocolates, and he poured two glasses.

'This can be our honeymoon.' They couldn't go away until after Christmas because of swim meets.

'Before the wedding?'

'Why not?' Sean made a toast. 'To us.'

'To us.' They knocked glasses.

After the sandwiches and several more glasses of whisky, Sean opened the chocolates, which had melted in the car.

'Come here.' He pulled up her T-shirt and smeared one across her stomach, then licked it off.

'Ow.' Katherine pushed his head away, but the remaining chocolate felt silky on her skin and Sean's tongue was rough – she liked the contrast.

She pulled Sean's shirt open and, taking a chocolate out of the box, smeared it across his chest. She pushed him back on the bed and licked. Some had covered his nipple. She sucked it into her mouth, he groaned.

'You like that, then?' She reached for another chocolate and smeared it on his other nipple. She straddled him as she sucked and licked it off. Sean lay back and watched her. She slid down his body and started to unbuckle his belt, seeing his penis starting to harden under the material of his trousers. She unzipped them and smeared another chocolate low across his belly. Sean started to move his hips under her, pushing them up, pressing her tongue harder into his flesh. He tugged at her T-shirt and she lifted her head and arms so he could pull it off.

Sean laughed as she lifted her face, and she could feel that she had chocolate all over it. She didn't care – she took another chocolate, pushed down Sean's underpants, and squashed it into his pubic hairs. She tried licking it off, but some of the hairs came with it and stuck in her teeth. She had to stop and pull them out.

Sean sat up then and undid her jeans, pulling them down as far as he could. He rolled her over so that she was on her stomach and rubbed a chocolate across one cheek of her bottom. His tongue tickled like mad as he licked it off, making her squirm. He then moved up to her shoulders, still licking but with no chocolate. She could feel the roughness of his pubic hairs against her bottom and the stickiness of the choclate. Sean reached her neck and was kissing and biting it, then he reached one hand around and grasped her breast, squeezing and kneading it.

Katherine could smell and taste chocolate. Her face and body were sticky with it, her head was filled with visions of bathing in it, like Cleopatra in milk. She turned her head and kissed Sean. Their tongues met covered in chocolate – sweet, sticky kisses. Sean was rubbing his whole body backwards and forwards, up and down Katherine's, the chocolate providing both lubrication and resistance.

His rubbing was getting faster and more urgent, and she could feel his penis between the cheeks of her bottom. He was going to come soon if she didn't do something, so she pushed herself up till she was on all fours and pushed her jeans further down to give her more room to move. Sean stayed on her back and started fumbling in his trouser pocket for a condom. He was breathing hard and fast and sweating. Katherine wanted to help him, but he was too heavy and she couldn't turn around. She realised he was going to fuck her in that position, doggy style. The thought excited her, and she remembered him talking about watching Phillipa and Matt in the bathroom. She felt her breathing start to quicken too, and she slid her fingers inside herself and started to rub them past her clitoris like Annette had done. She could feel the tension start to build inside her.

Sean had finished putting on the condom and sat back on his heels to watch her masturbate.

'Oh God.' He put his hand over Katherine's and she guided his fingers into her. 'Oh fuck,' he said when he felt how wet she was. He held his penis in his other hand and slid it in where his fingers had been. It was bigger than his fingers and Katherine had to move slightly before it would go in properly. It felt very tight, like she was stretched as far as she could go, but Sean was still pushing, wanting it deeper inside her. He pushed again and she gasped, it hurt. She pushed her bottom higher into the air and pressed her fingers hard against her clitoris.

Sean was getting into a rhythm, and each time he pushed it hurt less. She put one hand against the headboard to steady herself and dug the fingers of the other harder into her clitoris. Sean was pumping hard now, in and out of her, both hands on her shoulders, like he was riding a horse. She could tell he was close to coming. She rubbed her clitoris – if he could hold on just a little bit longer, maybe she would come too.

Sean thrust a few more times and then went stiff. Katherine tried to squeeze her muscle around him to keep him in there a little longer, but it was too late. He collapsed on top of her and his penis slid out.

'Oh, momma.' He rolled off her on to the bed and lay on his back, his limp penis lying across his leg. His body was covered in chocolate; he smiled at her. Katherine curled up beside him. She was covered in chocolate too, and now the sex was over, she felt sticky and dirty. Sean's eyes were closed and he seemed to be asleep, but as she carefully took off the condom, he opened his eyes slightly and then closed them again. She went into the bathroom and ran herself a bath, then lay in it, her fingers inside her, cupping her clitoris. She remembered Annette and how they had come within moments of each other, and Phillipa holding her from behind, coming as Katherine did, the evening of their threesome with Matt.

She got out of the bath and dried herself off, then climbed back into bed beside the sleeping Sean, trying to find somewhere that wasn't covered in chocolate. Sean turned over in his sleep and put his arm across her. She fell asleep and dreamed of Violet holding her as they slept in her single bed.

In the morning, the bed was sticky and damp and so was she. Sean was still asleep, so she went and had a shower, and when he was still asleep after that, she went outside to see if she could find anything to eat. The hotel was in the middle of nowhere at a fork in the road, and between the roads was Snowdon, sitting up amongst the clouds.

She had climbed it once as a child, with her mother and one of her many boyfriends. She remembered it being tiring and long and her mother telling her not to complain because she didn't want her to show them up in front of Steve, or John or whatever his name was. At the top, they could barely see two feet in front of them because it had come over misty, and Katherine had a tantrum because they wouldn't let her go down on the train.

It was cloudy today, too, and it looked like it was going to rain, but at that moment Snowdon looked clear and inviting. She went back to their room; Sean was in the shower.

'Where were you?' he demanded when he saw her.

'Looking for breakfast.'

He came over to her all wet and clean and gave her a hug. 'I'm starving.'

They drove down the road a little way and found a place that served up a huge breakfast and had a view of Snowdon.

'Want to go up?' Sean asked as he finished off his food.

'OK,' Katherine said. She was an adult now, and if she didn't like it she could stop and come back.

Halfway up, the clouds came in and it started raining. Katherine felt tired and heavy, like she wasn't used to moving through air as an element.

Sean was striding on ahead. 'Come on, slowcoach.'

She sat down on a rock and breathed in the cold, fresh air. She didn't need to go to the top, there would be no view and the cafe would smell of chips and be crowded with people who had come up on the train.

'I'm going back down,' she called after Sean. She could barely see him through the mist.

'What?' He stopped.

'See you back at the hotel.'

'But I thought . . .' He came back towards her.

'I changed my mind, but you go on. I'll do my essay.'

'But . . .'

'See you.' Katherine set off down hill. She half-expected Sean to come running after her, and hoped he wouldn't. A peaceful afternoon by the fire finishing her essay sounded like heaven.

The rain was heavier now, pouring down, drenching her through her jacket to her skin, turning the path into a little river and filling her boots. She felt much better, lighter, freer as though being wet made her move more easily.

Back at the hotel, she changed into dry clothes and got on with her essay, finishing it. Sean arrived back late in the afternoon, wet, cold and angry.

'This weekend was about us spending time together.'

'And we have done.'

Sean sulked about in his wet clothes.

'Have a bath, you'll feel better.'

'It's not me who's being difficult.'

'I wasn't being difficult, I didn't want to get wet and cold and for nothing.'

'It wasn't for nothing.'

'OK, but I had my work to do.'

'We might as well have stayed at home.' He stormed off to the bathroom and stayed in there for ages. When he finally came out, he seemed calmer, but they had a very quiet meal and he only pecked her on the cheek before turning over and going to sleep afterwards.

Katherine stayed awake and stared at the ceiling, wondering why it was so important to these men that they had to get to the top of the mountain and everyone had to go with them. She was sure there was something big and important in it, a metaphor there which, if she could understand it, would give her the key to understanding all men, but she was too tired to think about it. She closed her eyes and dreamed about swimming the Irish Sea.

TWENTY-THREE
Violet

Waking in her old bed, it seemed like her weeks in London hadn't existed and she was back having to get up to go to school all over again. Panic gripped her for a moment and then she rolled over and saw Belinda asleep beside her and smiled.

Her mother had apologised like mad for making them share Violet's single bed. Violet had tried to look annoyed but she could barely contain her glee, and when they went up to her room and shut the door, they both giggled like mad. If only her mother knew – but even when Violet had been expelled from school when she was caught kissing Patricia Masters, her mother didn't understand what the fuss was about. She would always be sweet Violet to her mother.

They had kissed again, starting slowly – they had all night and there was no hurry. Violet took off Belinda's jacket and then unbuttoned her shirt. When Belinda had pulled off Violet's T-shirt, they stopped to admire each other's bodies. Belinda's breasts were small and round; Violet could cup them easily in her hand and she did. Her stomach was a gentle swell between her hips and her pubic hair was the same pale colour as the hair on her head. Violet stroked it like she did the cats and Belinda's whole body seemed to purr.

Violet laid Belinda down on the bed and kissed every inch of

SWEET VIOLET

her skin, feeling its amazing softness under her lips, turning her over to kiss her bottom and back and then back again to suck in the pale nipples. Belinda watched her as she explored her body, stroking Violet's head and cheek, sighing occasionally when Violet touched a sensitive place.

Violet worked her way down Belinda's front to her pubic hair and gently slid her fingers in. Belinda closed her eyes then, and Violet rubbed her fingers in and out and her thumb around in a circle. Belinda arched her back slightly. Violet slipped her tongue in alongside her fingers and Belinda sighed. It took a long time, but Violet wasn't in any hurry: she worked her fingers and tongue backwards and forwards, pressing her thumb hard against the fleshy button until she felt Belinda swell around her fingers and then come with a high sigh.

She left her fingers in there and moved up to lie beside Belinda, who smiled at her.

'The patience of a saint,' Belinda said sleepily. She turned over, Violet's finger slipped out of her and Belinda sighed again. They fell asleep curled up together.

Violet smiled at the memory and touched Belinda's cheek. All that time she had been looking for Felicity and there she was right under her nose. Outside, it was pouring with rain. She looked at the bedside clock and saw it was 7.30, at least an hour before they had to get up. She snuggled in close to Belinda and kissed her on the ear, wanting her to wake up, wanting to stroke and kiss her again, slide her fingers inside her and watch her come again.

Belinda stirred slightly.

'Morning, gorgeous.' Violet whispered in her ear.

Belinda stretched and turned over to face her. 'What's the time?' she asked sleepily.

'Not time to get up.' Violet kissed her nose.

'Is it raining?'

'No, Mum's watering the garden.'

Belinda sat up and listened, then lay down again. 'It is raining! I get to wear my hat.' She rolled over and curled up. Violet put her arms around her and cupped her breasts.

'Don't think I don't know what you're trying to do.' Belinda said.

'I'll stop if you want me to.' Violet massaged her nipples.

'Oh no, carry on. I can sleep through most things.' Violet carried on, and as she kissed her neck and licked around her ear, Belinda pushed her bottom back into Violet. Violet stroked her stomach, feeling its rise from hip to hip, the softest skin Violet had ever felt. Belinda sighed.

'I thought you were asleep,' teased Violet.

'I am, and having the loveliest dream.'

'Oh yes?' Violet kept her hand moving and gently squeezed Belinda's breast with the other.

'Yes, this insatiable young thing has whisked me away for the weekend as her pretend date, Felicity, and is now trying to have her wicked way with me.'

'How awful, and will you let her?'

'Maybe, but there's something I have to do first.' She rolled over to face Violet and pushed her back on to the bed, then started kissing her, very softly at first, teasing little kisses, flicking her tongue in and out, not letting Violet catch it. While she was kissing her, Belinda pushed her hands into Violet's breasts, kneading them like a cat.

Violet was a little surprised and a little scared by this, and more than a little turned on. She had never let a woman take charge like this before and hadn't thought that Belinda had it in her. She tried to relax and let her carry on. Belinda was now holding both her wrists against the sides of her body and kissing her throat, nipping it with her teeth, and Violet could feel it tingling all through her body. Belinda slid a little lower, licking at her nipples, flicking them with her tongue. Violet had never felt anything like it, with all her being she wanted to push Belinda away, make her stop, but Belinda was holding her wrists tight. Violet squirmed, as she had seen women squirm under her. Belinda took her nipple into her mouth and sucked it hard. Violet drew in a sharp breath. She had done it often enough and watched the effect it had, now someone was doing it to her. She wanted her to stop, but at the same time she wanted more. For the first time in her life, she wanted to feel what all those women she'd had sex with felt.

Belinda had moved over to her other nipple and let go of her wrists. Violet wasn't sure what to do with her hands – she didn't trust herself to touch Belinda, whose hands were now on her stomach and working their way lower. Violet bit her lip, her body shaking from the strain of keeping still, of not pushing Belinda away. Belinda let go of her nipple and her tongue began to follow her hands down Violet's body, down to her hips.

Violet clutched the sheets and dug her nails into the bed. She felt hot, like she had a fever, she was sweating and shaking. All her attention was concentrated on Belinda's tongue and where it was heading. She had the feeling something huge was about to happen, something so big it would engulf her completely. She closed her eyes and threw her head back.

Belinda's hands started moving again, converging with her tongue on Violet's pubic hair. She felt one finger enter her and she was suddenly scared. She tried to sit up; she wanted to say 'no', but she couldn't get her mouth to work. Belinda put one hand up and rested it on Violet's stomach, which helped somehow.

Violet felt another finger enter her and then Belinda's tongue, hot and wet. She couldn't breathe, she gasped for breath, while Belinda was moving her fingers in and out, circling her tongue. Violet moved her head from side to side and her hands formed fists that dragged the sheet across the bed.

'Oh God.' She thought she was going to explode. Belinda was moving faster and faster, her tongue flicking from side to side. Violet's body seemed to be shaking faster and faster, in time with Belinda's movement. Violet had no control over her own body, she was a puppet and Belinda was pulling her strings tighter and tighter and then suddenly the strings snapped and Violet's body convulsed – shock waves started from her centre and radiated out to her extremities.

It only lasted a moment, no longer than a few seconds, then her body went limp, a stringless puppet. She slowly let go of the sheet, as a wave of emotion rolled up over her, a tidal wave of all the things she had ever felt and not expressed. It swept over her and she found herself in floods of tears, crying like a baby.

Belinda held her while she cried, cradling her protectively as she lay racked with sobs.

'It happens like that sometimes,' she said as Violet's tears calmed down. 'Especially the first time.'

It wasn't exactly Violet's first time, but she didn't say anything. It was the first time she had come with another person present. She lay quite still and enjoyed the closeness she felt for Belinda. After all the crying, she felt calm, serene almost.

'So, what do you think?' Belinda asked. Violet didn't understand the question. 'Shall I wear my hat?'

Violet laughed, hugged Belinda close and kissed her. When her legs were working again properly she went downstairs and made Belinda a tea and herself a coffee. When she got back, Belinda was leaning on the windowsill looking out at the rain.

'I love weather,' she said, not turning from the window. 'Rain especially – even the rich people get wet in the rain.'

Violet joined her. Her mother's garden was looking a bit sad, the roses drooping under the weight of all the water.

'What a day to get married on.' Belinda traced a raindrop down the windowpane.

Violet climbed back into bed. She had forgotten that was what they were here for. She watched Belinda at the window. This was the first time she had woken up with someone since Katherine. She felt a rush of warmth towards Belinda, she felt in that moment that she had found more than just her Felicity.

Belinda turned from the window and climbed back into bed to drink her tea. Violet noticed she stuck her little finger out as she drank, and laughed.

'What?' Belinda asked suspiciously.

'Nothing,' Violet said and kissed her cheek. 'You're just gorgeous, that's all.'

She wanted to kiss her properly and lay her down on the bed and do all the things Belinda had just done to her, but her mother came tapping on the door and insisted that they go downstairs for breakfast. She cooked them up scrambled eggs and toast. Violet put her hand on Belinda's leg under the table, but she gently pushed it off.

'Have you told your mother?' Belinda asked when she thought they couldn't be heard. Violet shook her head – she didn't think she would ever tell her.

'Told me what?' Her mother had overheard.

'Nothing.' Violet said, and she smiled at Belinda. 'Just that I've got a job in a gym and they are letting me instruct people already.'

'That's nice.'

'And I'm working for a removal company.'

'As long as you still have time to study.'

They showered and changed: Violet into black trousers and a black jacket, Belinda into the blue dress she wore at her reading and the same straw hat.

'Where's the wedding hat?'

'I don't have one.'

'But the poem?'

'Was only a poem. Come on, I don't want to be late. I want a seat up near the front.'

As they left, Violet's mother was washing the dishes. 'Have a nice time, girls,' she called out to them before starting to sing, quietly, 'Sweet Violet, sweeter than the roses'. Belinda stopped to listen to her and smiled, then she took Violet's hand and together they ran out to the car.

TWENTY-FOUR
Katherine

Katherine woke to driving rain against her window. She knew it was a bad thing for it to be raining because something big was happening today, something important, but in her just-awake state she couldn't quite remember what that was. She rolled over and tried to get back to sleep, then rolled back the other way and then sat bolt upright in bed – it was her wedding day.

She looked at her watch; it was 7.30. Her mother had promised to wake her at 8 o'clock with breakfast. She lay back down again. She felt sick and could feel a headache starting. She didn't want any breakfast, didn't want to have her hair done, or any make-up – she wanted to stay in bed all day and listen to the rain.

She heard her mother get up and go downstairs, then she heard Brian banging about in the bathroom. He did it every morning and she had no idea how or with what he made so much noise, but it really annoyed her. He was so untidy, inconsiderate, smelly and noisy, and Katherine hated having him in the house. After all the years of just her and her mother, she hadn't realised just how much time and space a man could take up.

She knew she couldn't get het up about it, as she was leaving soon to live with Sean in the flat that his parents were buying for them. Somehow that thought didn't cheer her up much. She had no idea what Sean would be like to live with. His room at home was immaculate, but then they had a cleaner coming in everyday.

Katherine put her pillow over her head, trying to block out Brian's noises. There was a tapping on her door.

'Katherine, love.' It was her mother. She pretended to be asleep. 'Katherine, something's arrived for you.'

She turned over and threw her pillow on the floor. Who the hell would deliver something at 7.30 on a Saturday morning? Her mother was standing in the doorway with a huge bunch of red flowers, so big, it barely fitted through the doorway. Her mother put them on the bed. Up close, she could see the flowers were a bit windblown and the card was wet, the writing run a little. She thought they were probably from Sean, which was sweet, but the card just said 'Good Luck' on it. No name, no initials even. If it had been Sean, he would have put his name on it.

Katherine ran through a list of who they could possibly be from. Annette came to mind first, but she was in America now, probably starting her new life as Claudia's trainer. Violet came up next, but flowers weren't really her style. Besides she would be too busy swanning around with her Felicity to be worrying about Katherine. Phillipa or Matt were possibilities, but they didn't seem likely either – they had already given her and Sean a set of towels as their wedding present. Katherine realised she had just run through all the people she had slept with and most of them since she was engaged to Sean.

'Well,' her mother demanded, still hovering around the door. 'Who are they from?'

Katherine shrugged. 'There's no name.'

'Oh, how mysterious, a secret admirer.'

'On my wedding day? I hope not.'

Her mother giggled. 'I'll go and finish breakfast.'

Brian was still banging about in the bathroom. Then he called 'The bathroom's free!' like he did every morning – as if they wouldn't be able to tell otherwise.

Katherine went to the loo and then stood looking at herself in the mirror. She looked awful: dark rings under her eyes, a red nose, spots on her chin, not the glowing bride at all. She splashed cold water on her face and then went downstairs.

'I was going to bring this up,' her mother said, gesturing at a tray she had laid out with strawberries and cream, orange juice and champagne. Katherine felt like crying when she saw it.

'What's wrong?' her mother asked. 'I though it's what you wanted.'

'It is.' Katherine did cry then, and her mother came over and gave her a hug.

'It's a scary thing, I know.' She held Katherine tightly. 'But you'll be fine – it's natural to feel a little emotional.'

Katherine heard Brian come into the room, and pulled away from her mother. 'I will have it in my room.' She couldn't bear the thought of Brian watching her eat.

'You go back up then, I've just got to do the coffee.'

Katherine climbed the stairs, she could hear her mother and Brian talking; it sounded like they were having an argument. She felt guilty: she tried to make an effort with Brian for her mother's sake, and she hated to see her torn between them, but he made her skin crawl. She put the flowers on the windowsill. They were very beautiful, exactly what she had wanted for her wedding before her mother and the florist had talked her into pale, prissy pink ones. She pulled one red rose out and pressed it against her face; it felt like silk and smelt of the rain.

Her mother came in with the tray, put it down on the bed and then hovered by the door.

'It's OK,' Katherine said. 'You don't have to stay.'

'It's just . . .' her mother started.

'I don't mind.' Katherine insisted, wondering if that was true. Her mother looked like she was going to say something, but instead she turned and left.

Katherine sat on her bed and looked at the food on the tray. She wanted to cry again; she suddenly felt very lonely. She drank the coffee and some of the orange juice, pushed the strawberries around in the plate and watched them leave red streaks on the cream, then made flower shapes with them. Then she went over to the flowers and looked at the card again, but she didn't recognise the handwriting. Who would send her flowers on her wedding morning? Someone wishing her well, or someone trying to unsettle her, because that's what they were doing, although Katherine knew she couldn't blame just the flowers.

She went and had a shower, washing her hair. She knew they would do it again at the hairdressers, but it made her feel better. Or rather it made her feel less, just the water pounding the top of her head and flowing down her body, washing away all thought with it. Her mother banged on the door and told her to hurry up. She dried herself off and put on her oldest jeans and a T-shirt, thinking she might as well be comfortable for at least some of the day. She stood and looked at herself in the mirror – not exactly the happy bride. Perhaps when she'd had her hair done and put the dress on, she would feel more the part. The outfit was hanging on her wardrobe door. She sat on her bed and looked at it, hanging there in its bag. Then she looked at the flowers on the windowsill: rich deep red roses; little flowers she didn't know the names of that looked like drops of blood; big fat flowers that started red in the middle and faded out to the palest pink on the outsides. She decided that she wanted to carry these flowers down the aisle, not the insipid bouquet the florist had prepared for her. It was far too big as it was, but she was sure her mother could do something with them. It would upset the florist, but she didn't care, it was her wedding after all.

Her mother came up and stood in the doorway, dressed in her mother-of-the-bride outfit, another new suit. This one was green and it made her look pale and tired; but maybe that was just the light, or the strain of having helped to organise the wedding – or maybe it was from being the barrier between Katherine and Brian. She felt a stab of guilt.

'Ready?' her mother asked.

Katherine nodded. They set off for the hairdressers, getting soaked on the way to the car and again from the car to the salon. Katherine had the flowers with her, but the bouquet from the florist was there waiting for her.

'I want these,' Katherine said.

'But I thought . . .'

'I'm having these.'

'But everyone else will have pink.'

'I'm having these,' she repeated. Her mother held up her hands in surrender, then pulled a face at the hairdresser.

'No hairspray,' Katherine said before they had even touched her hair. 'And no teasing it up.'

The hairdresser looked at her mother and her mother cast her eyes heavenward.

'I saw that,' Katherine said, in the tone her mother used to use when she was a child.

'She's just nervous,' her mother said to the hairdresser.

'I just don't want to look like a poodle,' Katherine countered.

In the end, her hair did look nice. The hairdresser put it in rollers to straighten it out a little and brushed it around her face. A manicurist did her nails – Katherine wasn't at all sure about it to start with, but once she relaxed it was lovely, and afterwards her hands felt so soft and smooth.

The hairdresser put some make-up on her too, no eyeshadow, just a touch of mascara and eyeliner and the lightest dusting of foundation and blusher. Katherine studied herself in the mirror and had to admit she looked OK. She didn't look at all like herself, but the person she was now looked almost pretty. They made her wear a plastic hat over her hair and sent her home.

They only had half an hour, once they got home, before Sean was due to pick her up. Katherine went back up to her room and closed the door, carefully took off her jeans and T-shirt and took the outfit out of its plastic bag. She tried on the trousers, but she could see her knickers through the silk so she tried them without knickers. It felt impossibly naughty to wear such sheer material with nothing underneath, but Katherine decided she liked it like that. She slipped the tunic on over her head, without a bra and she liked that too. The outfit completed the picture of Katherine being someone else. She tried smiling in the mirror, and the stranger smiled back. She looked a little sad, this stranger, even when she was smiling, but she definitely looked like a bride.

Her mother tapped on the door. She had made a bouquet out

of the red flowers and it was gorgeous, trailing nearly to the floor, which looked stunning with the outfit.

'Thank you.' Katherine kissed her on the cheek, too scared of ruining her make-up to make proper contact.

'You look lovely,' her mother said.

Katherine tried smiling again, but there was a wobble in it.

'Now we just have to get you to the church without everything getting wet.'

Brian appeared in the doorway behind her mother. 'Hey, sexy!' He whistled.

Katherine tried not to give him a dirty look. She knew he was trying his best, and was still upset that she didn't want him to give her away. He was wearing his suit, the same one he got married in, and Katherine was glad her mother had bought a new one, as it would otherwise have felt like a rerun of their wedding and that would have been too weird.

There was the sound of a car horn and her mother rushed off to get her things together, while Brian went downstairs to open the door. Sean came bounding in, loud and happy. Katherine stayed in her room, looking at herself in the mirror. She felt a total fraud, almost like she wasn't there at all – that she was sending this stranger out in her dress to her wedding and she was outside it all, watching from a distance. She wondered if that was how it felt when you died.

'Come on, Katherine,' her mother called.

She didn't reply. She wanted to stay in her room, watching this stranger in the mirror, and see what she was going to do next. She did wonder for a moment if maybe she was ill, if she had gone mad sometime during the morning and not noticed.

'Katherine!' her mother called again. She waved to the woman in the mirror and then turned from her, took a deep breath and stepped out of her bedroom door. She had a very strong feeling that she had forgotten something, that there was something of vital importance that she should have and didn't. She reached the top of the stairs and wondered if she could remember how to make her legs go down them.

Sean was standing at the bottom of the stairs. 'Oh, momma!' he said when he saw her standing there. 'You are gorgeous.'

This annoyed Katherine, though she wasn't quite sure why. Maybe it meant that he liked this strange woman more than he liked her. She put her hand out and held on to the rail, feeling like she was going to fall – not down the stairs but through them.

'Katherine?' Her mother was coming up the stairs towards her. 'Are you all right?'

Katherine tightened her grip on the rail. She tried to smile and nod, but she had no idea if it worked, since she seemed to have lost all control of her body.

'Come on then, we don't want to be late.'

Katherine couldn't understand what they were going to be late for; she had lost track of what this was all for. She tried to focus on getting down the stairs. She wished she was in the water, as she was sure her body would remember how to swim.

Her mother had taken her by the arm and was helping her down the stairs. Katherine kept her other hand on the rail, not quite trusting her mother, or herself.

'You look so beautiful,' Sean said as they reached the bottom. He tried to kiss her, but Katherine was still unsure of her balance and wouldn't let go of her mother's arm. Her mother put a coat over her shoulders.

'I was like this when I got married,' she joked to Sean. 'My legs just turned to jelly.' She put the plastic rain-hat on Katherine and tried to give her the bouquet.

Sean held open the front door. Katherine stared out at the rain coming down in sheets, bouncing off the pavement. She had never noticed before just how beautiful rain could be.

'Come on.' Her mother was pulling her outside. Sean was holding open the car door, getting soaked. Katherine smiled.

'Come on,' he shouted impatiently. She stepped out from the shelter of the front porch and stopped. The rain was cold and clear. She dropped the coat to feel it better, and it soaked through her tunic in a second. She wanted to stay there like that, but her mother was pulling her forward.

'What is wrong with you?' she shouted at Katherine, pushing

her into the car. She felt like she was six again and had just broken the front window playing hockey inside. She burst into tears.

Sean shut the door, came around to the driver's side and hopped in. Katherine could see her mother peering worriedly through the window. She waved to her and Sean started the car up and sped off through the rain. Katherine looked over at him – he was concentrating on the road, throwing the car around corners, speeding through orange lights, cutting up other cars. Someone had tied some white ribbons to the front of the car, and now they were stuck to the bonnet and water-stained, looking as sad as Katherine felt. She wanted to cry again, but by the set of Sean's chin, she knew that wasn't a good idea. She took a tissue from the glove compartment and wiped her eyes, pulled down the sun visor and checked her make-up in the mirror. The stranger looked back at her, wild-eyed and panicky, with smeared mascara and a silly plastic hat. She smiled at Katherine and Katherine smiled back. Suddenly, Sean braked hard and she was thrown forward.

'Bastard!' Sean yelled at someone through the window. Then 'Sorry,' to Katherine – though he didn't sound it.

He looked at her sideways and she tried to smile to reassure him she was OK, but she still wasn't sure her face was working. She found that she was shaking. It could have been the sudden stop, or because she was cold; then she looked at her hands, admiring their smoothness, and noticed they were shaking too. She tried to stop them but it only made it worse. She licked the tissue and tried to tidy her make-up, but Sean was off again, driving like he was in some international rally, so she left it. She would just have to get married with panda eyes.

When they arrived at the church, there wasn't anybody outside waiting for them and Katherine wondered if they had the right day. Sean got out of the car, came around and opened her door, but she didn't move to get out.

'Come on, Katherine.' His suit was gradually turning black from the top down where it was wet. Her mother appeared from nowhere and took her arm, helping her out of the car. She hurried her into the church porch and sat her down on the bench. She took the plastic hat off Katherine and dabbed at her mascara with her hanky. Brian arrived wet from having parked the car and stood around getting in everyone's way. Sean came in dripping wet and shook his head like a dog after a swim. Katherine's mother gave him some tissues to dry himself with, stood Katherine up and handed her the bouquet.

'You got the flowers, then,' Sean said when he saw them.

'It was you?' her mother asked.

'No.' Sean dried his hands. 'Her father.'

'Her father?' Both Katherine and her mother looked at him.

'You know, the man in Munich.'

'What man?' her mother asked.

'The journalist?' Katherine was shocked into speech. 'He's my father?'

'I didn't do a DNA test.'

'What journalist?'

Katherine looked at the bouquet in her hand. She didn't know whether to hug it or throw it on the floor and jump on it.

'What journalist?' her mother asked again.

The door to the church creaked open and the verger poked his head round. 'Good, we're ready then?'

They looked at each other. They weren't anything like ready: Katherine wanted to go back out in the rain, Sean wanted to change into some dry clothes, and Katherine's mother wanted to know who the hell the journalist was.

'Of course.' Her mother smiled at the verger.

'Then shall we? We have another wedding at three.' He opened the door.

TWENTY-FIVE
Violet

Violet heard the church door open, some whispering and then a pause. Katherine's mother and some strange-looking guy with thick glasses and no hair came through, hurried down the aisle and took a seat near the front. The organist started the wedding march; there was a long pause, the organist stopped and started again. A smallish fair man in a wet, grey suit appeared at the door and then, after another pause, Katherine appeared.

It was the first time Violet had seen Katherine since she had left her clutching the beanbag, her knickers down around her ankles, just short of an orgasm. She wasn't sure if she would have recognised her if this hadn't been her wedding – and there she was, all in white. She looked so different: her hair was straighter and she was wearing some make-up, but more than that, there was something in her eyes that was different, a wild, unfocused look.

She was walking unevenly too, leaning heavily on Sean's arm as though she was drunk or drugged. Violet half-rose out of her seat to go and help her – she had heard about the drugs they gave swimmers, maybe this was the side-effect. Belinda tugged on her hand to get her to sit down and Violet did. She looked around to see if anyone had noticed, but they were all too busy watching Katherine. Halfway down the aisle, she seemed to pull herself together, walking a bit more upright, not leaning so much on

Sean. She even smiled, but Violet noticed it didn't reach all the way to her eyes.

This had been the moment she had been dreading, seeing Katherine again for the first time. She was worried that what she felt for Belinda, so new and fragile, wouldn't match what she had once felt for Katherine. But instead of feeling anger at Katherine or jealousy, or any of the things she might have expected, all she felt was concern that Katherine wasn't well.

She looked at Belinda, who was looking back at her, the only person in the church not to be watching Katherine. Violet squeezed her hand, and Belinda smiled.

Katherine and Sean had reached the minister and stopped. All Violet could see now was the back of Katherine, who seemed to be standing unnaturally still. Two young people stood up and joined them. The man was good-looking, dark and well built. The woman was blonde and quite beautiful. Violet recognised her from one of the photos in the paper – they must both be swimmers. The four of them standing there in front of the minister with the dull light coming through the stained-glass window . . . it looked quite unreal, like a scene from a film.

The minister said something and everyone stood up – Belinda did too, and Violet scrambled to her feet. They sang a hymn, something about angels and heaven. Belinda seemed to know the tune and sang along, but Violet didn't even try. She watched Katherine instead, staring at the back of her head, willing her to turn around, wanting to see the expression on her face, still worried there was something seriously wrong. The hymn finished and everyone sat down – Belinda had to pull Violet's hand again to get her seated. Katherine turned her head for a moment and Violet caught that same wild-eyed look.

'There's something wrong,' Violet whispered to Belinda.

'Sh,' Belinda whispered back.

Katherine looked around again and Violet saw panic in her eyes.

The minister was talking again, but Violet didn't listen as she watched Katherine's back. She wasn't moving at all, not a single muscle. Violet knew that wasn't right: the Katherine she knew could barely keep still – she had pinned her against the wall often enough, to kiss her. Sean kept looking at her, obviously worried, and Violet warmed to him for that. The woman who was her witness put her hand on Katherine's back as if to support her, so she must be worried too. It was an oddly intimate gesture and it made Violet wonder about the woman.

A tall, thin woman stood up beside the organist and started singing, her voice high and forced like an opera singer. Violet didn't like it much but everyone else sat in rapt silence, Belinda included. The song seemed to go on for a long time and Violet tried to sit still through it. She watched Katherine; the beautiful woman whispered something to her and Katherine moved slightly. Sean reached over and took her hand, then the other man took out a hanky and handed it to her. She took it but didn't do anything with it.

The singer finished and Violet felt she should clap, but no one else did, so she put her hands back in her lap. There was a moment's awkward silence and then the minister stepped forward and started talking again, this time about the vows they were about to take. Then he said that bit that Violet thought they only said in films:

'If anyone knows just cause why these two cannot be joined in holy matrimony, speak now or forever hold your peace.'

The silence that followed his words seemed to echo around inside Violet's head.

Katherine

After the verger had opened the doors, and her mother and Brian had left, Katherine stood in the doorway. It felt like there was a great drop in front of her, a huge chasm that was drawing her in. She stood frozen by a fear so big that she couldn't even think about what it might be. Sean took her arm and tried to drag her forward, but she wouldn't move. She could hear them playing the wedding march, but it sounded like a funeral dirge, her funeral dirge. The music stopped and then started again.

'For God's sake,' Sean whispered in her ear, 'you're embarrassing me.'

Katherine looked at him: his hair was spiky and his suit dark across the shoulders where it was wet. His face was red and blotchy, exactly as if he had been masturbating, though she was sure he hadn't been. He took her arm again and pulled her forward and this time she let him. Her feet seemed to have forgotten how to walk, she leaned on Sean's arm for support, afraid that she would fall if she let go. She didn't dare look at the people sitting in the church, but kept her eyes fixed on the floor in front of her, aware that they were all staring at her. After a few steps, her legs started to get the hang of things and she straightened up a little, but still kept hold of Sean. She remembered she had left the bouquet on the bench in the porch, but she couldn't go back and get it.

Out of the corner of her eye, she saw someone stand up as they passed – it was Violet. She gripped Sean's arm tighter; she had forgotten Violet would be here, and with her Felicity. Violet was wearing a dark jacket and white shirt, her hair was really short and she looked older somehow, more of an adult than when Katherine had seen her last. She looked worried, though; that Felicity obviously wasn't looking after her. She caught a glimpse of Felicity, who, of course, didn't look anything like she had imagined. She was older than she had thought and not as pretty, although she wasn't ugly either – most of all she looked wise, like an owl.

Katherine stood up straighter. She didn't want Violet to see her like this, stumbling along, hanging on to Sean. She concentrated on making her feet work properly, and in no time at all they were standing in front of the minister. She felt herself start to shake again, from the cold of her wet tunic pressed against her skin. She wondered if the minister could see her nipples through it, then worried that everyone in the church would be able to see through the trousers and would know she had no knickers on. She found that if she tensed all the muscles in her body, then the shaking stopped. She was aware of Phillipa coming and standing beside her, which made her feel better.

SWEET VIOLET

The minister announced a hymn and she heard everyone stand and the organ start to play. She looked up at the stained-glass window in front of her, a scene of Jesus laying hands on the sick. She had seen it at the rehearsal when the sun was shining and thought it was lovely. Today it looked dull and depressing, the rain making everyone look like they were crying.

The hymn finished and there was the sound of everyone sitting down. She had a strong feeling that someone was looking at her, turned her head and saw Violet still standing when everyone else was sitting. She turned away quickly. She heard some whispering and knew it was Violet, just like she had imagined, laughing at her. She looked back but couldn't pick Violet out in the crowd of faces, all looking at her.

The minister stood forward again and started talking. Katherine could feel her legs shaking; she tensed her muscles again and concentrated on keeping them tense rather than listening to what the minister was saying. She could see his mouth opening and closing and caught the odd word.

'. . . good man . . .'

'. . . forever . . .'

She felt herself start to sway and then she felt a hand on her back steadying her – it was Phillipa's. She wanted to lean back into it and let its warmth spread over her whole body, but she was worried she would fall over.

The minister had stopped talking and the church was suddenly filled with a single voice singing. At first she thought it was the crying Jesus in the stained glass, and then she remembered they had organised some woman to sing 'Ave Maria'. Sean took her hand and squeezed it, and Katherine tried to smile at him. Phillipa leaned close to her.

'Your nose is running.'

Katherine sniffed and realised she was right, she was just so cold that she hadn't noticed it. Matt handed her a tissue, but she thought blowing her nose in a church was probably against the rules, so she just kept it in her hand for later.

The singer finished and Katherine was glad, as all those high notes were giving her a headache. There was some shuffling

239

behind her and the minister stepped forward again. He was quite young and Katherine had thought he was good-looking but he had a sour look today, like he had sucked too many lemons. Maybe it was just something that happened when he put his collar on. She watched his lips as he talked: they seemed almost obscenely pink and appeared to grow larger with each word he said.

His words seemed to run together. He was talking about her and Sean, and then he said: 'If anyone knows just cause . . .' And suddenly his words were very clear: 'Why these two cannot be joined together . . .' Her heart lifted and the shaking stopped and suddenly she was hopeful, waiting, holding her breath, '. . . in holy matrimony, speak now or for ever hold your peace.'

Katherine waited. Now was the moment when someone was going to save her – someone would have seen her and known her for the fraud she was. The silence seemed to go on forever. She imagined Annette bursting through the church doors, wet and out of breath, shouting 'No! She's mine, you can't have her.' Or Violet leaping to her feet, pushing Felicity to one side, racing down the aisle and sweeping her off her feet. Still the silence went on. She looked at Phillipa – surely she knew this wasn't right, that she didn't love Sean; but Phillipa was looking at the minister and smiling.

The minister opened his mouth to speak.

'Actually,' Katherine found herself saying. The minister closed his mouth again. Sean turned and looked at her. There was silence again, everyone waiting for her to continue.

'I mean . . .' She had no idea what to say; she looked at Sean. 'I love you, Sean, but I can't do this.' Sean's face seemed to freeze in a look halfway between surprise and horror.

There was silence for a moment and then she heard the congregation start to stir. The minister cleared his throat.

'Ahem, what exactly do you mean?'

Katherine didn't look at him; Sean was still staring at her.

'Maybe we should go through to the vestry.' He put a hand on each of their elbows. His touch seemed to spur Sean into action, and he threw it off.

'Katherine, don't embarrass me.' His voice was low and threatening.

She could hear the congregation murmuring as if to support him. Matt put his hand on Sean's shoulder, but Sean shrugged that off too.

'Don't,' he said again, more loudly. He looked wild, like he was going to hit her. The murmuring seemed to be louder now, like angry bees in Katherine's ears. She looked at the congregation. Some of them were standing, some leaning forward over the pews in front of them. Sean's mother and father were coming at her, looking murderous.

Katherine panicked then, threw off the minister's hand and ran down the aisle, out of the church and into the rain.

Violet

Violet's first instinct was to go after Katherine, but she saw Katherine's mother go, and the beautiful swimmer. An older couple who were probably Sean's parents rushed to him. The minister stood still, flapping his arms.

'Um, excuse me' he said, trying to take control of the situation. 'It appears the wedding is off.' He raised his voice but it was barely audible over the growing clamour. 'For the moment,' he added, as if catching himself. 'If you could all . . .' But what he wanted them to do was lost in the noise of outrage.

People were moving around, up and down the aisle, over the seats. Violet and Belinda stayed where they were, and Violet heard snatches of conversation:

'Far too young, I always said . . .'

'Drunk by the looks of her . . .'

'A waste of all that money . . .'

Violet didn't know what to think. Part of her was delighted that Katherine wasn't getting married, but she was also shocked at the way it had happened, and felt a little guilty, as if it was partly her fault.

The best man stood on a chair. 'Everyone, please, I know this is a bit awkward, but there's another wedding in here soon so we have to get out. I suggest we go to the hotel; the room's booked and there's food and drink, and it will be dry and warm.' People started to file out of the church.

Belinda looked at Violet. 'What do you want to do?'

Violet shrugged. She didn't want to go to the reception – Katherine would have been the only one she knew and it looked like she wasn't going to be there. The church was emptying out, getting quieter, but Sean was still at the front with his parents and best man.

'Come on.' Violet stood up; she didn't want to be the last out of the church.

Katherine's mother was standing at the door, dripping wet. 'I'm so sorry,' she was saying to people. 'I have no idea where she's got to.'

She stopped when she saw Violet and stood up straighter, pulled her face into a look of disapproval, but didn't say anything. Violet wanted to laugh, and she pulled Belinda outside.

'Come on.' She dragged her around the side of the church, until she found a reasonably sheltered spot. She pulled her in close to the wall beside her.

'What are you doing?' Belinda asked, laughing.

'I want to kiss you.' Violet held Belinda's face with both her hands and kissed her softly on the lips. Belinda kissed her back.

'You know something,' Violet said, looking into Belinda's eyes.

'No, what?'

'I think I do love you.'

Belinda laughed and they kissed again. Very faintly, as if from a great distance, Violet thought she could hear someone singing.

'Sweet Violet, sweeter than the roses.'

Katherine

Katherine sat on the tomb of one Michael O'Leary, 1882–1943, beloved husband of Bridget, father of Gerald, Patrick and Walter. Her tunic and trousers were now so wet that they plastered to her skin and had taken on its pink colour. She had picked up the bouquet of flowers on her way out, though she had no idea why, and it lay across her lap. She watched the rain form droplets on the petals and then run off them.

The feeling that she was a stranger, someone else, had gone. Now she just felt cold, wet and very clear-headed. She also felt very, very sorry for what she had done to Sean. She would find him later and try to explain it to him and maybe he would understand, and one day forgive her. She didn't feel anything for the others whom she could see filing out of the church, dashing for their cars. She hardly knew most of them and didn't care what they thought of her.

She was worried about her mother, how she was going to pay the money back to Sean's parents, as they certainly weren't going to pay their half now. She wondered what she was going to do now. She couldn't carry on living at home, and she doubted Sean would want her as a flatmate. She would have to find her own place and get a job to pay for it, give up college for a year or two, maybe.

She was thinking all this when she saw Violet come out of the church, with her Felicity. Instead of running for the car, they came around the side of the church towards her. Katherine ducked behind the headstone – of all the people there, Violet was the one who would probably understand what she had done the best, but she was the last person she wanted to see right now.

Katherine peeked around the edge of the tombstone, and saw Violet and Felicity leaning against the wall of the church, kissing. Katherine remembered kisses like that, up against the wall behind the pool. Kisses that melted her insides and warmed her through, kisses that only Annette had matched.

Katherine leaned back against the tombstone and pulled the head off one of the roses from the bouquet. The petals fell on to her tunic, settling against the silk as if they belonged there. She pulled another flower off and scattered the petals around her. She knew she couldn't sit there forever, scattering petals in the rain, but for the moment it seemed the perfect thing to be doing. Later, she could get up and face her mother and Sean, and more importantly, herself; but for the moment, she would sit in her wedding dress in the rain and pull the petals off the flowers.

She felt almost content, and she started singing the first song that came into her head.

'Sweet Violet, sweeter than the roses.'

SAPPHIRE NEW BOOKS

ALL THAT GLITTERS
Published in August 1999   Franca Nera

Marta Broderick: beautiful, successful art dealer; London lesbian. Marta inherits an art empire from the man who managed to spirit her out of East Berlin in the 1960s, Manny Schweitz. She's intent on completing Manny's unfinished business: recovering pieces of art stolen by the Nazis. Meanwhile, she's met the gorgeous but mysterious Judith Compton, and Marta's dark sexual addiction to Judith – along with her quest to return the treasures to the rightful owners – is taking her to dangerous places.

£6.99   ISBN 0 352 33426 6

SWEET VIOLET
Published in September 1999   Ruby Vise

Violet is young, butch and new in town, looking for a way to get over her childhood sweetheart Katherine. And there are plenty of distractions in 1980s London, as the rarefied big-city dyke scene is both sexually and politically charged – full of everything from cosmic mother-earth worshippers to sexy girls in leather.

£6.99   ISBN 0 352 33458 4

GETAWAY
Published in October 1999   Suzanne Blaylock

Brilliantly talented Polly Sayers has had her first affair with a woman, stolen the code of an important new piece of software and done a runner all the way to a peaceful English coastal community. But things aren't as tranquil as they appear in this quiet haven, as Polly realises when she becomes immersed in an insular group of mysterious but very attractive women.

£6.99   ISBN 0 352 33443 6

PREVIOUSLY PUBLISHED

BIG DEAL
☐ *Published in May 1999* Helen Sandler

Lane and Carol have a deal that lets them play around with other partners. But things get out of hand when Lane takes to cruising gay men, while her femme girlfriend has secretly become the mistress of an ongoing all-girl student orgy. The fine print in the deal they've agreed on means things can only get hotter. It's time for a different set of rules – and forfeits.

£6.99   ISBN 0 352 33365 0

RIKA'S JEWEL
☐ *Published in June 1999* Astrid Fox

Norway, 1066 AD. A group of female Viking warriors – Ingrid's Crew – have set sail to fight the Saxons in Britain, and Ingrid's young lover Rika is determined to follow them. But, urged on by dark-haired oarswoman Pia, Rika soon penetrates Ingrid's secret erotic cult back home in Norway. Will Rika overcome Ingrid's psychic hold, or will she succumb to the intoxicating rituals of the cult? Thrilling sword-and-sorcery in the style of Xena and Red Sonja!

£6.99   ISBN 0 352 33367 7

MILLENNIUM FEVER
☐ *Published in July 1999* Julia Wood

The millennium is approaching and so is Nikki's fortieth birthday. Married for twenty years, she is tired of playing the trophy wife in a small town where she can't adequately pursue her lofty career ambitions. In contrast, young writer Georgie has always been out and proud. But there's one thing they have in common – in the midst of millennial fever, they both want action and satisfaction. When they meet, the combination is explosive.

£6.99   ISBN 0 352 33368 5

------------✂------------------------

Please send me the books I have ticked above.

Name ....

Address ....

....

....

.... Post Code ....

Send to: **Cash Sales, Sapphire Books, Thames Wharf Studios, Rainville Road, London W6 9HT.**

US customers: for prices and details of how to order books for delivery by mail, call 1-800-805-1083.

Please enclose a cheque or postal order, made payable to **Virgin Publishing Ltd**, to the value of the books you have ordered plus postage and packing costs as follows:

UK and BFPO – £1.00 for the first book, 50p for each subsequent book.

Overseas (including Republic of Ireland) – £2.00 for the first book, £1.00 for each subsequent book.

We accept all major credit cards, including VISA, ACCESS/MASTERCARD, DINERS CLUB, AMEX and SWITCH.
Please write your card number and expiry date here:

....

Please allow up to 28 days for delivery.

Signature ....

------------✂------------------------

WE NEED YOUR HELP . . .
to plan the future of Sapphire books –

Yours are the only opinions that matter. Sapphire is a new and exciting venture: the first British series of books devoted to lesbian erotic fiction written by and for women.

We're going to do our best to provide the sexiest books you can buy. And we'd like you to help in these early stages. Tell us what you want to read. There's a freepost address for your filled-in questionnaires, so you won't even need to buy a stamp.

THE SAPPHIRE QUESTIONNAIRE

SECTION ONE: ABOUT YOU

1.1 Sex (*we presume you are female, but just in case*)
Are you?
Female ☐
Male ☐

1.2 Age
under 21 ☐ 21–30 ☐
31–40 ☐ 41–50 ☐
51–60 ☐ over 60 ☐

1.3 At what age did you leave full-time education?
still in education ☐ 16 or younger ☐
17–19 ☐ 20 or older ☐

1.4 Occupation _____

1.5 Annual household income _____

1.6 We are perfectly happy for you to remain anonymous; but if you would like us to send you a free booklist of Sapphire books, please insert your name and address

_____
_____
_____
_____

SECTION TWO: ABOUT BUYING SAPPHIRE BOOKS

2.1 Where did you get this copy of *Sweet Violet*?
- Bought at chain book shop ☐
- Bought at independent book shop ☐
- Bought at supermarket ☐
- Bought at book exchange or used book shop ☐
- I borrowed it/found it ☐
- My partner bought it ☐

2.2 How did you find out about Sapphire books?
- I saw them in a shop ☐
- I saw them advertised in a magazine ☐
- A friend told me about them ☐
- I read about them in _____ ☐
- Other _____

2.3 Please tick the following statements you agree with:
- I would be less embarrassed about buying Sapphire books if the cover pictures were less explicit ☐
- I think that in general the pictures on Sapphire books are about right ☐
- I think Sapphire cover pictures should be as explicit as possible ☐

2.4 Would you read a Sapphire book in a public place – on a train for instance?
  Yes ☐   No ☐

SECTION THREE: ABOUT THIS SAPPHIRE BOOK

3.1 Do you think the sex content in this book is:
  Too much ☐   About right ☐
  Not enough ☐

3.2 Do you think the writing style in this book is:
       Too unreal/escapist ☐   About right ☐
       Too down to earth ☐

3.3 Do you think the story in this book is:
       Too complicated ☐   About right ☐
       Too boring/simple ☐

3.4 Do you think the cover of this book is:
       Too explicit ☐   About right ☐
       Not explicit enough ☐

Here's a space for any other comments:

SECTION FOUR: ABOUT OTHER SAPPHIRE BOOKS

4.1 How many Sapphire books have you read?

4.2 If more than one, which one did you prefer?

4.3 Why?

SECTION FIVE: ABOUT YOUR IDEAL EROTIC NOVEL

We want to publish the books you want to read – so this is your chance to tell us exactly what your ideal erotic novel would be like.

5.1 Using a scale of 1 to 5 (1 = no interest at all, 5 = your ideal), please rate the following possible settings for an erotic novel:

       Roman / Ancient World ☐
       Medieval / barbarian / sword 'n' sorcery ☐
       Renaissance / Elizabethan / Restoration ☐
       Victorian / Edwardian ☐
       1920s & 1930s ☐
       Present day ☐
       Future / Science Fiction ☐

5.2 Using the same scale of 1 to 5, please rate the following themes you may find in an erotic novel:

    Bondage / fetishism ☐
    Romantic love ☐
    SM / corporal punishment ☐
    Bisexuality ☐
    Gay male sex ☐
    Group sex ☐
    Watersports ☐
    Rent / sex for money ☐

5.3 Using the same scale of 1 to 5, please rate the following styles in which an erotic novel could be written:

    Gritty realism, down to earth ☐
    Set in real life but ignoring its more unpleasant aspects ☐
    Escapist fantasy, but just about believable ☐
    Complete escapism, totally unrealistic ☐

5.4 In a book that features power differentials or sexual initiation, would you prefer the writing to be from the viewpoint of the dominant / experienced or submissive / inexperienced characters:

    Dominant / Experienced ☐
    Submissive / Inexperienced ☐
    Both ☐

5.5 We'd like to include characters close to your ideal lover. What characteristics would your ideal lover have? Tick as many as you want:

Dominant	☐	Cruel	☐
Slim	☐	Young	☐
Big	☐	Naïve	☐
Voluptuous	☐	Caring	☐
Extroverted	☐	Rugged	☐
Bisexual	☐	Romantic	☐
Working Class	☐	Old	☐
Introverted	☐	Intellectual	☐
Butch	☐	Professional	☐
Femme	☐	Pervy	☐
Androgynous	☐	Ordinary	☐
Submissive	☐	Muscular	☐

    Anything else? _____

5.6 Is there one particular setting or subject matter that your ideal erotic novel would contain:

SECTION SIX: LAST WORDS

6.1 What do you like best about Sapphire books?

6.2 What do you most dislike about Sapphire books?

6.3 In what way, if any, would you like to change Sapphire covers?

6.4 Here's a space for any other comments:

Thanks for completing this questionnaire. Now either tear it out, or photocopy it, then put it in an envelope and send it to:

Sapphire/Virgin Publishing
FREEPOST LON3566
London
W6 9BR

You don't need a stamp if you're in the UK, but you'll need one if you're posting from overseas.